Open Doors

written by

Beverly A. Burchett

www.blackcurrantpress.com

OPEN DOORS

written by Beverly A. Burchett

ISBN # 978-0-9817111-2-6
PUBLISHED BY BLACKCURRANT PRESS COMPANY. ALL RIGHTS
RESERVED.
COPYRIGHT (C) 2006 BY BEVERLY A. BURCHETT.
ALL RIGHTS RESERVED.

EDITED BY DENISE M. JOHNSON

CHAPTER ONE

I t was just the way he liked it, no noise, save the pull of his lungs on the Kools, the smacking of his lips at the bitter taste of the tar. He bummed three loosies from some guy off the street on the way over and enthusiastically smoked one before he made it to his quiet spot beneath the traffic under the bridge. After the first, his peace of mind slowly returned infusing him with the vacation from reality he sorely sought and needed. He could have done without being harassed but he knew that that was all part and parcel of the whole game being played. He was king of the shake down and almost laughed at them when it came his way. It was done abruptly but clumsily leaving him more annoyed than anything else. He could have smashed at least one of their heads in, the little one for sure, and sent the other larger guy to the hospital with a busted lip or blackened eye but something told him to be cool about it and remember what was at stake. He was high, which was a good thing. That entire scene could have gone down totally different had he been sober. He shook from the adrenaline rush that it gave him. The thing was so surreal. He felt like he was an actor playing a part in a movie. He was going to be the one left standing, 'That's for dang sure,' he told himself. His enormously opposing mass alone made them sloppy with fear but unbeknownst to them, he was afraid too. Not because he couldn't take them but because they were panicking in an uncontrolled sort of way. That made them less predictable and left him on edge. He liked predictability. He counted on it. He had won many fights that way knowing exactly how things were going to turnout step by step anticipating his opponent's every move. He used people's cowardice to his full advantage. He could always take any situation and make it prefer him no matter what it looked like from the start.

His eyes were shut for a moment as he mulled over the day's events. Nothing out of the ordinary occurred, other than the fumbling attempt at scaring him. 'So what I owe them money,' he laughed to himself, 'They'll get it when I'm good and ready to give it.' He didn't even see nor hear anything coming. Normally, at this hour of the night his senses were as sharp as an alley cat but he had committed the sin of mixing whiskeys with rums. When he looked out through the thick cloud of smoke in front of his face he saw something, or someone standing there. Their features were contorted, and shadowed by the cement and iron slabs of the bridge's old underbelly. Their hands were raised in shock and drool was coming out of their mouth. He followed their eyes down to his person, below his shoulders, above his rib cage, sticking out from his chest was a thick wooden handle, attached to a blade, now forced through his flesh. He hadn't felt a thing. He didn't know exactly what it meant either at first until his drag on his cigarette arrested in his throat and nearly choked him to death. It was agonizing. His chest didn't swell on the inhale. It just froze slag in mid inhalation. The cigarette slipped from his hand. In slow motion it fell to the dirt. He watched it sailing down wanting desperately to pick it back up for one last puff. It was his favorite part where the tobacco had disappeared leaving a wet cushioned filter that burned the edges of his fingers. He tried but couldn't move. They both stood in silence for a long while staring at one another, both helpless, one for causing the injury and the other for suffering from it. He swaggered back, just in time as the hideous faced assaulter was about to retrieve his weapon from out of his heart. 'Ain't this a blimp,' he thought, 'I'm the victim of some random, ass crime.' He didn't have much time to access the irony of his predicament. He had to think fast. Like his cigarette, his sense of humor and his patience were gone. He wasn't going to let that happen to his life.

CHAPTER TWO

This is based on a true story, *unfortunately*. His name was Jimmy. According to the Coroner, Ms. Vicky Loretta Talbot, his death was a particularly brutal, vicious crime. That assessment being given in New York City may not mean much to the general public but to those who knew him — well it still managed to shock and amaze. It was the summer of 1975. Clark Green was just turning fifteen years old, living in a city that was on the verge of bankruptcy, but with a music scene that reflected on the earth like stars from heaven. It was a decade long party with clubs like CBGB's hosting Blondie, Talking Heads or the Ramones. Disco was practically a right of passage at Studio 54 and one might actually bump into Prince on the street or see Chaka Khan live and up-close in a free concert at the Pier. The New York Philharmonic Orchestra would play Central Park on the open lawn, while Springsteen was holding his own across the river in Ashbury Park. It was that time in the City's history where it was blissful to be young and alive. Patsy Mae asked her youngest and most impressionable child, Clark; one who had just proclaimed that she was an atheist, to go and find her wayward, step-father, Billy Earl. Clark loved the way she could tell just how upset Patsy Mae was with him by how many names she'd call him. Normally, she'd just say 'Earl' but that afternoon she used all four of his God given names and some that were none too holy.

"Go and get that goddamn low down man of mine Billy Earl Slocum Platt from down that there street, would you honey? Tell him I need to speak to him right now, you hear me," Patsy Mae stomped.

Clark went sailing out of the house always in need of an escape from the confinement of a daily routine. She would have done anything to leave even if it meant raking the yard or taking out the trash and for a family of six that would have meant more than a day's labor. Plus the vacant stare Patsy Mae gave her at her latest declaration gave her great cause for concern. Point blank she had informed her mother that she would not be attending church with the family any longer. She knew that Billy Earl's absence took precedence but Patsy Mae would soon enough remember to continue their little discussion. It wouldn't be pretty either. Clark knew that her mother would raise all kinds of hell to get her back to going to church again, but Clark would employ every weapon at her disposal too. Mainly, she'd bring up the fact that she was becoming a young woman and therefore should be able to make up her own mind on the subject. If that didn't work, she'd simply tell her mother that if God was who he claimed to be then he would be more than capable of understanding that some people didn't believe he existed. With those thoughts in mind, there she was forgetting the original errand no sooner than it was given but outside and away from her mother's disagreeable gaze at last. She couldn't retain anything lately, what with being so distracted. Once outside, she had to pay careful attention to the front door diagonally adjacent to hers for that was where Alfonso lived. She wasn't sure if he was Black or Hispanic, smart or dumb, lazy as a mule or spry as a racehorse. All she knew was that she was in love with him. Someone pushed back a curtain whilst she stared transfixed at his redbrick single-family attached home. She wasn't at all embarrassed for gawking either. In fact, she was sure, had it actually been him at the window that he wouldn't have even noticed her at all. He probably thought she was a little too school-girlish for him. At least that's what she told herself. He was out all night most nights even though everyone else their age had school the next morning. She couldn't really figure him out and she desperately wanted to. He was long becoming a delicious daily mystery to her. She wanted to be a part of his life in the worst way and wished that she could simply step into it like an old pair of dirty but comfortable shoes that had always been there.

Ray Brown's joint was just across the street also, which, once she came to her senses, was where she was supposed to be heading. Clark could hear what she knew to be Al Green's "Let's Stay Together" playing faintly on the jukebox. She couldn't for the life of her understand why every older person's club, record player, or radio played this particular song. Patsy Mae played it all the time too.

> *Why, why do people break up?*
> *Turn around and make up?*
> *I just can't see*

Clark strolled over to the entrance never completely taking her eyes away from Alfonso's house. Finally in front of Brown's place, she had no desire to go in but if Billy Earl was anywhere, he was at Ray Brown's in the middle of this hot sticky summer afternoon having a sip of something. She walked in quickly to make sure no one saw her go in then stood at the entrance taking her time checking every stool and booth. The place seemed deserted, save for some jackets slung over chair backs but there were no behinds in the seats. Clark rolled her eyes in the air and wondered why she had to walk all the way inside just to tell Billy Earl to come out. So, instead she yelled, though her voice was not made for producing loud noises. She was cute and petit all over. Besides, once inside, Al Green was up way too high for this hovel and it was competing with or concealing some sort of commotion in the back room. Clark didn't like the place at all and was old enough to know why the floor was sticky and the furniture well worn. She turned and took another look at the daylight outside before walking all the way into the darkened bar. She scanned the bottles on the counter. They all looked aged and dusty. There was a mirror that stretched the length of the entire back wall. It too had marks and handprints all over it, so stained that one could scarcely see their reflection in the glass. As Clark walked further down the aisle she got completely grossed out by the unevenness of the floorboards directly beneath what could only be described as carpet, threadbare and lathered in gook. There was a really thin curtain separating the front room from the back and there was definitely a party of sorts going on beyond. Clark could hear women and men back there and one voice in particular sounded vaguely familiar. She approached but couldn't see anyone just what sounded like scuffling. She touched the filthy curtain with the edge of her shoulders and nearly fell out from what she thought were boogers on the trims. That's when she got a good look at what was taking place in the little back room. Clark could just make out two people, at first, both naked from nose to toes. Initially, all she saw were limbs; just shiny, Black body parts moving around. They were lying on what appeared to be a bed, or table; one male on the bottom and one female on top of him. It is utterly amazing how much information could be retained from a glance. The woman was an enormous mammoth mass, giggling and flopping upon a fragile looking, skinny man who was also extremely giggly or drunk or something. Clark stood frozen, eyes bulging and mouth agape. She blinked out of a need to refocus, reassess – reason. That's when she made out the voice that she heard earlier while walking towards the curtain. It was definitely, Jimmy, their obviously secretive houseguest who lived in the basement. He, it would seem, was supervising this disturbing display of lust while it seemed the others were hungrily awaiting their turn. He saw her. She paused; then she quickly observed the other men circled watching this repulsive ritual. 'Good,' she thought, 'my daddy's not a member of this club.' Then she turned on her heels and ran without ever looking back.

Once Clark's front door was firmly shut, her back to it and the outside horrors securely latched and behind it, her breathing slowed a pace and she began to feel normal again.

"Is he coming or what?" Patsy Mae barked at her.

"What? What?" she stammered.

She could have substantially said her name if asked but not much else.

"Girl, what's wrong with you?" Patsy Mae placed her hands on her hips and glared at Clark.

Clark tried despondently to recuperate. She didn't really have words to describe the loss of innocence that she had just endured. It would be years before she could articulate the effects of a mere glimpse at wickedness so up close like that. She noticed that she was shaking and flustered but didn't want to admit to these emotions especially to herself and without a single doubt she wouldn't utter a word of it to her mother. She froze in her deer in the headlights stance, the one that says, "I don't know," with shrugged shoulders in bewilderment. Patsy Mae studied her evenly, controlled and silently. She exhaled and thought hard about children being a blessing.

"Well, did you see him or not? Is he coming or not?" she asked while rushing to check on her lasagna, which had just caught on fire.

It was obvious that Patsy Mae didn't want an answer so much as some acknowledgement that Clark still possessed the power of speech. Clark breathed a little easier once Patsy Mae's exit created some distance between them. Clark could still, however, hear Patsy Mae expressing her wonder of Clark's mental abilities.

"How hard is it to do a simple thing? I guess I'm supposed to do everything around here, is that it. I cook the food, put it on the table, and pay the goddamn bills. He got paid today and where the hell is he? I suppose I'm supposed to go track him down too so we can keep a roof over our heads, is that it...?"

The tirade would not end for quite some time and everyone within earshot began to slowly become scarce. It was interesting how fast Patsy Mae could clear the house without even trying. They wouldn't be far though because supper was almost ready. Clark could hear her sisters and brothers upstairs pretending to be busy when Patsy Mae called from the kitchen, "Ya'll come on down here now and get this goddamn charcoal food!" It would be a very, very silent event this dinner. Clark didn't want to be the first one at the table either but Patsy Mae had one eye on her and they both knew that the kitchen was right at the end of the hallway. Clark acted as if her feet were made of led yet she still made it before her siblings appeared at the top of the stairs. Clark slumped into her usual seat, in the middle, to be pinned between one older brother and one older sister. She determined to eat in extreme stealth mode if at all possible. It seemed as if everyone had taken that same tactic while Patsy Mae continued to argue with the steam off the crispy tray of pasta.

"What ya'll waiting for? Do you want me to put it in your mouths too?" Patsy Mae said grouchily.

They had to laugh at the thought of that but it was disguised as coughs and the clearing of young suggestible throats. Patsy Mae was a natural, born comedienne. Even she smiled unwittingly while piling her plate with food. She made her usual drink, ice-tea with a mountain of sugar and flip flopped into her room, which was adjacent to the kitchen. Snickering ensued as soon as her feet hit the threshold, then they all got up to get some dinner.

"Save some for that fool, all-right?" she mumbled, mouth slightly full of noodles.

Everyone knew that by 'fool' she was referring to a now very tardy Billy Earl.

Otherwise, it was a typical Friday. There was still some daylight left and they would make the most of it by sneaking out into the streets until they could only see the whites of each other's eyes. Patsy Mae preferred them to go outdoors as long as the blackened night didn't catch them there. She'd stand in the doorway and yell, "Melanie! Melanie!" Clark's older sister, "Mel, ya'll…" 'Ya'll' meaning everyone else, "…Ya'll get in here now!" It was as if the night held all the critters and creepy crawlers within and once darkness fell, they'd slither to greet it and trouble would ensue. Clark was afraid of it unless others were about. Unfortunately, she'd learn early on that there were things that sunlight couldn't quench and hold captive and childhood monsters didn't always lie on their bellies at one's feet.

Before they all sprung outdoors leaving Tara, Clark's second oldest sister to wash their dirty dishes, Miss Beatrice, Patsy Mae's best friend and next door neighbor, swung in through the back screen door. She had juicy news to tell, this showed in her fat, red, round face like a balloon about to pop. What news? No one cared save her. Even Patsy Mae wasn't fond of hearing all the many tidbits that oozed frothy mostly denigrating bile, so indelicately named gossip, out of her mouth. Patsy Mae put up with it, as it were, because she didn't want to hurt Miss Beatrice's feelings by sounding self righteous in saying that it bothered her that Miss Beatrice seldom offered any good news. Miss Beatrice bounced into the moderately sized kitchen lightly bumping into all the furniture with her cushioned curves. She looked cute to Clark, almost like a little girl with an enormous secret. Everyone noticed that there was something in the air and slowed apace except for Marlin, Clark's oldest brother. He headed straight for the family room where he would sit for a good portion of the entire weekend watching basketball, baseball, football, or anything ball related. Tonight was a recast of the *NBA Game of the Week* where Earl Monroe, Spencer Haywood, Walt Frazier, Bill Bradley, and Phil Jackson would be showing the other team how basketball is done with Red Holzman, of course, cheering encoded strategy from the front line. Marlin would not be disappointed. He'd yell at the screen baiting it to yell back or until Patsy Mae threw her shoe at him so she could get some much needed sleep. Her internal clock was permanently set four to five hours faster than anybody else's. If she got up at three in the morning, by 9:00 am it was lunch time, by 1:00 pm she would prepare for dinner.

"I've got to tell you some-thing," Miss Beatrice teased, "Did you know that, uh, that, uh…girl, Jimmy's dead," Miss Beatrice said bluntly while rushing to the stove to ladle some lasagna out of the pan and then settling her backside into Patsy Mae's side chair.

Patsy Mae tried not to let it show that she heard the chair squeak and yield to accommodate the heavy weight. Then there was a distinct chorus of "Dead?" "Dead?" "Dead?" "Dead?" "Dead?" "Dead?" "Dead?" "Dead?" "Dead?" "Dead?" "Dead?" "Dead?" coming from all her kids. Then there was silence from everyone, what with the straining to overhear Miss Beatrice describing the incident in second and third hand detail. Apparently he was murdered, "…brutally murdered," she said, "…stabbed." The word 'stabbed' hung in the air ever so indecently. It had painful hidden all over it no matter how it was uttered but Miss Beatrice's Southern drawl dragged it across the room as if it were a wet mangy dog on a leash squatting to stay put because he hated being pulled. Everyone got the impression that Miss Beatrice was relaying the story word-for-word from the Post rather than from the eye witnesses, where the newspaper cover page possibly had his bloody body sprawled across it with a caption that read, 'BUTCHERED, BLUGENED, BLOODY, BIG, MANGLED DEAD MAN!!'

"The body was unrecognizable. Say it could have been that serial killer who done it. Ya' know, the one that they call the '44-caliber killer.'"

There was a long stretch of quiet following Miss Beatrice's last statement. Clark couldn't help but realize that she had just seen him no more than an hour and a half ago. Patsy Mae was in some kind of shock. Her mouth hadn't closed since Miss Beatrice said the word dead, but she managed to sit upright so she wouldn't choke while chewing with her mouth wide open, not to mention her bulging eyes.

"Does Earl know?" Patsy Mae managed to ask.

That was her way of trying to see if Billy Earl was all right without actually admitting to anyone listening that she cared. She wanted to maintain a healthy 'attitude' towards him so he could receive the full magnitude of her disapproval about his recent disappearance.

"I don't know. All I know is that it's going to be a closed casket," somberly spoke Miss Beatrice.

She was clearly intrigued by the gore of it all.

"Isn't a 44-caliber a gun?" Patsy Mae asked rhetorically being firmly familiar with weaponry.

She possessed two shot-guns; one was loaded and propped up betwixt her bed and the bureau drawer at that very moment and the other was underneath the bed also loaded and ready.

"What?" Miss Beatrice asked despondently.

She wasn't paying attention any longer. Her face was glued to the television set now as Tom Jones began to sing, "It's Not

Unusual." Patsy Mae and her children would have loved to be so preoccupied too but they had just heard that their boarder, housemate, free loader, wasn't coming home due to a sudden lack of life within his body. Patsy Mae's mind began to race with thoughts of going downstairs and having to go through a dead man's things. She wasn't sure if he had a family, friends or anyone resembling loved-ones. What was she going to do with all that stuff? Jimmy was a hoarder, who actually had accumulated some fairly nice belongings, worth a few hundreds of dollars, at least; though nothing of which Patsy Mae wanted or cared for. Having buried one husband already, she was unenthusiastic about the entire business of making funeral arrangements, and placing middle of the night calls and listening to those who regarded him dearly weep without ceasing. Meanwhile, Miss Beatrice rocked from side to side snapping her pudgy fingers to the music.

"We're all going to church this Sunday to say a prayer… and gottdamnit, I mean it!" Patsy Mae yelled into the kitchen to all of her children but especially to Clark.

Clark resolved to make an exception in this case only, of course. Patsy Mae could hear all of her children sighing and stumping in protest. She knew them all too well. In their minds, Christmas and Easter visits were more than enough. She allowed them their moment of believing that they had a choice. Then she placed her plate on the dresser top thinking that she'd eat the rest of her dinner at three or four in the morning, that is to say, for breakfast.

CHAPTER THREE

Ms. Vicky Loretta Talbot used her twenty-nine dollar Sanyo micro-recorder as a notebook observed Detectives James Robert Miller and Susan O'Neil of the New York City Police Department, Robbery-Homicide, who were both present for the autopsy. Vicky took her time. Detective Miller especially noticed that particular fact too. Ms. Talbot liked to simply look around the deceased and make a general external assessment. This helped her size up the amount of work she would have to do later. She placed her attention on the numerous wounds, more than thirty counted at a glance, mostly centered in the upper portion of the torso of his rather large frame. By the angles of the incisions it could be surmised that the killer had a tough time disabling his victim. Talbot had a pretty good hunch, though, that it was the very first strike that had ultimately ended his life. Just by the location of and size of the incision she could conclude that it penetrated his aorta and probably ripped it apart. At that time the deceased probably leaned forward allowing the blood to continue flowing temporarily through the tube but it was just a matter of time before the rupture widened separating the passageway completely. She could also see that the killer did not yank the blade out. She came to this conclusion because the blade was definitely pulled out slowly and painstakingly. The killer would have just dislodged it without discretion. Talbot conjectured that the deceased possibly slid it out himself. It gave her a shiver. Obviously, he was a strong man. She conjectured

further that while he was preoccupied with one hand on the knife
handle, the other was probably blocking his assailant from other
attacks. She made this assessment by noting that his left hand
was marked with more than a dozen incisions alone while his
other hand was virtually clean. Also, she could tell that the other
incisions on the decease's body were made by something else,
possibly something that broke on contact. Unfortunately, for the
deceased, he eventually lost this furious struggle and as a result
his body was covered with stab slashes, cuts, and abrasions. She
felt sorry for him. Talbot regarded any stiff on her table as her
patient of sorts. Although none of them could physically walk
or talk anymore, she knew that eventually she and her forensic
team would allow them the ability of speech from the grave.
After some fourteen years she also knew that they all had a
unique story to tell. Judging from the sheer severity of this
crime, this Autopsy Report number 96-05134 a/k/a Jimmy
would not stop talking until his killer was found. Detective
Miller rolled his eyes to the ceiling waiting rather impatiently
for the compression click of the play-record button of Talbot's
Sanyo.

Vicky Talbot pretended not to notice and began speaking
rather slowly into her recorder, "Autopsy performed on the body
of DuBois, James P., at the Department of Coroner New York,
New York on August 10, 1975 at 0730 hours." Detective Miller
yawned, breaking her concentration. Then he waved as if to say
continue.' Vicky Talbot continued as she was rudely instructed
but spoke even more slowly than before, "From the anatomic
findings and pertinent history, I, Vicky Loretta Talbot, ascribe
the death to multiple sharp force injuries due to or as a result of

Roman Numeral One, Incised wound of chest: a) transaction of
the center of the aorta, b) transaction of left atrium, c) transaction
of left pulmonary artery, d) incision of left pulmonary veins, e)
incision of left ventricle, f) transaction of interior vena cavag)
transaction to right membrane of sternum." She paused. She
was finished with the heart but was distracted by the incisions
she saw on the epiglottis, and hypopharynx and the left and right
internal jugular veins. He had stab wounds of the neck and even
at the base of the scalp. She continued, "The neck shows sharp
force injury to be described below, and the larynx is visible
through the gaping wound." She pointed to the open wound on
the neck and then continued, "The Notes and Procedures on this
subject are as follows: 1. The body is described in the Standard
Anatomical Position. Reference is to this position only; 2. Where
necessary, injuries are numbered for reference. This is arbitrary
and does not correspond to any order in which they may have
been incurred. All the injuries are antemortem, unless otherwise
specified; 3. The term 'anatomic' is used as a specification to
indicate correspondence with the description as set forth in the
textbooks of Gross Anatomy. It denotes freedom from
significant, visible or morbid alteration. The body is that of a
well-developed, well-nourished Black male stated to be thirty-
seven years of age. The body weighs 360 pounds and measures
78 inches from crown to sole. The hair on the scalp is brown and
the irises are brown with the pupils fixed and dilated. The
sclerae and conjunctive are unremarkable, without evidence of
petechial hemorrhages on either. Both upper and lower teeth
are natural, without evidence of injury to the checks, lips or
gums. There are tattoos found above each shoulder blade and
upon each pectoris, transversely oriented and measuring three

and one half inches in length." She paused again. She wanted to know who this person was before her. Usually, she had odd questions that would pop into her head without warning leaving her feeling as if she might be going crazy. Suddenly she thought, 'I wonder how he liked his coffee,' or 'Did he have a happy life or did he just go through the motions.' She didn't like being distracted like that but sometimes it moved her to feel some kind of kinship with the deceased or at least she liked to think that maybe she was someone who was acquainted with them. "From the rate of rigor mortis, time and temp," she went on, "it can be determined that he died twenty-four to thirty hours ago." Detective Miller scribbled this information into his notebook. Talbot placed her recorder down and rolled him onto his side with the help of both detectives in order to examine the exterior of his back. She pushed record button again, "Examination of the posterior surface at the trunk shows some excoriations compatible with postmortem injuries on the upper back, right side, on the medial aspect of the right scapula and on the lateral aspect of the right scapula (compatible with ant to insect bites). An abrasion above the left scapula measures 3/4 x 1/2 inch and is red-brown in color and appears antemortem. Otherwise, the lower back and remainder of the posterior aspect of the body shows no evidence or recent injuries."

"Look, which wound actually killed 'em?" asked Detective Miller in a huff.

Vicky motioned for the two detectives to help her roll the body back over.

"I have to examine the chest cavity more closely," Vicky calmly told him while taking a scalpel to cut through the epidermis on the deceased's chest. She slid the blade easily down the front of his abdomen. Detective O'Neil tried to hold back a giggle when she saw Detective Miller turn and threw-up on the floor and on his shiny loafers. He quickly pulled a handkerchief from his breast pocket to cover his mouth and nose. Vicky knew all too well how the smell alone could cause one to lose their composure. She was, of course, used to it as she was with witnesses who mixed their vomit with the odor of the dead. Vicky placed the scalpel back on the tray and slowly pulled the skin back on both sides of the chest cavity of the deceased. Detective Miller tried to maintain his footing as he leaned towards the table in horror. He had viewed many autopsies in his career but with a Tequila hang-over it was hard to stomach this one – literally.

"Death is attributed to multiple sharp force injuries, including a deep incised wound of the chest and multiple stab wounds of the neck. Sharp force injuries led to transection of the left and right common carotid arteries, and incisions of the left and right internal jugular vein causing what could have been fatal exsanguinating hemorrhage," Talbot told them.

"Wait. Wait. What do you mean by *could have been*?" asked Detective O'Neil while erasing what Vicky Talbot just said.

"Well, that wasn't what actually killed him, I don't think. I just wanted to make sure those were recorded," answered Talbot then continuing with her recording, "Also, there was a sharp force injury to the scalp which was superficial and also non-fatal."

Detective Miller forced a long exasperated sigh into the air. Detective O'Neil stepped away from him all the while fanning her hand over her nose from the staleness of his breath. Talbot took the scalpel and made another incision to the chest cavity fully exposing the heart. She leaned into the body twice slowly and conscientiously before speaking again into her recorder. Detective Miller shook his head from side to side wondering how long all of this was going to take. He was more than a little ready to run out of there.

"Judging from the depth of the penetration of this wound here…" Vicky pointed to a section of the aorta closest to the left pulmonary artery, "…mind you we would still have to send this to Toxicology for a routine workup, but I would say that this is your fatal blow."

Detective Miller hesitantly scribbled what Vicky said into his notebook.

"Injuries present on the hands, including the incised wound of the left hand are compatible to defense wounds. Routine studies will be ordered," continued Talbot.

Detective O'Neil kept her eyes on Jimmy's chest.

"What else can you tell us on the chest wound? I mean, can you tell what type of weapon was used?" she asked.

"Well, it's true that the depth and shape of a fatal stab wound, fixed during an autopsy, may give a clue to the type of weapon used. And the track of a weapon may be very clear in fleshy areas. See this here?" Talbot pointed to his skin near the heart. "However, when a weapon penetrates inner organs, its track may not be all that accurate. Inner organs change in shape and position after death and when a body is moved it really gets distorted. Also, a strong stabbing force against a soft area like the heart can depress the area, making the wound deeper than the true length of the weapon. Likewise, a longer blade may not penetrate its full length at all. Then the wound path is shorter than the blade," Talbot shrugged out her answer.

"Can't you give us anything? I mean, really! I had two hours sleep for crying out loud," Detective Miller mumbled through his hand which was still covering his mouth.

"Well, I do have some good news. A homicidal stab wound often penetrates a victim's clothing and I took special care when removing and checking the victim's clothes. Many times the clothing matches the real width of the weapon better than the wound does," answered Talbot proudly.

Detective Miller was growing weary of Talbot's forensic lesson, "And...?"

"And, I would say that, preliminarily speaking and judging from the clothing and the shape of the wound, the tearing pattern here and here, that it was just a plain old ordinary six-inch long, one-inch wide kitchen knife. Mind you, I need more time to measure the tear in the clothes but my guesses are pretty on target most of the time," Talbot said very modestly.

"And your *guess* is six-inches long and one-inch wide, right?" smirked Detective Miller.

"Yes, Detective Miller, that is correct," replied Talbot seriously and sternly.

Talbot about faced and began picking out minute fragments from the deceased's scars.

"What in the world! What's that?" asked Detective Miller sharply.

"Glass, Detective Miller. Glass," Talbot held up a piece in the light and looked at every corner of the tiny shard.

"What can you determine from that?" asked Detective O'Neil.

"I believe judging from the amount of these little chunks imbedded into his skin that this was the secondary weapon," answered Talbot calmly, "Yeap, look at all these tiny pieces."

They all leaned in as Talbot shined the overhead light closer to the body.

"What the heck?" shouted Detective Miller.

The deceased's body glistened with a faint residue of green.

"He's glowing!" giggled Detective O'Neil nervously.

"He got hit with that, didn't he?" said Detective Miller while shaking his head from side to side.

"I believe you are correct and it smashed all over the front of his body. Then he was repeatedly hit with whatever was left of it," Talbot kept picking away with her tweezers and dropping the pieces of green glass into a tin bowl.

"A vase? A bowl?" asked Detective O'Neil.

Detective Miller shrugged, "Nah, more like a bottle of Colt 45."

"Exactly," replied Talbot, "Exactly."

Talbot referred to a bowl in a miniature glass door refrigerator on another table.

"From the stomach content, there was heavy drinking involved. Eighty-five percent of his stomach was filled with an assortment of liquors and something that my guess would be bar nuts," Talbot informed them.

"Bar nuts, huh," Detective Miller echoed.

"Yes," replied Talbot as if she no longer noticed that the detectives were there.

CHAPTER FOUR

I t wasn't as difficult as one might imagine. In fact, it was a lot like waking up from a deep troubling sleep. Sure there was pain involved but it was just the early morning kind, a slow unyielding yawn. His muscles pulled and tore in a way that made him feel as if he were being fed through a shredder but that agony subsided like the after effects of an excruciating pinch. Certainly, during those moments whilst he was dying, he cried out inaudibly like an abandoned, hysterically lost and hungry child. That was to be expected. His entire soul was heaving and spewing and stretching so as if it were escaping through every teeny tiny pore. He literally spilled out of himself or the self he was quite used to, quite fond of.

Dying

Dying

Dying

Yet all that remained was a brilliantly piercing fear and that fear slaughtered him more than the sharpness of the cold metal blade or the slow ebbing away of air from his lungs, his heart, his brain, or even the shaky numbness at the loss of his own blood. All the while the *thing*, the murderer that was before him finally made its way out of the darkness and into his sharp positively clear vision. He grinned knowingly at the recognition, just another low life he had encountered along the way. That way he once trod merely happened to be his life. It didn't much matter though. At this point he just saw this person as yet another horrible thing. He was apathetic and ready for it, but simultaneously not necessarily jaded as in life or cool or confident anymore in any human sense. He was renewed. He was transformed.   Now he was suddenly connected to everything in the universe and embracing it all with a reaffirmed grip, with fervor, welcoming it even. He was no longer his old cynical self. Then he all at once soared into the sky. He was a god, lifting high above pesky mortality, towering over everything including what he had just encountered and witnessed. If dying gracefully was the measure of a man he'd say he died nobly. Though up until the time he involuntarily began to surrender to it, he believed he could still maintain his footing on earth. Forever the fighter he was sure that he could overpower his foe.   There was nothing in his mind save destroying his combatant. He maintained human status and was in sound mind up until his spirit pulled and fled away from his body. Thusly, he lived until his very last breath. That fact struck him and stuck indelibly in his remembrance.

Still even then looking down with an aerial view upon his own face, he still felt alive somehow. There was thought and presence of being. There was consciousness. Other than the reality that he was presently without body he sensed that he was fine, astoundingly, better than fine. All pain had vanished. He was unexpectedly invincible. With that thought in mind he quickly ascended above all he used to hold dear, Ray's bar, Billy Earl's house, Jamaica, Queens…earth. He didn't know where he was traveling to. He just loved the sensation of being able to ascend amongst the birds and look down on what used to be his whole dreary, dismal life. There was a comfort and a peace that wrapped itself around him. Every inch of him was drenched in it. He couldn't believe how empowered he had become. He was without a single solitary worry, ache, level of indebtedness nothing but hilarious freedom. He was absolved even of all his past hurts both those he wrought and those committed against him. It was a high like none other he had ever experienced, no alcoholic beverage or drug could induce this exquisite sense of relief. He was released from any harm that could befall mere mortal man. He was lord over it all, pettiness, longings, meager trifles. He saw the pitiful little creatures below all rushing along to and fro. He howled in laughter at their ridiculous fragile pursuits. He was no longer subject to their imperfection. He was superior in every way. He had no idea that dying could be so liberating. He began to understand what the preachers were talking about when they said that man was made in God's own likeness, for he could finally embrace that concept. He was now immortal and all powerful too.

Then in less than a blink, he was at his body again. There it was draped over a lowered stretcher. He perceived a remarkable bond to it as if at any moment he would slip back into what now appeared to be a dull, empty canvas bag. Something literally drew him there as if by tugging on an invisible cord connecting his spirit to his flesh. Once there he saw two very diligent paramedics pushing down hard on what used to be his chest. They were extremely persistent yet by all accounts ineffective. He wished they would stop. It was futile. Having a small taste of this awesome emancipation, he was no longer interested with the living and he resented being tied down in this manner. Obviously they were more fascinated with his human form than he. He had so enjoyed being one with the heavens. Meanwhile they pressed and pressed and pushed and pushed literally assaulting his remains. He held there in mid air watching and waiting. He figured that that's what one does at one's passing, watch over one's carcass. It was not as he thought it would be. He wondered if he should be more emotional, mournful like at the losing of one's favorite pet. It was not like that at all. He was but a passive observer. All he could do was be patient until every inch of him died. He didn't recognize himself either lying there oozing out onto the ground. His flesh was gray and slack and lifeless. It was gross and absurd. Yet it was the last look on his face that made him halt ever so briefly. It actually caused him some concern. In fact, it troubled him. To make matters worse, the expression seemed larger than life as if frozen in time by the skilled hands of a sculpture. It was cauterized for eternity and unmistakable. He moved closer to his body to be sure. Yes. Yes, there it was. He couldn't believe it. He wouldn't have if he did not see it for himself. He, the proud and fearless person that he portrayed in life, was unmistakably scared at the time of his death. Though the paramedics had graciously closed his eyes and mouth, the expression was still there in every line and at every angle. It was true. To his dismay, this final representation showed severe terror in every wrinkle and shadow within the eerie matte finish of this marble statue of a face. It made him utterly melancholy. The sadness ripped through him like a tidal wave of sentiment. It grieved him so that his spirit which moments ago seemed enormous began to truncate. As he shrank, his sorrow slowly turned into rage. Then his spirit felt as if it had been set aflame. He looked around to see where this new phenomenon was coming from. It didn't take him long to realize that it was indeed coming from within. It was pure anger, the hot burning kind. It was a type of sickness, a madness of sorts. It was the kind of anger that's raw and prickly, the brand that consumes and engulfs and blinds. He began to stride back and forth, growling like a lion, weaving in and out of the crowd that had gathered to gawk and ridicule. He hated every single one of them but especially the buffoons cracking what used to be his rib cage.

"Stop!" he roared at them.

At that he saw fire shoot out of the place where his mouth used to be. It hit the air and acutely vanished on contact. Then a strong gust of wind blew pass the paramedics' ears and forced them to cease and desist pumping momentarily. One fell off his knelt knee and wavered unsteadily to regain balance. The crowd backed off wondering what had happened. Then after a brief peculiar pause everyone resumed activity, though cautiously and guarded. Just the way Jimmy liked it. He was satisfied with having everyone feel his presence. He felt like his old self again, intimidating. He had learned a new and useful trick too, no doubt one of many of the newly dead - haunting. He could send the air flying where he purposed. He truly loved that. He was once again in control. He pushed his way through the crowd. Some people shuttered as he passed through them. They could sense something slithering betwixt and between. Others were hopelessly clueless. As he discerned the essence of weakness in all of them, his spirit bore a smile that stretched him back to his enormous size. He was free again. Plus the paramedics had forced every last bit of air out of his old home, cell, his confining space called body. He would have died a long time ago had he known he could feel this good.

CHAPTER FIVE

"Poor Jimmy," came up at least once at dinner but only in passing. There was probably a moment of silence following but Clark wasn't one hundred percent sure of anything around her house anymore. It might have been the kind of silent time reserved for seriously chomping down on Patsy Mae's bar-b-que chicken cutlets and collard greens without annoying chatter, rather than a sincere time of commemoration. All Clark knew was that in several trips to the basement in order to bring up can goods for Patsy Mae it proved creepy and weird for her young soul. She began to believe it was more than just her impressive imagination that someone was watching her down in the gallows of their pit of a basement in the process of being finished for the past eight years if not more. Billy Earl had other things on his mind, of course, besides adorning Jimmy's bachelor pad. At least that's how it was when Jimmy was alive. The drop ceiling framing was up but half of the tiles were propped against the partially finished wall at the side of the staircase. Two-by-fours were neatly stacked along each side of Jimmy's makeshift closet which consisted of a broom-stick and an old fitted sheet. Now that he was deceased, Billy Earl insisted that one of Jimmy's friends come and collect his affects so that he could finally give Patsy Mae the basement she deserved. Billy Earl knew full well that this request would buy him some more time, possibly a year or two, before he would have to go down there and actually finish the job. He knew this because Jimmy, though seemingly liked by all, earnestly didn't have any real friends. He had acquaintances only. Billy Earl observed this flaw in Jimmy's character especially when it came to women. They were practically interchangeable as far as Jimmy was concerned. Billy Earl would see him call number after number to ascertain which one was available for any given evening. Sometimes this list was quite long and Jimmy would accidentally call a few more than once. He'd forget names and faces, as that wasn't what he focused on regarding these individuals. He enjoyed all of the seven deadly sins but none more than lust. Billy Earl would shake his head in disbelief questioning why Jimmy's chorale of females never caught onto this obviously self-centered manipulation.

Clark took a curious look around at all the many somewhat splendid things Jimmy left behind. She was more than a little tempted to snoop around in all of his personals herself. She wasn't trying to pry into his life necessarily. She was just looking for loose change. One thing she did know was that older people kept their money hidden under mattresses and such and she thought she'd just try and un-earth some of the treasure. Though, as she walked towards his bed, she could have sworn she heard someone sneaking up behind her.

"Marlin, quit playing around," she shouted into the air.

When she turned to find that no one was there, "Marlin, I know that's you hiding behind that couch. Stop it!" she said and looked quickly behind the sofa.

When she did not find Marlin scrunched down between the wall and the sofa back, she was more than a little spooked. She immediately ran quickly towards the can goods, grabbed anything within reach and hauled tail back upstairs. She slammed the can down on the counter top and slid into a chair at the table to rest a moment and to catch her breath. She decided not to move a muscle until her goose bumps were all gone and she could stand without wobbling. Patsy Mae stood still and observed her for a long while before she said anything.

"Girl," she paused, "…does this look like corn to you?" she asked her calmly.

Clark tried not to show panic on her face as she swept her eyes over to the counter. There, with the label facing her was a rather large plastic bag of black-eyed peas. Clark could have sworn that she had her little fingers around a can of something. Sure, she just grabbed whatever she could and ran but she thought that luck was on her side and that it would be something that Patsy Mae could use. Patsy Mae waited for a response. She tapped her foot on the Linoleum floor tile and drummed her fingers on the marble-like finish Formica…nothing. Clark was frozen with fear. She didn't want to enter that basement ever again without an escort and she was petrified that she'd be asked to do so.

"I suppose I have to go and get the corn myself now too, right?" Patsy Mae uttered rhetorically.

Patsy Mae picked up the peas and tossed them back and forth from one hand to the other and thought about the meal she had planned.

"I guess we could have peas with the Whiting I'm making," she shrugged, "…but I did have a taste for some sweet corn." Pause. "I really did."

Patsy Mae eyed-balled Clark shrewdly. She was trying to gently persuade her into going back downstairs to get the corn.

She could have simply ordered her to do so but something told her to leave well enough alone. Patsy Mae knew her children. She already could see that Clark wasn't coping so well with the fact that there were clothes of a dead man, among other things, in their basement. Patsy Mae, in truth, was none too keen in going down there herself. She would prefer to send one of her children or Billy Earl. Though she also knew that sooner or later she wouldn't have the luxury of their assistance and would have to eventually go and clean the place out. She perished the thought. It actually gave her chills. She was never particularly fond of Jimmy and only allowed him to stay because he begged her. In some ways she knew that she said yes out of pure spite. Billy Earl didn't like him much either and told him that if he could convince Patsy Mae then he could stay. He made sure to convince Jimmy that Patsy Mae was the one who didn't want a boarder in their basement. Patsy Mae fixed Billy Earl, all right. After Jimmy moved in, Billy Earl had a constant companion, a running mate, a drinking buddy. Patsy Mae was none too pleased with her decision but she refused to allow either one of them to irritate her. Though Jimmy was, in deed, a bad influence on Billy Earl, Billy Earl always knew as a pure fact how angry Patsy Mae would be if he took anything they were doing too far. Patsy Mae was his conscience and his judge and jury and without any doubt in his mind, she could be his executioner. Billy Earl would say, "I don't know Jimmy, Pat might not like that," chuckle, chuckle. At that, Jimmy wouldn't insist on Billy Earl's participation in any activity that would leave Billy Earl in trouble and him possibly out on the street. Jimmy was shrewd. He had managed to live rent-free practically his entire life. He had acquired that many acquaintances, all willing to give him shelter for next to nothing because they either felt sorry for him or because he convinced them that he would be an asset. Jimmy was a big man and having one of those around the house did surprisingly come in handy, if for nothing else, security. Jimmy also had a gift for fixing things. Patsy Mae had a radio that would mysteriously change stations without being touched until Jimmy opened up its back, fiddled with something and *voila* it was repaired. Patsy Mae watched his big hands fumbling with the delicate mechanisms of her little AM/FM transistor and figured he'd break it and have to buy her a new one. She couldn't believe her eyes when the dial held itself steady at WWRL, her favorite station. From then on, every time she turned on that radio she knew that Jimmy had earned himself another day in their home.

"I guess I could put some fatback in these peas and make something out of it, huh," Patsy Mae told Clark while reaching into the refrigerator and pulling out something that looked like a big old dirty frozen foot. Patsy Mae always had a little inside snigger when it came to the way Clark saw things. Clark twisted her lips up and jerked her head back in repulsion.

"You'll like it once it's thawed out and cooked," Patsy Mae told her.

"Yeah…well…" Clark broke off in a whisper under her breath.

She had a lot to say to Patsy Mae on the subject. However, she didn't want to sound too sassy, what with Patsy Mae not forcing her to go back downstairs and all. Patsy Mae just laughed out loud and tossed the fatty meat into the sink.

"You want to help me cook today or you got better things to

do than to hang out with yo' Mama?" Patsy Mae joked.

Clark smiled wide and bright loving this alone time with Patsy Mae. She liked being treated like she was one of the girls just cooking in the kitchen as if that's what they always did. Patsy Mae would always pull out something that was just for the two of them. She reached back into the refrigerator and took out two bottles of Coca-Cola. She bumped the cabinet drawer open with her hip, took the opener and flipped both bottle caps off in a quick twist of her wrist. When she handed one to Clark, she could see her smile shimmering and glowing.

"Let's see if my show's on," Patsy Mae said while seemingly gliding into her room and switching on the television set.

Clark knew that she was not allowed in Patsy Mae's room with food but she wasn't quite sure about drinks. Patsy Mae opened her small folding table and placed it beside her side chair.

"You can come on in," she told Clark.

Clark hesitated a little before walking in and taking a seat. She just loved it, Patsy Mae's side chair, ice cold Coca-Cola, girl talk and a table to rest things on, she just didn't think life could get any better. Clark didn't care what was on television or how many times she'd be asked to get up and change the channel. She was in heaven until, "So…" Patsy Mae began, "…no more church ugh…?"

Suddenly, Clark squirmed in her seat feeling altogether trapped.

"…Don't believe in God?…umm…" Patsy Mae uttered in a sing-song fashion, which belied its overall intent.

Clark wasn't quite sure if it was a question, an answer, or a statement. She didn't know what to say in return and felt sure that her mother was truly searching for at least some speech to come from her all too dry mouth.

"…ah…" she muttered, and then gulped down the cola. "Nothing to say, huh?" Patsy Mae asked.

"…ah…ah…" Clark repeated.

"Well…God sure believes in you…That's for sure. He believes in you," Patsy Mae told her as if she had some secret shared just between her and God.

Clark was glad that there was a period following Patsy Mae's last statement and not a question mark. She was safe for the time being, that is until Patsy Mae had more to say on the subject. Then Clark would have to come up with some kind of theory to support her original declaration. She would have to think on something stronger than "ah…ah…."

CHAPTER SIX

The trial schedules at Queens Borough Court can be two to five years backlogged. Bernard Jeremiah Kennedy, Jr., a Court Officer of thirty-nine years, thought about that fact as he entered the name James P. DuBois into the record book. The pages were already yellowed and the edges threadbare and frayed of the thick, only one month old tightly woven leather bound book. Bernard wrote as he always did, slowly and legibly. He would be retiring early as he had always promised himself and didn't want a misspelled name to come back to haunt him later on. Therefore, from day one he swore an oath to C.Y.O.A. a/k/a 'cover your own ass' that was as iron-clad as a judge's ruling. All he needed was a gavel. His 'c.y.o.a.' decision wouldn't be overturned nor appealed until someone was dead and that did not necessarily mean him. Otherwise, Mr. DuBois was just another nameless, faceless entry into the journal to Bernard and all he had to do was assign him a Case Number - 012567. Bernard didn't need to know anything else about this latest case save the six digit code that would be permanently affixed to it and the events that followed. Bernard smirked at the thought of the 'events' and there were always *events*, issues, problems, drama that followed every single case number he applied to those pages. If he had a dollar for every time someone acted a fool in court, he would be retiring a wealthy, wealthy man. As he continued with his filing, he didn't give another thought to this latest case. And why should he? A very long time ago he had become an authority in the reality of his career choice; and that reality was that every single trial involved a murder. These case numbers were only assigned when someone died as a result of someone else killing them. Though that fact alone used to horrify him, he had adjusted to it a lot quicker than he had originally imagined. At first, he wasn't sure he had made the right decision of working in a courthouse. He was like any other normal, red blooded human. He'd look at the exhibit photos and lay awake night after night wondering if some murderer was coming to get him too. He had times when he'd think that any footsteps behind him were those of some killer. For years he couldn't and wouldn't watch any type of police drama on television. And to this day he applied a particular emotional safety technique to reading the newspaper. He reads the cover page first then the last page, usually that's the sports page, then he reads the second page then the second to the last page and so on and so on until he eventually finds himself in the center of the newspaper where the fashion or celebrity pages are. This way he doesn't have to think that the whole city is filled with criminals. Rather, he can go to bed believing that everyone is socializing and having the time of their lives.

In the absence of murder, mayhem and destruction on his brain, he was then able to find humor in the courtroom proceedings. He was an equal opportunity kind of guy. The judges, juries, witnesses, the attorneys both prosecuting and defending, were all equally comical to Bernard. He often thought that holding court would play out better if it took place in a boxing ring. Regardless of the specifics of the case, there was always a knock down drag out brawl beneath the surface of polite 'counselor this,' or 'judge this or that.' Bernard had seen it all and was even there for some that were televised. He was bored with it all too, jaded, done. He looked forward now to putting his fishing rod at the stern of his Prosport and launching out and it didn't much matter where. Though docked in his own back yard, he had only had it on open water once. Now he thought that as long as he had a six pack of something cold and his hydraulic steering didn't rattle too badly, he would be fine for hours with no one and nothing to disturb his peace. A smile grew across his creased face and the wonder of the ocean appeared to be reflecting in his tired eyes or was it paperwork. With a sigh he began the sometimes tedious task of assigning this latest case number to a trial judge. Once the case had a date on the trial calendar the difficult part of his job was over. He couldn't complain about that. Most companies had a-hurry-up-and-wait attitude and justice was no different. It would be a year or two before Case Number 012567 came up for air and when it did Bernard wanted to be long gone.

CHAPTER SEVEN

What really surprised him about his current state of affairs was how everything looked. He had observed some of these things throughout his entire lifetime and they meant nothing to him and yet somehow now they were altogether special. Each item took on a peculiar fascination for him. He paused often to study objects that he would have never given a second glance before. In life he had always regarded the things he saw with cynicism and loathing. It was a feeling so pervasive that it transferred itself to humans as well. There was a constant dullness that he believed permeated the whole world and covered over even the most dazzling natural wonders. If a delightful, colorful butterfly flew across his nose he wouldn't think twice of swatting it to kill it with his bare hand. He had no patience for such things as beauty, loveliness or life itself. That's why it was so unlike him to be so transfixed by these things at present. For instance he found himself staring for hours at an over-stuffed, filthy trashcan. It was literally filled to the rim with discarded rotting food and soiled newspapers from dog walker pick-ups. It would be considered gross by most. Yet to the new Jimmy, it was a rare delicate bird flapping its wings in the breeze. It was the rolling sea crashing into the shore at dusk. It was the brilliant sun cascading its rays across a vibrant blue sky.

This change in him began when he had recalled one of his old haunts at the backside of Baisley Park, a favored spot amongst him and his thugs. It was not a place where law-abiding citizens parked or benched necessarily. The slowest of strollers ran pass and joggers sprinted by like front runner marathoners. It was dank and smelly for all the moss clinging to the surface of the dirty water and the flies and bees swarming, no one really wanted to linger there save Jimmy. He and his friends would actually meet there for a smoke to discuss the goings on of the day. It was usually filled with riotous laughter or for the divvying up of their latest spoils. He remembered those times fondly. Of course, Jimmy assumed the role of parceling out the loot whether he helped perjure it or not. His portion was always the same too, more than he legitimately deserved. His group of ruffians and transients responded submissively to massive size and a resounding baritone voice. No one ever questioned Jimmy because no one ever wanted to fight him, the fact that no one ever witnessed Jimmy in a fight, notwithstanding. The fact of the matter was that they hadn't a visual reference of his true capability. He'd launch forward with his hands curled in enormous threatening fists and with an intimidating growl that was usually enough to send an average man running away with his tail between his legs. It was at these gatherings, that anyone who had fallen victim to the group's schemes got an honorable mention and a tribute of thanks for donating to the cause. The so-called cause was a euphemism for drugs, booze or alcohol and of course for their occasional meals.

Thus there he was, enamored by the garbage before him. Each piece of paper's stain seemed to gleam in the sunlight. It was curious how his sight showed the truest hue of reds and yellows, grays and blues. They were vivid, sharp and rich with tone. Then there was the green grass. He had to meditate in awe at the sight of the grass. It stunned him. It overwhelmed him. It mesmerized him to his core. It shone with such a picturesque quality that it took his breath away, that is, his will shriveled in acquiescence to it. It danced before him this grass with verve and vigor. It swelled when the wind blew and contracted as if bowing down from the gods itself. Jimmy remained still in order to capture it all with such a significance of pleasure that his spirit felt as if it were weeping. Though he liked this new sensation that welled up inside him, he absolutely abhorred the wimpy reaction it ignited. He wasn't a helpless female or child in the spirit or otherwise and yet there he was vulnerable to mere blades of grass. He didn't under any circumstances like this revelation. In fact, the whole experience began to disgust, thus ultimately annoy him. He wasn't necessarily enjoying this particular side of his character. He found it to be a weakness, this much exquisiteness. Then he began to brood about this obscure renovation within him. He decided that it was not an improvement. It was then that it occurred to him that without the presence of the other senses, sight must have taken them all in sum total. He could currently see as if there was something beyond grasp and comprehension. It was as if he were the most powerful of all telescopes and the most penetrating of all microscopes at the same time. This was obviously yet another gift he had acquired in this cosmos he'd entered. He knew some place deep down that this would eventually come in handy but at present he had to redirect his focus elsewhere. He didn't want to sulk around all day or be upset, though he concluded that this was a side of him that would have been better functioned had it been buried with his corpse.

So he concentrated on his old home and in a flash he was there. All was quiet and still in his old room, the basement, save Melanie ironing one article of clothing after another, profusely sweating and all the while fussing about the laziness of others. She had been at it all day, he could tell. It showed in the completed piles of folded shirts and pants covering the sofa. She was proud of all she had accomplished. This showed too in the way she'd turn and admire the fact that there was no room left to sit. Her shoes were tossed to one side and her thick hair clung to her neck and shoulders. He watched her for a few moments with the same intensity he gave the trashcan but was momentarily distracted when her younger sister, Clark, came sauntering down the steps. She startled him at first, making his spirit surge and flutter. Then before he knew it, his aura had completely changed color at the sight of her. An almost superhuman pull had induced him to gravitate in her direction. He remembered suddenly that he had had an enormous crush on her in life though then she was only a child. Now, older, and he free to do as he pleased; he was positively smitten. He could feel himself turning into something resembling jelly. She had an inescapable effect on him that literally transformed his figure and made him long to engulf her as if he were a predatory shark and she were squid. He was in rapture and hovered beside her gawking and ogling everything about her, her hips and thighs, her hands, her fingers. Her innocence also actually propelled him towards her. It was intoxicating, this girl with her exciting youthfulness. He had always liked the young ones best with their adorable lack of experience. He loved that he could say whatever he desired to them and they would heed every word. They were just too naive to skillfully argue a point.

He looked over at Clark again. He liked the roundness of her face and the way it glistened. Her dimples were so deep that they sank into her cheeks and made her smile seem to be extending across practically touching her delicate little ears. She bounced when she walked too. He liked that too. There was a dance going on as if music accompanied her like a chaperon. The beat was all in her head but it displayed itself in her exuberate gait. She was filled to overflowing with the essence of springtime. It was contagious to be in her presence. Once there he felt totally alive. She reeked of it like a noxious odor that shadowed and penetrated into the fabric of things. Her ebullient smile warmed him. Her doe-like eyelids fluttered in his direction and cast a spell upon him. She was yet another thing that he was now seeing as if for the first time. In truth, he had thought her cute in life and had stolen more than a few wicked glances at her on the sly. However, he had no desire to tangle with the likes of Patsy Mae. So he made sure she never caught him at it. He knew that Clark was unaware of it as well because she didn't change her behavior in any way when she was around him. 'She was filling out nicely,' he'd say to himself from time to time. He was always surprised at how the natural order of a woman's body was designed to attract a man. As far as he was concerned, it was indeed her fault that he even noticed her at all. Clark made him react in a way that was reminiscent and familiar to the crux of who he was among the living, covetous. Now, he had to have her, to possess her.

It seemed that the differences separating them, however thorny, certainly had no effect on his way of thinking either. He wanted to own her, to ravage her, to impregnate her with what he believed to be his undying love and devotion, though he was incapable in life of loving anyone other than himself, notwithstanding. He had always been the equivalent of a little devil; wanton, lustful, gluttonous and unremorseful. So, like the new emotions he had experienced in the park, he began to harbor some new emotions towards Clark. Now he was as giddy as a schoolboy. He even began to change his form for her more into something that he imagined she'd like. He also began to cling to her. It occurred to him that being near her intensified these feelings of being in a flurry of unabashed excitement. This was an awesome reaction to the living that totally took him by surprise. It dawned on him that he must be head over heels in love.

CHAPTER EIGHT

C lark waited patiently for Alfonso to make the first move. Though she was firmly based in reality and knew that he didn't even know her name, she hoped beyond hope that she was wrong just this one time. The music was ear-piercing and the bass parts pounded through the gigantic speakers with such force that they pitched from side to side. As she scanned the room for familiar faces, her heart stopped when she noticed that he was beginning to walk in her general direction. She quickly angled herself in such a way in order to mentally record his every little step. 'Wow,' she thought, 'look at how well he walks.' The spring of his tread on the floor as he bounced off the left foot and landed squarely on the right made her dizzy with anticipation. All the while she imagined, 'Maybe he's coming to see me.' Meanwhile, her friend, Lisa, who dragged her to this particular soirée, yammered on and on about how she simply wanted some privacy in her house of fifteen. Lisa couldn't understand how her mother and father allowed her only slightly older brother, Alan, to bring his girlfriend and their two babies to live with them in her parents' small one family home. She was sick of him, his lover, the high pitch squeals of the constantly crying tots, the pungent odor of dirty diapers everywhere, not to mention the infantile bickering of her brother and his lady, but mostly she was tired of having to clean up after them all. Her mother insisted on polished floors, dust free surfaces, empty hampers and kitchen appliances that you could see their reflection out of. This would be achieved, of course, not by those making the mess, oh no, but by those who sarcastically according to Lisa, had nothing better to do. Lisa longed for the days when doing her homework was the hardest chore on her list and mind-numbingly boring was the description of her household.

Clark struggled to hear just enough of what Lisa was saying in case she'd be asked her opinion all the while with her eyes fixed on Alfonso's shirt buttons. They shun in the dim light of the single overhead naked bulb. Every time he smiled, Clark assumed her heart had stopped completely and that her feet had levitated a few inches from the floor. As the distance between them tightened, Clark became more and more off balanced. His very presence stirred up a host of emotions that she had not known she possessed. Lisa was completely oblivious to the fact that Clark wasn't paying attention to her conversation. She went right on without pause.

"The girl was raised in a barn. She doesn't even flush the toilet half the time. Can you imagine?" Lisa said nodding and shaking her head from side to side in utter disbelieve.

"Yeah, yeah," managed Clark through her love trance.

"And the other day when she cooked grits for Alan, she stirred too hard and actually scrapped and mixed in some of the bottom of the pot," she laughed, "The grits were black by the time she finished."

Lisa laughed until she coughed. Then she scanned the room searching for cute boys for a moment. Having nothing worth observing, she continued her brief tirade of Alan's babies' mama.

"But don't let her leave the house without looking like a

model or something; no, all hell would break loose. The girl spends about three hours just taking a shower. And when she's finished, you can't get in there without a hose. Honestly, how could that little thing collect that much dirt," she queried.

Suddenly, Alfonso was standing right beside them. He was conversing with one of his friends, a hoodlum really. Clark couldn't understand why someone would want to replace a perfectly good tooth with a gold one. The friend's hair, which shot in every direction at once, stood at least three inches tall from his scull and was adorned with a plastic afro pick embedded and leaning to one side. When he smiled, Clark squinted from the glare off the metal teeth that clashed with the gold inscription, 'Brute Force,' necklace he was sporting. Clark felt dangerous just standing next to Alfonso and friend and loved every minute of it. If Lisa could just keep quiet for a brief spell, Clark would have enjoyed and savored that moment a little longer before the lights went out. As it was custom, Lisa informed Clark, these *over the bridge parties*, as they were called, always had several periods of absolute darkness. These dark periods allowed the boys to grope and feel to their hearts content without prying eyes and inhibited girls. Clark and Lisa made sure that their backs and fronts were covered by pressing themselves against the wall and folding their arms across their chests. Lisa tried to make it seem as if she was used to this sort of thing by continuing her speech about Alan's girlfriend. On the other hand, Clark was reticent about the whole ritual.

"All I know is that I make sure that when she's around, I'm no where to be found. One day I even hid in the garage just to get away from all of them. And you know how dirty that garage is. Mama acts like I'm everybody's personal slave. It's always Lisa this and Lisa that. What do I look like to them? The girl is practically my age but since she has kids now that don't automatically make her no adult. She's been drinking my Daddy's beer too. Can you imagine? If I touched his precious beer, I would be thrown out of the house and I'm his flesh and blood," she said with a sneer.

A match was struck and held in front of Lisa's face. It was gold tooth himself and that was his way of asking her if she wanted to dance. She blew out his match and chuckled out a 'hell no.' Clark loved Lisa's direct approach and was nervous about gold tooth coming her way. She knew that she would probably accept because she didn't have the heart to say no and besides, she actually wanted to dance. Then another match was struck, this time it was Alfonso and he was standing directly in front of Clark. She accidentally exhaled and in her excitement extinguished his match. Her head was still shaking with shame when the next match was lit. She hoped it was Alfonso again and to her delight it was indeed.

"You did that on purpose?" he asked her jokingly.

Clark could barely speak. She had decided to hold her breath as not to put out another one of his flames.

"Wanna dance?" he asked her and reached out his hand for hers.

Clark knew that she must have walked into the middle of the dance floor especially since suddenly she was there. She must have taken Alfonso's hand when he offered because he was certainly holding hers delicately in his. She also knew that she must have put her arms around Alfonso's neck because suddenly they were there clasped and supported by his chest and shoulders. She must have moved in close to him too because without warning her body was pressed against his. He smelled delicious to her, a mixture of motor oil and Ivory soap. She sunk into him as if she had been lost her whole life and he, her savior, had found her. Her head tilted and rested upon his shoulder. She could hear him breathing and him grunting every time she moved to the music. The more she relinquished control of her own body into his, the more he grunted and groaned as did most of the boys on the dance floor. His arms began to encircle her waist and rub her back and neck. Then his lips began to lightly brush against her cheek. She didn't know what was happening to her as they melted into one another so effortlessly. Now the loud music seemed to be muted. Earth, Wind and Fire's, Philip Bailey, seemed to be way off in the distance somewhere. She heard him echoing over and over again, *"...the reasons, the reasons, the reasons...."* She had no idea what he was talking about. All she knew was that her knees were shaking and her throat was dry and cracked. Her palms were sweaty and her clothing clung to her skin as if they were another layer. Her heart throbbed against Alfonso's as if there was only room for one as their bodies fused into a single being. Their legs intertwined in a wrapping, weaving snarl. Clark could scarcely feel anything except pleasure and exhilaration. Before she knew it, she was moaning right along with Alfonso. Every time she did, he'd kiss her neck and cheek hard like he was starving for her. Then his lips periodically swept across and his teeth gently nibbled and pulled at her skin. She didn't think that she would be able to withstand the new sensation that this inspired in her. It was painfully sweet like someone tickling your toes in slow motion. Then a scorching heat rose off of Alfonso and engulfed

Clark. It was so hot that she wanted to pull away and just for a second she did, only to realize that she actually missed him when he wasn't right beside her. Alfonso gently pulled her back like a puppy longing to be walked.   He had some kind of enchantment over her. She felt drawn to him. She could not stay away much longer. The air between them just intensified their desire for one another. Clark wished she could retard time and hold this moment as a keepsake. In the flesh, he was actually better than she had imagined he'd be in all those many months of watching him from afar. She was finally in his world, a friend of sorts. She felt like she knew him. She wanted to touch every inch of him and apparently he wanted to do the same to her because when they did finally come back together again, that's what he began to do. He rubbed her legs and arms, her neck, back and her fingers. His hands seemed to be everywhere at once as were his lips.   The nibbling and the kissing of her neck was Clark's favorite part. Then his mouth poignantly found hers. She lost all track of space and time when they did. As they embraced, all of her energy merged, locked and welded itself into that kiss. The taste of it, the total consuming power it had over every muscle in her body, the surprising familiarity of it all struck her core and liquefied all of her reserve. His mouth was so supple and positively irresistible. His skin reminded her of running her fingers through velvet or silk. She couldn't bring herself to think of anything else save Alfonso, Alfonso, Alfonso…Al…fon….so.

Rudely, the lights popped back on. When they did, instead of the dim one from earlier, there were five stark, glaring white lights extremely irritating to the pupils. Simultaneously, and by design, the music abruptly stopped as well with the needle scratching across the vinyl. This prompted disapproving *ahs* and *why fors*. Clark didn't know where to look first when Alfonso released his hold of her in a tender but firm jerk. Then he quickly made eye contact with gold tooth and the two of them sprinted towards the door. Clark could still taste the chewing gum and funny cigarettes that Alfonso had transferred into her mouth by way of his tongue. She momentarily felt ridiculous standing there alone watching his back from the middle of the now practically deserted room. It was Lisa who informed her that the party was over by bumping shoulders and pushing her forward. She knew she was in trouble for she could barely string together words as they both exited out to the street.

"I...ah....well...ah, ah..." she stammered all the while pretending that she wasn't looking for Alfonso, Alfonso, Alfonso...Al...fon....so. Every boy she saw with short cropped curly hair sent her into a state of love sick that tingled down from her neck to her stomach. He was no where to be found. She wouldn't have known what to say had they met but she wanted to at least muster out a 'good night' and tell him her name. Lisa was rather noticeably quiet about the whole thing. She told Clark that her feet hurt and that she was tired. Clark had to suspend disbelief of Lisa's reason for her sudden change in demeanor. She hadn't the energy to delve into anything besides a warm bed. Fortunately for them most of the party goers lived on the other side of the Van Wyck Expressway too and provided lots of company as they strolled in silence back over the highway bridge. Lisa kept peering at some of the girls who were putting their tops back on and wiping off excess make-up.

"They must have fallen off on the dance floor," Lisa joked.

"Yeah, I guess," Clark replied though she wasn't interested in any of the girls' transformations. Her eyes were peaked steadily searching for Alfonso, Alfonso, Alfonso...Al...fon....so. Then as their journey came to an end, she felt sure that her heart was going to break in two if she didn't see him again that evening. 'Where'd he go?' she kept asking herself. She wondered if he had one of those topless girls pinned up somewhere at yet another party. She was hollow now as if he had emptied her of anything remotely resembling herself. He had stolen it all, all of her oomph, her will to live, her very soul. 'Where could he be?' she lamented. Then she tried not to think about it and instead concentrated on their dance. Yet those memories proved to be as elusive as him. It had been an hour since and she felt certain that she must have dreamt the whole thing. She barely said good-bye to her friend Lisa as she rounded the corner to go home. Lisa muttered something about all the lights being on in the house and how she didn't want to have to talk to anybody; she just wanted to go straight to bed.

"Night," she offered while turning her key in the lock and pushing her way inside.

Clark turned onto her block and saw that the streets were full of people, all coming and going from other parties she assumed, and very wide awake. Apart from the nightfall, it appeared to be mid-afternoon rather than after mid-night. Clark refused to consider Patsy Mae's opinion on the subject. She knew that she, Patsy Mae, would not be pleased. Clark hoped that she was sound asleep. Her thoughts then only lingered on Alfonso, Alfonso, Alfonso...Al...fon....so. She couldn't help herself. Though she told herself not to look, she glanced across the street at his house. The curtains were drawn and the house looked asleep. Several motionless, torturous minutes later of watching and waiting she figured that he was probably asleep inside too. She walked up the steps of her house unsatisfied and reluctantly went in. 'What else can I do?' she thought. She couldn't very well go over to his house and knock on the door, could she? Although, after such a passionate and personal time together on the dance floor, wouldn't she be afforded at least a proper introduction? She wasn't going to do that though, not at one thirty in the morning. She would never presume that he was now *that* kind of friend.

She made it all the way upstairs to her room skillfully avoiding Patsy Mae. Her calf muscles were sore from climbing the steps on the tips of her toes, but she dared not stop to relieve the pain, what with Patsy Mae's bionic hearing and her tendency to make numerous trips to the bathroom in the middle of the night. So she crept soundlessly until she reached her bed and finally there collapsed upon it. It only took a couple of seconds for her to realize that she wasn't the same girl that she was earlier that day. It wasn't just the euphoria of Alfonso... Alfonso... Al...fon...so, which was sweet, awesome and acutely splendid. There now was something all together different, something deeper at work, something slightly unsettling. She noticed that her head felt heavy and weighted down upon the mattress. It sunk so far downward that she couldn't see peripherally in either direction. Too tired to get up and investigate this awakening particularity, she just remained. Her body began to feel light and then ever so slowly it pulled itself away from the mattress. She felt a sudden coldness underneath her legs and thighs. At first this was a relief to the sweatiness she had earlier, and then a sensation of dampness swept across leaving her cold. She knew inwardly that she was separated from her bed and that although in a dream state, she was still afraid of heights. The uneasiness continued as one of her eyes slowly opened allowing her to see that she was indeed at least two feet from the bed. She froze, terrified. Her breath was caught and swelled within her chest. Then slowly, eerily she began to drift towards the window left open on account of Tara's asthma. There was just enough space for Clark to go right out and dangle in mid air above the pavement, two stories below. Clark could taste the saltiness of her own tears trickling into her mouth. This was hardly the evening closer she expected. She wasn't sure if it was the elation of dancing with Alfonso or the marijuana transfer or what. She looked around and tried to focus on the moonlight, which shone clearly upon her head. She wouldn't look down less her body plunged against the sidewalk. Her limbs were completely stiff all save her face. When she decided to close her eyes, she sensed a slight shift in positioning taking place and before she knew it, she was back inside above her bed. Then inch by inch she descended back upon the covers. Unable still to move a muscle for the severe, crippling fear, she fainted into a comatose sleep.

CHAPTER NINE

Bernie was still fuming over the fact that his entire family had poor, dirty, rotten, good for nothing gums, especially his.   They bled, they swelled, they divorced themselves from their root bones, etc. Bernie and his family had routinely visited his suspiciously happy dentist two to three times a week, months at a time for a veritable assortment of procedures; root canals, periodontal surgery, tooth extractions, bridge work and a whole other host of things he couldn't repeat, nay he couldn't pronounce. He didn't want to delve too deeply into the details ever because that would remind him of all the money he'd spent, the tooth aches he'd tolerated and the hassle of it all at nauseam. Instead he would just say, "It's the burden we bear," and leave it at that. If people didn't understand why he couldn't eat an apple without screaming they just didn't understand. He'd fasten his eyes on them real mean-like until they changed the subject. His wife, Lillie, say, "Bernie, you's just a bastard sometimes I think." Bernie would smile and tell her that that was the only way to keep stupid people out of their business. Lillie, a woman of few words, and a proper lady would never say anything bad about another human being. So if she swore at him, he knew she was most probably right. He thought about that very fact as he sat in the courtroom trying deliriously hard not to laugh at the goings on. If he did, he knew that his temporary false front teeth would go flying out of his mouth landing squarely in the jury box or worse yet on Judge Binghamton's freshly polished mahogany bench. He tried to muffle the air that burst up his windpipe by squeezing his entire face up like a shriveled prune but the vibrating breath still traveled up to the top. His under-exercised stomach muscles were no help either in keeping the laugh squat in his belly where it belonged. Before he knew it, his falsies hung over his bottom lip and made him look like a rabbit. Juror number seven glanced over at him in wide mouthed horror. As their eyes met, the middle aged lady shifted and nearly fell off her seat and that guffaw almost made Bernie lose total control. He wondered what Lillie would have said had she seen him squinting invisible anger darts at this particular lady's head. The wise woman slowly slid more erectly into her chair carefully paying stricter attention to the prosecuting attorney's next question, rather than being sneered at by the crazy man in the drab puke green court officer uniform.

"So, are we to believe that you did not know the deceased, a Mr. James P. DuBois? Is that correct, Mr. Brown? Are we to understand that that is what you are saying?" mused Jason Spitzer, Esquire.

Raymond Brown scanned the courtroom, then nodded and shook his head up, down and horizontally all at the same time.

"What's that you say? Yes or no, Mr. Brown? Did you or did you not have a relationship with Mr. James DuBois? The court is waiting for your answer, Mr. Brown. Yes or no," asked Spitzer patiently.

Brown, "Yeah, yeah. I mean no, no, I did not know 'em."

"I see," Spitzer said with his nose pointed up towards the ceiling and his eyes glaring at Brown over it.

Spitzer sauntered back to his table and picked up a stack of pictures from it. He started shuffling them in his hands. He took his time perusing each one individually before waving them before Judge Binghamton and the court.

"Exhibit thirty-nine, your Honor," he stated loudly for the court recorder.

Then he carried them over to the jury box and spread them out across the front of the partition. The jurors sat up on the edge of their seats in order to get a closer look. Those in the back row stood and leaned forward to view them. About a minute later, they all, little by little, one by one, turned and faced Mr. Raymond Brown. Bernie could hear the visitor's section whispering and conjecturing about what the jurors had apparently discovered. All eyes were on Brown. He squirmed uncomfortably in his seat and tried focusing on anything other than returning stares to the now entire courtroom. He didn't even know why he lied. In retrospect it just sort of came out spontaneously-like. Now, in hindsight he sure would have preferred that it hadn't. How was he going to explain his true opinion of Jimmy? He knew deep down that poor ole, fun-loving Jimmy was not the type of person that you ever, under any circumstances, wanted to admit to knowing and that was a plain truth. Jimmy was acquainted with all kinds of people and most of them were like something out of 'Night of the Living Dead'. They hid in dark shadows, slithered around town seeking chaos and destruction and by and large were on no account up to any good. Most of them had never worked a day in their lives, not for honest pay anyway and they always had some scheme, scam, flim-flam they were running on some unaware sucker. Brown kind of figured that that was what probably got Jimmy killed. He didn't want the same thing to happen to him, by association, he thought. Right now, however, he would have to face the court and speak to them with absolute candor. He hung his head down ashamed remembering the pictures they used to take with his favorite Polaroid, right there in the back room of his bar, good times even. He completely forgot about the officers who went through his place with a fine, tooth, comb grabbing anything that wasn't nailed down. He didn't know from collecting evidence, incriminating or other wise. He assumed that his words would save him as they had in the past.

"Well, well, well, Mr. Brown. What do we have here?" Spitzer goaded.

He scooped up the photos one by one loving the dramatic effect of this line of questioning. One could never tell what would happen during jury deliberation but imaginary points were won moment by moment, day by day whilst in court. Spitzer knew that. He was also smart enough to know that he was winning. He had this obviously bad liar on the stand, which made all of his questions look in-depth and him intelligent. Jurors normally liked attorneys who are razor sharp. Spitzer was no dummy, he was astutely aware that he was just incredibly lucky but he could live with that especially if it meant a win. He held the photos out in front of him, dangling them so Brown could get a little peak before he handed them over to the Judge. Brown felt an uneasiness that he couldn't even describe as those memories passed his face and yanked at his psyche. What in the world was he thinking? Those were the pictures that were taken at his sixtieth birthday party. Jimmy arranged it, bought the cake, invited the guests, etc., etc., etc.

"That must not be you with your arm around Mr. James P. Dubois, I presume?" Spitzer teased.

Bernie had to rock back and forth in order to hold back the flurry of chuckles that bubbled to the surface when suddenly he saw water trickling down from the witness box. It was the smell that hit everyone else. The jurors knotted their noses up to their eyes and glowered at Mr. Raymond Brown then they swung their heads in Judge Binghamton's direction.

"I have no further questions, your Honor," Spitzer spat.

Bernie saw Judge Binghamton jump up from his chair right after he nodded for him to give Mr. Brown the boot. Bernie's side was splitting observing Ms. Janet Cummings, the stenographer, who showed a startling surprised look of disgust at witnessing up close the moisture that leaked onto the paneled floor. She jumped from her seat and backed away from Brown as did everyone in his path. Spitzer was the only one who didn't move in some way as Bernie escorted Brown from the witness stand and out of the courtroom. He was enjoying this moment of victory. He made a grown man wet his pants. In his book, that was most definitely a win. Brown couldn't even look at Spitzer as he was leaving and he was assuredly leaving. There was a strict unwritten rule in the courtroom. Any disturbance of any kind got the eighty-six, eliminated, arrested, in other words, thrown out on their butts. Bernie was just the man to do it, but somehow this particular day it was difficult for him to do his job without bursting out into hysterical laughter. He knew it was partly due to the painkillers his dentist prescribed and possibly due to the raucous nature of the entire court that day. Judge Binghamton had already decided to retire to his chambers refusing to return unless the urine smell also vacated the premises. Bernie just had to hold it together for another couple of minutes, just until Brown was securely out of the Judges' courtroom. Brown looked pitifully fragile holding his hands out to his sides trying not to touch his own wet clothes. Bernie actually felt sorry for him. He knew that Mr. Raymond Brown didn't even realize that he was a very minor character in this whole sorted case, and that he probably imagined Bernie was throwing him in the slammer. Bernie wondered if he thought it would be for lying under oath or for pissing all over the witness stand, either reason would be the super's choice. Tony, the superintendent had been on the maintenance staff for fifteen years and never, ever been called into the courtroom. When he was summoned by radio he assumed he hadn't done something correctly the day before, only to drag his slop bucket down the aisle of some wildly out of control spectators; he couldn't even make his way clear to the now empty box. No one looked at him; instead they went on and on about some poor slob named, Brown. Tony didn't get the connection even when he saw the lawyers all gathered at the prosecution table. Even as he was mopping the booth, he just figured that Judge Binghamton's glass must have toppled over into the witness stand. He finished up, glanced over his shoulder as he was exiting and still after seeing a full glass of water sitting perfectly on the bench, he could not put two and two together. Bernie greeted him just outside the courtroom door also smiling, as was everyone else.

"What? What?" Tony inquisitively pressed.

Bernie tapped him on his shoulder and pointed towards the witness box and held his nose.

"You didn't smell that, man?" he asked him.

"What, man? What?" Tony asked again and again.

Bernie realized that for one, his teeth couldn't withstand any more laughter and two; Tony hadn't a clue to what had just transpired. Bernie straightened up before continuing.

"Tony, man. That was pee you just sopped up," he whispered, in case there were any prying eyes and ears.

Bernie didn't want to be the one caught gossiping about the cases. He had his c.y.o.a. to consider. Tony's eyes popped wide and he dropped his mop handle with a crash to the floor.

"Yuuuccckkk!" he screamed angrily and then began a complete discourse in Spanish.

Bernie didn't understand a word but figured Tony finally had.

CHAPTER TEN

L ife was not turning out the way either of them had expected. Clark would be going to school in Manhattan, while Lisa had opted to stay at home and continue her work at a local Macy's. Lisa's selling point being that it was in walking distance from her house. Clark knew better than to argue with her. After all, Patsy Mae was not *her* mother. If she were to go to college or not to go to college, wouldn't be an option. It would be a flat out fact. Either Patsy Mae's children were going to school or they were going to the hospital to have her foot surgically removed from their backsides. Therefore, if a child lived under Patsy Mae's roof during the week daylight hours, they had better have their behinds in some institute for higher learning. It didn't much matter the area of discipline, so long as her children came away with some means of supporting themselves other than staying at home with her. In fact, her exact words were, "You ain't staying home with me," quote end quote. Marlin went to a trade school to become a better automotive mechanic. His girlfriend Karen together with Patsy Mae made sure he attended each and every class. It wasn't exactly college but at least he could make a decent living and would be able to some day support a family. The latter part of that equation really appealed to Karen, for she had already decided for the both of them that she would be his future wife. It would be several years before Marlin would become privy to this minor detail. By then it would be too late.

Suddenly, both Clark and Lisa felt anxious, neither knowing what to make of their apparent, current differences. As far as they were concerned, weren't they supposed to be friends for life? Now, that idea seemed out of place somehow as they walked together down Sutphin Boulevard for what might be their last time.

"So Alan finally moved out? How did that happen? I thought they'd be there for life…no rent and all…" said Clark.

"Girl, if you could have seen the look on his face when Daddy gave them the hee ho…It was all I could do to keep from passing out," Lisa laughed hard enough to cry.

Clark joined in just for the sheer joy of sharing Lisa's triumphant moment.

"Girl, I was holding my knees together to keep me from sitting down right there on the floor. I couldn't faint, just couldn't. I wasn't going to miss a single, solitary minute of it. You hear me? They looked like…" she showed a face of complete shock, "Then Daddy said, 'The dishes are never cleaned and the bathroom is filthy…This is my house!' Told them flat out to leave by the end of the week. Yes, he did," she giggled.

Clark giggled too at Lisa's delivery of the facts complete with her father's expressions and that of her own. They had to pause their strolling several times in order to howl a little longer, and then compose themselves. There they stood on the sidewalk holding onto their sides and leaning forward so they could breathe.

"You should have seen *her* face," Lisa said slowly as if she was getting to the best part.

Then she shared a knowing glance with Clark. By 'her,' she

meant Alan's live-in girlfriend, one of whom Lisa couldn't stand the sight of.

"That lazy behind child had the nerve to want to argue with Daddy," Lisa informed Clark.

"What?" Clark asked.

"Yes," Lisa confirmed.

"What did she say?" Clark inquired.

"She said she didn't have no-place else to go. Count of the children, her mother doesn't want them coming back to live with her either," Lisa could barely get it all out for the laughter.

Clark and Lisa both shook their heads in disapproval.

"'Wrong answer,' that's what Daddy said, 'Wrong, goddamn answer.' Then he walked back down the hallway as if to say that this little conversation was definitely over. Left them both standing around staring at the walls. I had held in the laughter for so long that I finally had to just leave. It was like my stomach had a cramp, girl. I tried not to laugh as I passed them though, 'cause I knew that that would have started a fight," Lisa said grinning from ear to ear as they continued walking further down the road towards their favorite local candy store.

"What now? I mean where will they go?" Clark asked now a tad more compassionately.

Lisa shrugged her shoulders, "Don't know. Don't nobody want 'em."

"That's messed up," Clark said.

"Daddy always say that if you do what's right, you'll be accepted. Says that's what the Bible say," Lisa told her.

"Hum," Clark expressed seeing as she didn't believe in any of that but was fine with Lisa's decision to believe in it, if she liked.

"Guess they didn't do what was right and now they got to go," Lisa giggled some more.

They paused again to have another round of laughter. Then just as they were straightening back up a homeless woman approached them.

"Spare some change?" she asked.

Lisa looked her over annoyed that she smelled worst than she looked. Meanwhile Clark dug into her pocket. She wasn't more benevolent than Lisa. She just figured that was the quickest way to get rid of the woman. She found two quarters, pulled them out and dropped them into the woman's hand. As she did so, suddenly, the woman grabbed hold of her. And, Clark tried and tried but couldn't get her loose.

"Hey, what's wrong with you old lady?" Lisa shouted at her.

Clark stood in amazement not knowing which way to turn. The woman was insistent.

"You have something…something…" the homeless woman began.

Lisa pushed her, yet she held onto Clark even more. This time she hissed at Lisa making Lisa feel disoriented for a moment. She couldn't believe that this old woman had that kind of gumshone.

"…dear, dear…" the woman continued on, looking as if she'd seen a ghost while staring adrift into Clark's eyes.

Lisa pushed again, harder this time and managed to severe the hold that the woman had on Clark. The old woman stumbled back wheezing for air, appearing even more haggard than she did when she first approached them.

"Listen, I'm trying to tell you something important..." she spoke only to Clark, as if Lisa wasn't there.

Lisa took offense but backed off when she saw that Clark was generally interested in finding out what this stranger had to say.

"Let it go, Lisa," Clark told her.

Clark reached over and helped the woman steady herself. Lisa rolled her eyes up wondering what was wrong with her best friend.

"Listen..." the old woman began again, then paused.

Both Clark and Lisa stared at her then each other waiting for the woman to say whatever it was in her scrambled head.

"Yes?" Clark finally asked.

"Yes, well..." she began again and again paused.

Clark reached into her pocket again and this time pulled out a dollar bill. Lisa wrapped her arms around her body and eyed the woman with a frown, as Clark handed the bill over to her.

"Well?" Clark asked this time with extreme impatience.

"Well..." the woman said straightening up and looking physically better all of a sudden.

Lisa looked over at Clark and both of them shared a silent laugh.

"Well," the old woman said again and this time gently took Clark's hand and turned it over with the palm facing up.

Lisa almost burst out in tears of laughter.

"You have it," the woman said knowingly.

"It?" Clark questioned.

"You have a way of seeing into the realm of the heavens. Gifted, you know," the woman told her, "You can see things, beyond this world. You will travel too, to many, many places in your lifetime."

"Famous?" Lisa asked the woman.

"Well…maybe…" the woman answered.

Lisa and Clark smiled.

"…maybe not," the woman further clarified.

"Hum," Clark thought out loud.

"That's not what I mean. You can see in the spirit," the woman told Clark.

Clark seemed less than thrilled with that particular skill, as it were.

"That's better than being famous," the woman told her.

Lisa looked at her as if she had two heads.

Finally the woman let Clark's hand go feeling satisfied with herself for having given her such wonderful news. Then Lisa stared at the woman for a moment hoping to have her palm read also.

"What about…mine…?" Lisa asked hesitantly.

The woman grabbed Lisa's hand and turned it over to the palm.

"Two kids, a boy and a girl, not married," she told her despondently.

"Huh?" Lisa shrugged, not particularly amused with the reading.

Lisa snatched her hand away from the woman and reached into her pocket pulling out a nickel.

"Keep it," the woman told her, "You're gonna' need it…I don't see any money for you either."

"What?" Lisa said indignantly.

Clark put her head down and tried not to giggle.

"Well," the woman said once more, this time a forward before parting words.

"Well," Clark said, also a forward before good-bye.

"Well," Lisa said too, definitely a good-bye with a good riddance attached.

The old woman bowed her head to both of them then walked away. Lisa and Clark took a long moment to register what they had just heard and seen. The old woman walked a few yards then turned toward them again.

"You need to stop talking yourself out of your blessings," she told Lisa.

Lisa stood frozen, like the old woman touched a nerve.

"And you need to wear more dresses," she told Clark.

Then the old woman about-faced, then vanished within the crowd leaving both Lisa and Clark standing frozen in the middle of the sidewalk. Each had a quizzical look upon their face. Each mulling over the old woman's predictions.

"Two damn kids and no damn husband?" Lisa finally mouthed under her breath, "Is she out of her damn mind? There is no way I'm dropping a bunch of kids so I can take care of all of us by myself. Now, you know she crazy."

Clark burst into laughter, then Lisa followed suit.

"What is the world coming to that these nuts are offering their delusional advice to people right here on the street anyway?" Lisa asked to no one in particular.

They both laughed some more.

"Two damn kids….no…damn husband…she nuts alright…" Lisa stomped.

They walked on some more.

"Let's get on to the store before all hell breaks loose," Lisa advised.

"Look at what she told me…'seeing things that aren't

there'…okay," Clark grinned as if to say which is better, what she told Lisa or what she told her.

"We both know she was talking about herself on that one…" Lisa said soberly, "…obviously."

"'Wear more dresses'?" Clark repeated the old woman's advice.

"'No money,' isn't that what she told me, 'no gotdamn money'," Lisa repeated the miserable forecast for her apparent future, as if to say, which is better still, Clark's or hers.

Clark couldn't stop laughing about that prediction.

"It doesn't sound good," Clark finally looked up from being doubled over and agreed, but still smiling broadly.

"Maybe I should go to school because that old crazy lady might have a point about that," Lisa said seriously.

"Hum," Clark agreed.

"You know, these old people see things that no one else can. I'm here to tell you that my grandma was like that. Look right through you, yes, she could. I didn't trust her for that, you know. I could say something down the block, damn if that woman wouldn't repeat it like I said it directly to her," Lisa strolled squinting her eyes as her grandmother might be hiding around any given corner, "Nope…didn't trust her. Loved her, but you couldn't trust her for that, nope."

CHAPTER ELEVEN

"**D**o you think this is funny, Miller?" growled Lieutenant Hall, "Oh, I will give you something to laugh about don't you worry about that."

He waited for any sound to come from Detective Miller. If he so much as blinked too loudly, Lieutenant Hall would have grabbed his big fat head and smashed it through his newly Windexed double plated glass door. He was sick and tired of smart mouthed detectives who assumed that every word from their mouth was tantamount to a commandment. He was about to show him a glimpse of God from the bottom of his size twelve polished Police issued shoe, squarely placed on his soft out of shape behind. Miller scrunched up his face and bit his lip.

"I guess you like it when the Mayor, the Commissioner and half the City wants to use me as their personal punching bag," he continued, "Koch may seem all diplomatic but that doesn't mean he doesn't have his foot up my ass! Well, I've got myself a little plan. I'm gonna' pass the buck right on over to you. How would you like that? Get this Miller, they can have you for less than the price of a cup of coffee from the street vendors, especially when they find you out there on foot patrol. What do you think of that?" The Lieutenant waited again for Miller's response and none came, "I thought so."

O'Neil tried her hardest to keep her face blank and with a thin veneer of fear showing. Yet she wasn't in the least bit afraid. She knew all too well how this all was going to pan out. She and her far too comical for his own good partner would be in full uniform in the worst part of the City up to their eyeballs in common variety bad guy sludge. That she was sure of.

"Do you have anything to say, O'Neil? I see that look on your face," inquired Lieutenant Hall with a chill in his voice.

O'Neil shook her head indicating a firm 'no reply'. She knew better than to say a single, solitary word, for anything and everything spoken could and would be used against her. This was not the time for answering questions and offering opinions. This was the time for getting answers. She wished she were out on the street finding clues, gathering facts and the like instead of getting her head chewed off in front of the whole Precinct.

She was glad that mostly everyone pretended to be too busy to notice the very loud public spanking once she and Miller exited the Lieutenant's small office. Lieutenant Hall continued to wear out the carpeting behind his desk. He looked like a mean, hungry lion stalking his prey. No one wanted to be next. It may have meant the end of their career. O'Neil didn't even glance over at Miller. She had had her fill of testosterone for one day. She hurried back to her desk and started right away on her dwindling witness list. Raymond Brown was one of her witnesses turned prime suspect until he got up in court and lied and peed. She almost laughed at the thought of him sitting in there squirming but couldn't because she was supposed to be deep in introspection and hard at work solving this bazaar case. The only people on her list were semi-close friends of the deceased. That was not a good sign considering that none of them had motive. They actually seemed to like the guy. She was now completely out of ideas and since the Judge threw the case out of court, this really was not a good sign. She would have to pull a rabbit out of a hat in order to settle this one and she was no magician. Miller was humming underneath his breath. This was usually not a good sign either. O'Neil hated it when Miller hummed. She hated all things male at this point but especially this finicky idiosyncrasy. It meant he had something, something that he would not in a million years want to tell her willingly. She would have to stumble upon it accidentally by riffling through his desk or, worst of all, she would have to ask. This troubled her greatly. This would mean that she did need him. She wanted to be the one that got the next bright idea. She wanted to be the hero today but no. She would have to bow down, bend over and generally humiliate herself. He would gloat, brag, strut and generally on purpose be a pesky nightmare for the rest of the day. She hated her job sometimes. She queried ever so lightly, "So..." Miller kept his head down as if he hadn't heard her. 'Great,' thought O'Neil, 'Now he's ignoring me!'

"So?" she snapped almost in a yell.
When Miller finally, slowly lifted his eyes he made sure to keep one on her and the other on a thin slip of paper within a plastic baggie he was waving backwards and forwards in front of his nose. O'Neil was in the worst sort of mood for this type of game, the one that says catch up with the expert if you can.

"You got something?" she asked nonchalantly, hating herself every moment for doing so.

What did she have to lose, though? She was practically back on a beat. All of her cramming for tests and promotions, not to mention salary increases were about to do a ninety degree about face. For all of her complaining at this level in her career, she liked where she was and didn't want to go back to square one. So she sunk her pride down to a new low and asked again.

"Something important?" she poked.

"Could be," Miller teased.

'Ooh!' she hated that more than anything else. That's what had them in the Lieutenant's office for half the morning in the first place. Miller had to open the gaping hole in his face he called a mouth. He had to pour salt on the already deep wound. He just couldn't leave well enough alone. He had to be the one to say what was literally on every body else's mind. Her dubious partner, Miller, had stood up and in a loud resonating voice blurted out that the deceased probably deserved what he got and that he didn't see what all the fuss was about. Everyone else already knew, heck even five year olds knew, that if Mayor Edward I. Koch wanted to make a federal case out of every single murder case then no one under his jurisdiction would be allowed to do any packing it up and going on home. The Mayor could make tourists believe that he resurrected victims from the dead just by saying 'We've apprehended the assailants and he/she is serving our swift justice.'

Everyone thought that the Lieutenant's head was going to jettison clean off as he turned it all the way around to scowl at Miller. There were quite a few rookies who took quite a few steps back just to make sure that the Lieutenant didn't lump them into his tirade. O'Neil couldn't believe that Miller had the nerve to sit across from her after all that he wrecked that morning and still be in some kind of playful mood.

"Miller, what the hell are you up to?" O'Neil asked, temper flaring, restraint gone.

Fellow detectives within earshot snickered but dared not look in O'Neil's direction. She was their quintessential female cop with something to prove and nothing to lose. More importantly she was one of two female detectives who knew karate. Her parents enrolled her in classes after her very first mid-term dance recital with the Miss Petra School of Ballet at the tender age of five. O'Neil never got to see her debut video-tape because her father and mother exposed it to light, accidentally they told her. To this day, O'Neil could not understand how such a thing could happen what with tamper proof packaging but she realized that they obviously had their reasons. She had discovered that she could barely bob her head to any given rhythm and had to stick to the one two step for any given dance. She couldn't understand why her mother would always say, "At least my child will know how to defend herself." It was the 'at least' that made her feel uneasy. For whatever the reason, O'Neil knew that this was where all of her training would come in handy though. She'd flip Miller out of his chair, poke something sharp in his eye, and if that didn't do the trick, crack a few of his ribs. Then as she's being tossed into a cell and the *officers* are hurriedly throwing away the key, she would remember to sincerely thank her parents for their obviously good judgment and marvelous foresight. She stared at Miller's ears and wanted to rip them from his head. She caught a glimpse of Lieutenant Hall staring at Miller's ears as well. There was obviously something about Miller's head today that awestruck the both of them. There he was waving that piece of paper in the air bating her. The nerve endings at the base of her neck shot up. So help her, she wanted everyone to see him getting his butt kicked by a woman.

"Patience, patience, O'Neil," Miller grinned, "All in due

time."

Then Miller stood up, put back on his suit jacket, smoothed out the wrinkles and adjusted his tie. O'Neil jumped out of her seat and threw her jacket back on as well. She didn't know what he was up to but she didn't like the smell of it. He looked too cheeky and too pleased with himself. Then, of all things, Miller nodded for her to come and join him back in the Lieutenant's office. O'Neil was inches away from him and still couldn't grab him to stop him. She leaped across two desks, sliding and pushing papers, telephones, and confidential document files in her path and still could not secure a single finger around Miller's neck. Her colleagues caught on quickly to her quest and tried to assist her by blocking Miller's pathway to Lieutenant Hall's office. Unfortunately, Miller was a step ahead of everyone and O'Neil was a step or two behind him. She could have killed him if she were not an officer of law with a lifetime pension to take into account. She wondered if he was a glutton for punishment. She wondered if he wanted to be back on foot patrol. She wondered if the Lieutenant would determine that her presence meant she was in cahoots with him and therefore stopped approximately three feet from the Lieutenant's door. Miller slid inside the Lieutenant's office and sensing O'Neil's apprehension closed the door in her face. O'Neil could feel every eye in the place on her back. If she could have she would have just stood there until Miller exited but detectives were supposed to always be in absolute control, knowing every right move to make, confident, etc., etc., etc. She turned and business perked to a bubbling start again complete with heads bowed in silence. She quietly assisted in helping to pick up the items she sent flying to the floor and mechanically returned to her desk. Once seated, she pretended to scratch her head whilst stealing a glance at Miller in the Lieutenant's office, when suddenly she saw the door swing open and the Lieutenant thundered out.

"O'Neil, get in here!" the Lieutenant barked.

She wished she could just start this day all over again. She would hit the snooze button and roll back underneath the covers. She walked hesitantly all the while trying to encourage herself. She wanted to be, above all, prepared for what was coming next. She felt blind-sided throughout the day and just wanted a little bit of that alleged control back. She'd stand firm and await her fate allowing every reprimand to bounce off without synching her soul. Should she be sent back on the beat she would tell everyone who'd listen that her dumb partner sent her there. She'd make sure that his name, rank and number was strategically written in every bathroom stall. She didn't care. If she was going down, he was going further down.

She approached the door and still couldn't see the expression on Miller's face. He hadn't turned around or in any way indicated what was going on since he walked in. O'Neil imagined that he had a look and pretense of absolute admiration towards the Lieutenant with his lips in a pucker. She took a deep breath and opened the door. For all her posturing, she was scared. The door elbow in need of oil squeaked shut behind her. She didn't know where to look first, so anxious to get it all over with. The only thought that resonated was, 'Miller, what have you done now?'

"Sit," Lieutenant Hall ordered.

So O'Neil pulled out one of the two most uncomfortable

chairs in the entire precinct. No one could figure if it was the unyielding hardness of the leather or the fact that the Lieutenant sat directly across. O'Neil was not in the mood to debate the issue. She adjusted herself as best she could and sat down.

"So, O'Neil, Miller tells me that you two may have solved this case," the Lieutenant started.

O'Neil tried hard not to show her literal disgust of her partner Miller. How could he do such a thing to her today of all days? She knew that she would not forgive him ever.

"Is this true?" he asked.

'Is this true?' O'Neil thought. She was ready to tell the Lieutenant, Miller and every-freaking-body where they could go.

"Lieutenant, I…" she began all the while wanting to choke the life out of Miller if he didn't jump in to save her. Miller shifted in his seat but didn't say a word.

"Lieutenant, I don't really know what the f…" she stopped herself and took a long hard deep breath, "Miller, if you got something you want to say, you better say it," O'Neil told Miller.

"What O'Neil is trying to say is that this piece of paper right here that I have in my little hand just so happens to be…" Miller didn't realize it but he was on thin ice.

Lieutenant Hall cleared his throat in a manner that told them both he carried a gun too.

"See, we thought all this time that it was just a simple receipt…We bagged and tagged it and threw it into evidence and really didn't give it a second thought after that…" Miller offered to seemingly bored faces.

O'Neil squirmed in her seat looking for a way of escape.

"...But it turns out, it isn't a receipt at all...but a marker...Apparently, Mr. James Dubois owed somebody quite a bit of money," Miller finally concluded.

CHAPTER TWELVE

J esse was the younger brother of Clark's dance teacher, Karen. Karen taught African, modern and jazz dance out of the Queens Youth Center. All of the neighborhood kids hung out at the Center, so it was called. There was so much to do there, cooking classes, full court basketball, board games, dance, karate and more, and all with minimal supervision. This was during the time when the latest political agenda was to prepare the youth of America and integrate them into the work force having skills and a trade. Clark lived right next door and was there along with countless others day in and day out. So much so that Patsy Mae began to euphemistically refer to Karen as Clark's second mother. Clark didn't know from jealousy and couldn't understand why she always got an argument from Patsy Mae whenever she asked to go to the Center.

"*Can I go?   Can I go?*" Patsy Mae would say, "That should be your middle name, 'Can I go?'"

All Clark knew was that she just loved, loved, loved to dance and that she could do it to her heart's content at the Center. It was the ultimate in freedom for her, one for which her body was shaped and formed. She didn't have professional training, and she didn't need any. It all came natural. When the music started her legs and arms would meld themselves around the tune, the structure, the rhythm and the beat of it. She couldn't help herself. It was in her blood. She'd find out much later in life that her real father, Mann Green, Jr., was in fact a musician. She'd get completely lost in the music as if each song were a place that had texture, contours and a destination to it. Karen brought in songs that gave lessons and meaning to the kids like "Black Butterfly" sung by Patty Labelle. Patty would go into the stratosphere with her voice and Clark would sail along with her in movement. Clark knew that if she opened her mouth Patty's voice wouldn't come soaring out but her delicate whisper might, of the same song. No, Patty was perfect, so Clark would merely interpret her songs through the dance. Nina Simone was another one Clark took pleasure in. Simone sang the blues out of "Strange Fruit" and "Four Women" and Clark would have to hide her face for the tears she'd shed just listening to the coarse truth of her raspy tenor.

> *Strong enough to withstand the pain*
> *Inflicted again and again*
> *What do they call me*

Clark's head would be twisted to one side unable to show how deeply she suffered with each syllable and note. She loved Nina and Patty and Stevie Wonder and anyone else Karen chose to introduce them to. Clark loved everything about the Center, or home away from home, according to Patsy Mae. She'd dance there all afternoon and evening most school nights, and all day Saturday, or at least when she was finished washing and cleaning to Patsy Mae's rigorous specifications. Clark would dust the living room mostly and clean the bathroom, both of which she hated to do.

Jesse always hung around the Center too. In an adjacent room to the dance studio was an old pool table where the boys, who didn't dance or who didn't like any particular girl, gathered. Some days Clark would hang out at the felt table, especially if it was too hot to do anything else. Karen would say, "Okay that's it," having sweated herself into a puddle. Even if they hadn't finished a routine, all dancing would cease and everyone had to high tail it someplace out of her immediate sight. Clark leaned on the table one such specific day and wondered how the game was played. She didn't really want to ask any of the boys because then they would spend the greater part of the day explaining. It wasn't that interesting to her, she was just slightly curious, more bored than anything else. Jesse must have sensed that in her and began engaging her in conversation.

"The highs are the ones with the stripes and the lows are the one without," he said as if he were reading her mind.

Clark turned and smiled at him. She always had some kind of connection with him that neither could explain. Jesse always reminded her of one of her older brothers without the jokes and constant ribbing. She actually regarded him as if he were somewhat a part of her family in a cosmic way. She and Karen were together six days a week which meant they were just about related, that is again according to Patsy Mae. Though length of time together was not the qualifying factor for Clark, for her it was how Karen spoke to her. Karen was nine years her senior and Clark definitely respected her and treated her as an elder but Karen never treated Clark like she was just a child. It gave Clark something she never had at home – a voice, an opinion, a sense of self.

"The eight ball is the last one to go in," Jesse informed Clark.

Clark always got the impression that she was safe around him. He was indeed like a big brother. The other boys either ogled her or ignored her but not Jesse. He was always so gentle and kind to her. Clark had heard all kinds of things about him that she knew he didn't really want anyone to know. Karen would express certain things that Clark never repeated but also never forgot. She'd say, "Jesse is a real genius." He was elected into Bronx Science with a grade point average that was higher than that of any student in the entire region. He also had a rare blood disease that kept him indoors most of his life. Karen said that when he was younger he was not allowed outside for months at a time. Clark didn't have a clue as to what that all meant. She foolishly stayed away from him sometimes because she didn't want to make him sicker or, at the very least, uncomfortable. Yet when she was in his presence he was one of the sweetest people she had ever met.   She'd even unconscientiously gravitate towards him wherever he was in the room. Even if they never spoke, they always knew where the other was and with a silly grin exchanged, they'd say everything that needed to be said.

"Hold your hands really steady when you shoot.
Remember don't let go of the cue until the ball goes where you want it to. That's right," he instructed warmly.

She awoke on her Manhattan apartment futon flushed and curiously thinking about Jesse. He was a good-looking guy she remembered. Even with the thick glasses and full head of messy hair, she could see the potential of the man he would eventually become. It was a magical feeling as if she were actually back there with him playing that same simple game of pool. She could smell the lazy summer air and hear the chatter of the boys and girls clumsily getting to know each other. There was Karen stretching on the floor, head leaning over one leg for what seemed like hours. The traffic, the faint footsteps overhead of the basketball players on the second floor, the tenable remembrance of youth and its empowerment were all present in this unbelievably real life seeming dream. Then, as she opened her tired eyes, she could have sworn she saw him, Jesse, sitting right there at the edge of her bed. And he was saying something to her that sounded like hello? When she wiped the gook out of her cloudy lens, just like that, he vanished. Then the phone rang loudly startling her to her feet. She didn't recall picking it up, just a strained voice on the other end and what was said.

"Clark, it's Karen," long pause, "Jesse died," she plainly stated.

"..hat…What?" Clark managed but Karen's words didn't need to be repeated.

Though, it had been three years since they last spoke, Karen spoke as if picking up a conversation from yesterday. As Karen went into the details of Jesse's passing, Clark thought about all the catching up they would have to do in order to bring each other up to speed. She heard rumors that Karen was now a Dean at a middle school in Queens and that everyone respected her in the community. Clark had heard that she was doing really well; well that is except for this now latest tragedy. It was nice hearing Karen's voice, though the content of the conversation made Clark's head spin. She hadn't thought of Jesse in all these years, but there he was in her mind that morning like a fathom. He looked just as he had so long ago at the Center too, quiet and gentle still. Clark realized that she had just been visited by him not that she really knew what that meant. He was saying good-bye to loved ones possibly? That made her smile in a way that he would have thought of her at all. 'He must have really liked me or something…maybe,' she thought.

"You know, he always had a crush on you," Karen told her through the harshness of dried tears.

Suddenly Clark felt a gush of cold wind sweep across her face. It was more than a little bit eerie, spooky even especially when Clark maneuvered back over to her bed and noticed how warm it was in her apartment. She wasn't quite sure what to make of someone visiting her from beyond. Having just had that experience, it was not as comforting as some people make it out to be. Clark said something to Karen, something that people say to those who are in mourning. She tried to sound as authentically sincere as possible with practically letter perfect responses.

"He's in a better place now," Clark told her.

She wished she were right. She wanted to immediately tell Karen what had just transpired but what do you say? 'I think I just saw your dead brother? We had a marvelous chat about playing pool and then like childhood he just disappeared?' she thought.

She spent the remainder of the day in a fog. She remembered the homeless woman's words, calling it "a gift," like it was unique and wondrous. For Clark it was not so reverent. For her it was down-right frightening. Then she reasoned that, 'It could have been nothing more than an ordinary dream,' although, she couldn't fully reconcile that notion on account of the coincidences. If she didn't see him the same night of his death, if his sister hadn't called that morning maybe she might be more inclined to disbelieve. She lingered over the way everything in her past showed so picturesque and perfect. She was there. It was categorically a transportation of her very spirit to that place and that time, something out of body. It was more than just a vision, not that she knew what that meant either. It was so real. She blew off her Theater History class. She couldn't distinguish between *Commedia dell'arte* and dramatic prose if her life depended on it that day. That day she sat in the cafeteria with her head in her cup of cold coffee instead. She needed to do some personal research. She needed some personal answers. When the only spiritual friend she knew entered the room, she immediately went over to pick her brain. Arlene, a Puerto Rican spit fire, had expressed to her in confidence once that she had experienced some rather interesting occurrences too. Clark never paid it much mind until now. Now, it became clear that Arlene was quite possibly the only person she knew who could help her. It didn't take Clark long to realize that she was very much mistaken.

"Oooo, girl, then what's been happening?" Arlene asked leaning in so tightly that she forced Clark to the far side of her chair.

"Well, I...I..." Clark stuttered, suddenly afraid to continue.

Arlene was louder than Clark would have preferred especially since they were delving into the occult in a basically Catholic college. Plus the Chapel sat directly across from them, not that either ever went inside.

"Meda, sister, we can talk, ra-ight, ra-ight? I've seen things, you know," Arlene told her.

"Really? Like what?" Clark asked interestedly.

Though she wasn't completely sure that she really wanted to know.

"Look, ah be lying in the bed, you know and then all of a

sudden, whoosh, something or someone come through the wall like and I be like, 'what the hell was dat', you know. Is that a ghost, ah ax myself. Ah say, 'Arlene, you be seeing sum-in. It's real scary, you know. Ah hold my breath until they go away back through da wall, you know. Ain' ah don't be telling my man or no body na-thing. Who believe you, you know. Who believe you when you see sum-in like dat, you know," she trailed off in a whisper audibly slurping her orange juice through a straw.

Clark thought about Arlene's last statement, 'Who would believe you? No one from the grave has come back to tell anyone what it's like and yet there are these stories, near death experiences and all. They claim to have seen the light, whatever that is. They've claimed to have seen their family members and were welcomed home.' It was just a bit too nutty for Clark. Sure, she had an imagination same as everybody else, but life after death didn't make sense to her. She figured that when someone died, that that was the end of that. There was a cycle in place. Ones remains sunk into the earth and became part of its nourishment. Trees would be strengthened, minerals would be fortified, other plant life would be brightened and spring forth flourishing flowers. The rest of the body would have completely decomposed like rain evaporating on a windshield, the end.

"You got to stand up to them you know. What was it wearing?" Arlene asked.

'What was it wearing?' Clark repeated in her mind. She wished she could just go to her class now but she would be late and that would require a lie to her professor. She was a horrible liar. She'd formulate one in her head perfectly sound but by the time she spoke it would descend into a guilt-ridden pile of horse crap to the listener. She'd have to endure Arlene a little longer, just enough to be polite.

"Well, I don't know, something plaid, I think," Clark guessed.

Arlene shook her head, "Good. Good, girl."

With that, Arlene turned around pondering plaid. Clark tried not to look at her. When she did she was reminded of a witch stewing something in a caldron.

"That's good. That's good," she said.

'Yes, yes, yes, plaid,' Clark thought, 'What in the world is she talking about?'

"It's a soothing color, you know," Arlene told her.

Clark nodded yes whether she believed that statement or not.

"If it was nice to you, which ah bet it was, because of the color, then that's okay," Arlene went on and on and on and on.

It was crystal clear to Clark. She had to get away from Arlene. She had learned all she cared to for the day and was in no mood to gather any more "information" on the subject. She realized that she might be on her own with this particular, pesky problem. As scary as that was for her, she sort of thought that if Arlene could handle it then she might be in good shape. Arlene, however, did say something that unusually stuck for many years. She told her that if a person died a miserably painful death that their spirits were said to walk the earth until their souls were settled and that she would then have to see a shaman in order to get rid of it.

CHAPTER THIRTEEN

That night, Clark awoke to see a lone figure, resembling a man, hovering directly above her. He is, in fact, on top of her, just a silhouette, a breath really, a cloud. Even staring up at him, she can't figure out what she's actually seeing. His body is formed with chiseled angles, sharp, enormous and flat. He looks a little like a marble sculptured image of Adonis made out of white smoke. And there's a small scant grin titling his square shaped lips to one side. He is completely rigid, though by all accounts, a spirit. Unbeknownst to her, it's Jimmy and he's been with her many times before. In fact, his daily routine is thusly…waiting for her to come home, for he loves her. Though his capacity to love has never fully matured with his age nor anatomy and now even in death he still doesn't genuinely know what love is. Unfortunately for Clark, only the living are afforded the opportunity for growth. Jimmy's death cauterized him wherever he was in development, hence the statuesque quality. In life, he only possessed lustful thoughts towards those he admired and this was a considerable sum of individuals, anything that moved, anything female. They were beautiful if they stayed and obeyed, gorgeous if they submitted to all his carnal appetites. He didn't see the whole person ever. It was as if his eyes lingered only on those parts that could pleasure and please. And now, his latest conquest, he would say his greatest, for even unto death he clings to her, is Clark. She was a gentle flower, budding in the freshness of youth when they met. She'd embarrass easily from those bulging eyes of his as he noticed her breasts enlarging as puberty pushed forth. Her hips rounding nicely as only athletes do. All those years of dancing gave way to well-developed calves, arms and legs.   Only Jimmy would see her transformation into womanhood as an invitation. While others, more decent men, would have noticed without intrusion, Jimmy didn't see the clear line of respect that shouldered the moral, the conscious.   He saw what he wanted, to hell with the consequences. As in life, he never thought twice about what comes next. So here he waits, appearing and reappearing at will in Clark's small apartment, obsessively pretending that she is coming home to him. Before she enters, he has the house cleaned out of any other spirit who dares trespass on his domain. He likes it empty like his heart. Plus, he wants her all to himself especially since he couldn't have her in life that way. He'd be damned if he would not have her in death. In some ways he feels tied to her very soul. And he can't get enough of her. Overnight she has become his reason for being. Though he does occasionally roam to and fro and about to his old haunts and wreaks havoc whenever and wherever he chooses, his absolute peace comes wherever Clark can be found.

Sometimes he places himself on her body while she sleeps. He stretches himself across her, head to toe and holds there all night. He imagines that he is her lover or her husband and that they are so happy together. And just as a husband has rights so Jimmy contrives that he too is so endowed with those same privileges. He kisses where he pleases with remembrances of things long past. He touches with unnatural hands where his used to be and where hers still are. Though she can't feel him, he is there. He often wishes that he can gather up all of his energy and strength in the pit of his being and push her out of her body so they could be together forever.   Because he has prospered so from this unique experience, having left his remains behind, he wants a companion for the journey. His choice is Clark.   When Peter was about, Clark's live-in boyfriend; Jimmy grows angry and tries to force him away from Clark by sheer will. Suddenly Peter will lose all interest in Clark favoring a good night's rest instead. He'd roll over and fall into a deep disturbing sleep, never realizing that both he and Clark have company. Clark would wake to find that something was wrong in her very being. She couldn't quite put her finger on it but she knew that there was a stench in the air. Sometimes she'd have cuts and bruises about her body that she just couldn't explain. She'd awake bleeding from scratches on her legs and thighs, similar to those of a woman who had been raped. She'd have these wilts on her knees and on her shoulder blades as if someone had been forcing her in a position that twisted her unnaturally. She just couldn't make heads or tails of any of it and most times didn't give it that much thought. It was mostly shadowed somewhere beyond her level of comfort.   She reckoned that possibly her nails were too long and decided to keep them shortened at all times. Then she began to believe that it was Peter and the focus of her discomfort took on his face. She thought that perhaps their love-making was rougher than she remembered and decided to make those encounters fewer and fewer. Jimmy would laugh at this and knew that it was only a matter of time before Peter would be gone like all the rest. Peter was more difficult to get rid of because there was a genuine bond between Clark and him that was a lot more solid than the one night stands and mere boys who didn't want to commit themselves to Clark completely. With the others, Jimmy would treat them like the silly mortals he knew them to be and blow his fiery hatred into their faces. Clark would slowly witness them disappearing from her life one disturbing utterance at a time. She thought there was something wrong with her, why men didn't stay in her life for longer than a heartbeat. Yet, Peter was still not her husband and this fact gave Jimmy hope for a way into her life. Oddly, Jimmy never had this wide an entrance before Peter. He would not let this opportunity pass him by. He would once and for all find some way of putting Clark's beautiful body into her grave. This way they could be together forever, she his bride and he, her adoring husband.

CHAPTER FOURTEEN

P atsy Mae left a message on their answering machine. She hated the fact that she had to listen to Peter's voice telling her that she needed to wait patiently for the beep. She was equally annoyed with Billy Earl who would not stop asking her what she was cooking for dinner.

"Man, get out of my face. Stop playing. I'm trying to leave Clark a message on this daggone machine. Man, what's wrong with you? I'll be in there in a minute. Who says you don't like string beans? That's a lie. You'll eat what I fix," long pause with sounds of someone moving around. Then, "Baby...baby...I'm not sure if this thing is recording. I didn't hear the beep. Billy Earl, I know what I heard and there wasn't a beep. I didn't hear the beep. I was too listening," long pause, "Baby? Clark? It's your mother," long pause, "Call me."
Clark and Peter always had a good laugh when her mother or when his granny called. They were opposites in every way, one black, one white, one fifty something, the other eighty something, one modestly poor, the other three floor penthouse with separate maid quarters rich. Yet they had two things in common. They loathed their loved ones' mate and neither understood new technology.

"Your mother called," he greeted Clark with a kiss as she walked in.

Jimmy gave her one also but when his cold chill passed by, both Clark and Peter thought it was coming from each other. To break their awkward silence, Clark listened to the message, at first laughing then thinking of its implications. She and Peter had some serious issues on their hands that needed moments of humor to remind them why they still cared to include family in their plans. It was the holiday season once more and a decision would have to be made as to whose house they'd be going to and more importantly for what length of time. They both knew that his mother would not be the problem, or his father. Peter was the product of a divorced home and for his parents the holidays were reserved for getting things done around the house or for going on the vacation with their new lovers. Peter was long used to it. After many years of therapy he was even prepared for the excuses that would come. That's why he really had his heart set on going to meet Patsy Mae. He knew her only in theory and he was dying to see if what he pictured was in deed the real thing, a cross between Aunt Jemima and Scarlet O'Hara. Clark was more interested in going to his granny's house. It was after all on Park Avenue overlooking the entire world of Manhattan. She wanted to meet the woman who danced her way through the great depression while sipping fancy Champaign and hopping from night spot to night spot with friends in toe traveling in her chauffeur driven Rolls Royce. That kind of wealth needed an introduction into Clark's life. She was not at all materialistic but a taste of Brie cheese combined with Bosc pears imported from Belize resting delicately on English water crackers while sitting, legs loosely crossed on the roof top garden meticulously manicured and designed by an expert; beat the heck out of Patsy Mae's two by two vegetable garden in the far corner of the back yard equipped with raw green tomatoes and collard greens so dirty that Clark had to clean them with detergent. The fact that granny hated blacks, and thought that they were only useful for cleaning her eight or nine toilets notwithstanding, did not deter Clark. She was fully immersed in Peter's stories about her intriguing life and longed to meet someone of her caliber up close. She would first have to take a lesson in table manners and speak without all of the many uh ha's that seemed to precede every answer to any given question. She thought that she could pull it off though for at least an hour or two especially if Peter sat real close and held her hand the whole time.

Peter knew his granny well and knew that it would probably be more than he could bear. She would let Clark into the spacious, ornately decorated, quasi-art museum without much fuss for the sake of her precious grandson. However, Clark would not be allowed to see much more of it. Hopefully, they could make it to the drawing room for some tea but anything beyond that might need the enlisting of his father, granny's first born. However, since his father longed for a romantic weekend with his significant other rather than the chaperoning of his son and black girlfriend, Peter knew that their visit to granny's might end up in the fowler and no further. No, he would prefer Patsy Mae's. She was after all colorful and lively and spoke her mind at all times. He had first hand knowledge of this aspect of her character every time she called and he'd answer the phone.

"Hel-lo," she'd say firstly.

"Hello," he'd answer as if he were from Mr. Rogers Neighborhood.

"Oh," she'd reply, disappointedly after recognizing Peter's voice immediately, of course.

"Miss Green, it's…" he'd try.

"Well just tell her I called," she'd hang up before the d in the word *called* fully formed in Peter's hearing.

He'd hear the disconnection click just as he was about to say, "How are you?" He never took it personally, bless his soul. He figured it was his duty to be strong for the sake of Clark, whom he adored. If she could take his intolerant bigot of a little old granny than he could endure the dull miserable abandonment of a hang up.

Patsy Mae had interesting ways of showing her disappointment to Clark as well. Clark had no idea that she even meant that much to her. She would never believe in a million years that Patsy Mae could feel loneliness or empty nest syndrome. Clark always remembered her throwing her and her brothers and sisters out of the house. It was Melanie who called to say that Patsy Mae wanted to know what she was doing for Thanksgiving. Clark didn't know quite how to answer. She wanted to meet granny in the worst way instead of going back home but somehow she knew that family obligations almost always overruled personal wants and desires. It was granny who ultimately settled the issue. She requested, requested, requested the presence of her grandson for hors d'oeuvres not dinner, not dinner, not dinner. She was planning on resting for dinner as she was up there in age and required plenty of rest even on holidays.

There Clark was shaking with apprehension in the taxi ride over. She and Peter lived in a six-floor walk up in Harlem and granny was in the East seventies. It took only a second to get to granny's house, to Clark's dismay. She wondered how she could feel grown enough to live with a man and yet too young to handle a simple pâté and cracker with his family. She was at best starkly inadequate and at worst fidgety and uncomfortable. A faceless maid took her coat. Clark felt undressed and embarrassed by the dress she'd worn and suddenly had the desire to run home and change. There would be no running home to do anything as they could not be too early or too late. Granny would not hear of it. She was the grand dame and everyone obeyed her every order carrying each detail out to the letter. Clark asked an all too relaxed for her taste Peter how she looked. To which Peter answered with a shrug, "Fine." Clark had to resist the urge of feeling like she'd been deserted. So far he was no help and she hoped that that behavior would not continue throughout the evening.

They sat in the library filled with too many antiques for Clark to count, which looked more like an eclectic museum had a yard sale. There were three Mahal Persian rugs strategically placed over the wide cherry wood planked floors. Charles Large Italian imported sofas flanked the doorways at each end of the room together with carved engraved end tables. Each item was unique and nothing matched exactly as she was so used to seeing in every other home she'd entered. Yet everything blended together perfectly. There was harmony that she thought sure if someone was watching her would know that she was definitely the *thing* out of place. Clark was indeed afraid to sit down.

"Sit," granny ordered.

The couch had no give to it. It was probably centuries old at a time when people used bricks as pillows. Clark felt like she was royalty just with one cheek on the edge. She wanted to be able to maneuver easily in case granny decided to change positions. Another faceless maid served tea. She was in and out of the room so quickly that Clark scarcely could identify her presence.

"Drink," granny ordered.

With that, Peter, Clark and granny drank some of the bitterest tea and some of the hardest biscuits, which reminded Clark of cookies.

"Sonny tells me you sing…uh…uh," granny started.

"Clark, granny. Her name is Clark," Peter jumped in gallantly.

Though Clark wished he hadn't. She was dying to know if she even knew her name. She would have allowed her to stumble at it all night if need be.

"Yes," Clark simply answered.

She did not think herself a particularly good singer but if granny wanted to hear a tune of two she felt she could muster something up. Granny rang a little bell and yet another faceless maid came out of nowhere and as if she could read granny's mind helped and escorted granny into another room. Peter raised his eyebrows way up indicating that they should follow granny and they did. They all went down a long hallway also decorated through and through with everything an art collector could possibly desire. Then they entered the entertainment room. Clark saw at least seven other rooms suitable for entertaining but this was the only one with a signature grand piano given to her by Duke Ellington and his Duke Ellington Orchestra. Clark's knees didn't wobble too badly until she saw someone who looked vaguely like a musician standing right beside it.

"Well, I'd like to hear something," granny told her.

Clark looked over to Peter who seemed as if he wanted to hear something too. Clark could have killed him. She wanted him to suggest otherwise but he sat down next to granny as if they were an audience. Even the maid lingered and waited for the first note. Yet, Clark couldn't remember a single lyric to a single song. She thought her brain had decided to take a vacation. She looked up at the ceiling trying desperately to will a song up in her system. Nothing was coming for the longest time. Then the pianist sat down and started playing something. Clark thanked heaven that he had because trucks could have been driven through her silence. She smiled a nervous smile to him and he smiled back. Once she relaxed a little she realized that he was playing a song that she did know. She couldn't quite figure out exactly what it was but she knew that she knew it somehow.

"You want to try this?" he asked her, "New York State of Mind?"

Clark began to sing. She was so happy that she knew the words and that he followed her whether she sang it correctly or not. He was a real professional and she knew that he knew that she was not.

"Some folks like to get away take a holiday from the neighborhood…" she sang.

Granny sat up straighter listening intently.

"…Hop a flight to Miami Beach or to Hollywood…" she went on, "…I'm taking a Greyhound on the Hudson River Line…I'm in a New York State of Mind."

Granny was absorbing every iota of the song. She was being transported back to a time when all of the greats frequented her house and jammed to the wee hours. Her eyes were twinkling and moist. Once the song was over she even applauded. Clark had done real good, real good, real good. She had managed to do something that Peter and she thought impossible. She had won over bigoted granny. From then on Clark was invited to everything. With granny she had dined at The Four Seasons, in their private suite, had ice-cream at Lutéce, at the owners' table and had seen practically a full season at the Metropolitan Opera House, front row seats. Granny could barely walk but she did know how to have a good time.

CHAPTER FIFTEEN

ernie had to hand it to them. This might actually be a real honest to goodness trial. It started off with Detective Miller being called to take the witness stand. He sauntered over to it with the serious gait of a man sure of himself, a man who was on top of his game. He slammed his hand on the Bible with authority and provoked the trainee court officer to swear him in.

"Do yu' 'ear to tell the tru..th da' whole tru..th sooo help yu' Godd," said the very young, very traumatized court officer.

"I do," swore Detective Miller as if he were cursing.

Then he took the seat as if he were straddling an untamed horse of which only he could control. He was cocky and wanted everyone in the building to know that he didn't want to be there but had no choice. He also wanted everyone to know that he was the only one who had all of the answers. Bernie surely wished someone had. He was tired of having to endure work lately. He was ready for retirement. He glanced momentarily at the jurors as the defendant's attorney, Andrew Harrison, III, Esquire, was riffling through a mountain of papers to find one piece in particular. The jury, by and large, was made up of mostly professional people who seemed anxious to get on with their lives. Not one of them had asked Bernie about how much they would be paid for their civic duty but rather just how long was all this going to take. Bernie got to know them real well by their surprising lack of chat chit and by how they generally turned their noses up to everything and everyone including him. The spectators, though few, sat calmly and attentively waiting patiently for the trial to begin.   Obvious to everyone in attendance was the fact that all of the attention was beyond a shadow of a doubt upon the rough-neck over at the defendant's table.

He was indeed a sight to behold. Bernie had counted at least twenty gashes on his face alone. The one that stretched down from his left ear to just below his chin looked as if it had been sewn up by hand with a Dollar Store sewing kit. His name was Mr. Clinton James Thomas, his friends called him Busta, his occupation, professional criminal. His wrap-sheet was thicker than the Bible. Apparently, he began his illustrious career of crime at the tender age of four, wherein he killed his neighbor's pitbull because it barked at him. He waited until everyone in the house was asleep, then crept into his neighbor's backyard and stabbed the poor dog in the eye. A witness to the offense, the neighbor's ten-year-old son, said Mr. Thomas laughed while watching the dog yelp as he bled to death. Mr. Thomas was the most menacing creature Bernie had ever seen in life. Besides his looks, he had no morals, no remorse and no guilt whatsoever. When Harrison said good-morning to him, as he was being led into the courtroom, Bernie could have sworn his reply was, "…fuc…mornin'…" slurred and angry like someone just woke him up. It was 10:30 am! One could barely look at him without wanting to hurl for what appeared to be dried blood stuck in the cervices and groves of the sores surrounding the random, patchwork stitches. Several wounds were definitely fresh. Then there were the knuckles that too had dried blood or some sort of human matter upon them. There was cracked skin everywhere about them. It was as if his hands had suffered a massive sun burn that left the skin purple, scabbed and raw. Bernie thought he looked like he was falling apart but it was his eyes that stopped him from feeling pity for the man. His eyes were the most threatening shade of green with a hint of gray, just like a ferocious tiger. His eyebrow skin rested over them so heavily that all one could see was a faint essence of the color. Though thinner than thread, a rumor circulated that he was powerfully strong and had to be chained to his seat. Bernie heard that he could use anything as a weapon and therefore, nothing was placed on the table in front of him. His own attorney and associate attorney sat at least a yard and a half away from him. If looking at a person and telling the whole story were appropriate, Bernie would have summed it all up by saying, "damn scary." That's what he told Lillie, anyway, not wanting to frighten her but just to say that he might not be coming home for lunch as per her request. It was a dark day in court. The sky was over cast and gloomy and everything and everyone was in a foul, miserable mood but none more so than Judge Binghamton. He was just fit to be tied. Try as he might he could not dislodge himself from this particular wretched seemingly never-ending case of one James P. DuBois a/k/a Jimmy. He had gone so far as to bring Judge Reingold's wife a bouquet of Daffodils, her favorite flower, in an effort to butter her up so she could then persuade her husband to switch cases with him. In hindsight he realized that it was an exceptionally foolish thing to do because Reingold was a notoriously jealous man. As was Reingold's practice, he took the entire gesture of a peace offering, before some major begging the wrong way. Reingold saw the lovely arrangement and assumed that Binghamton was trying to seduce his wife right there in front of him and in his own house no less. Binghamton yelled back at him when Reingold insisted that there was foul play afoot.   Then Binghamton was just shy of saying that Reingold's wife's face looked like the wrinkled behind of an old dirty pig when Reingold took him by the shoulders and pushed him out of his front door.   Needless to say it did not go well and hence, Reingold was Binghamton's last resort having asked every other Judge he could find already, there he was on the bench muttering obscenities into his clinched fists all day long. Bernie tried not to let any of it get to him. Though now he had two people he had to contend with, the delinquent defendant and now the jacked-up Judge. He didn't know which was worst. At least with the defendant he would only be concerned for his life and the welfare of others should something go down but with the Judge he had his pension, his job, his wife and kids, his livelihood and to top it all off his sanity to consider.

After the preliminary questions were asked, name, rank and Precinct, Andrew Harrison, III, Esquire was ready to get down to the true business at hand, winning his case. He showed Detective Miller a thin slip of paper.

"Recognize this, Detective?" Harrison asked waving it about like a carrot before a rabbit.

Detective Miller smirked out a nod. Then he showed the slip of paper to every single member of the jury. Bernie felt a little agitated as did Judge Binghamton when some of the jurors couldn't see it and had to get out their glasses. Then they couldn't figure out what it said and gestured that they had some questions.

"Let's move it along," rudely shouted Judge Binghamton.

Bernie knew that it was never a good sign when the Judge started yelling this early on, especially not for the attorneys and the defendant definitely didn't have a chance.

"Let's see now, how did you come about this particular piece of paper, Detective Miller?" Harrison asked.

"We found it in the deceased's pocket…" Detective Miller answered but was cut off by Harrison.

"…In his pocket or by his pocket?" Harrison queried.

"Huh…in his pocket, sir," barked Detective Miller with the 'sir' sounding like bastard.

"What's that you say, Detective? In his pocket or by his pocket?" Harrison asked again.

"Well, once we emptied his pocket, it was by his pocket, but…" Detective Miller answered curiously.

"…Sooooo, it was by his pocket at the time you found it? Is that cor-rect…?" Harrison interrupted as if he'd stumbled upon the truth.

"…Hey, look now…That's not what I was saying…" Detective Miller interrupted right back.

"…But you just said by the pocket, did you not?" asked Harrison, as if he caught Detective Miller in a lie.

"Wait a minute now…" Detective Miller jumped up and stood over Harrison like he was going to hit him.

"Counselors," long pause, "…approach the bench," Judge Binghamton ordered sternly.

Both attorneys hustled forward to Judge Binghamton. Judge Binghamton took his time with his next statement to them. He wanted to make sure that there was no misunderstanding. They each had to know that he would confess to the crime himself if that would end the hell of this trial he was enduring. As the cops drug him to his private cell, he'd have a smile on his face knowing that at least he wouldn't have to preside over the murder trial of one James P. DuBois a/k/a Jimmy any longer. Bernie had to take in a deep breath as not to laugh because he knew, after so many years with Judge Binghamton, what was coming.

"I'm going to tell you this only once, okay? Can both of you hear me because I'm not going to repeat myself without canceling this trial first?" he asked in a simmering whisper.

They both nodded yes hesitantly.

"In the pocket, out of the pocket? If that's your gottdamn damn defense we're going to be here all gottdamn night. Do I look like I want to be here all gottdamn night? Do I sound like I want to be here gottdamn all night? What might I do to you if you were in my company all gottdamn night?" he bore his eyes into both of them but especially into Andrew Harrison, III, Esquire.

Harrison took a step back and hung his head down.

"Look at me, Counselor," shouted Judge Binghamton.

Harrison's head snapped back up and he gave Judge Binghamton his full attention.

"When I said move this along, gottdamnit, I meant it! Now move this along! Counselor, you have one more question for this witness," proclaimed Judge Binghamton.

Harrison looked like he wanted to reply but that was only a look. No sound came from his lips. Bernie had never seen Judge Binghamton interfere to this degree with the attorneys but it was only fair after that crazy line of questioning. No one in the entire state could understand what difference it made.

With their marching instructions from the Judge, the attorneys made haste to their post. Harrison approached Detective Miller again. He paused thinking of his next question for it would be his last. He wanted to review his notes but thought better of walking back to his table and thereby extending his time with this witness. He knew that he just had one chance to convey what his notes said fifteen questions would do. He wasn't particularly good at thinking on his feet. It wasn't his custom to do courtroom magic tricks. He was a methodical thinker. He liked to draw everything out then mull it over and only after several drafts introduce it anew. Alas, he didn't have that kind of time. Judge Binghamton looked threateningly over at him. Harrison wasn't afraid of him. He just didn't want the Judge's irrational anger to compromise his case.

"Detective Miller, did you yourself witness this piece of paper coming out of the decedent's pocket?" Harrison finally asked.

Everyone began to understand what he was eluding to when he asked that question. He was trying to sever the connection of his client from the evidence and therefore evidence from the deceased. He wanted it to seem as if the officers collected everything at the crime scene and inadvertently picked up a few stray pieces of garbage. Bernie thought that that was a reasonable assumption until Miller answered.

"Look, I took it out myself. And before you ask, yes, I wore Police standard issued gloves," said Detective Miller very much on the defense.

"Oh, huh, no further questions," said Harrison with a tinge of uncertainty over what had just transpired.

CHAPTER SIXTEEN

It was a typical night except that her roommate was snorting so loudly that it sounded more like roaring. That was part of what woke her. The other was purely cosmetic. If she didn't wash her hair before morning, she doubted she'd have time later on or that she could show her face in public. They would be on the road all day heading south towards Memphis. She couldn't wait because touring Elvis' home was definitely going to be on the agenda even if she had to see it in between acts. She glanced over at *weirdo*, so she was called, her new roommate. She was ostracized by everyone in the cast having cursed out a few for no apparent reason, and left a couple of nasty notes for others affixed to their dressing room mirrors. She did interesting things on stage too. She'd look one way at the audience then turn up stage making abnormal faces at her fellow actors. Clark wasn't fortunately in any of her scenes hence she was placed in a room with her in this lowly run down hotel in southern Illinois. Clark thought she was a *weirdo* too but refused to say so when asked by the road manager. She wanted to play team and to stay employed. It was a good job for someone new to show business and she wanted to prove that she could be a real actress. Besides she thought this all would make a good story one day when she told people how she paid her dues along the way to becoming a star. In truth, she didn't, in fact, think that *weirdo* would hurt her but she did honestly believe that some of her weirdness might rub off.

She rolled from side to side on the mattress dreading the idea of rising before dawn for any reason least of all the work it would take to tame her wild head of hair. She wore it natural the whole tour, which meant all over her head. She swung her feet round and scampered into the bathroom. She sat on the toilet for a good five minutes before realizing that her feet were wet. She didn't have the energy to speculate why because she was too busy contemplating whether to wash her hair in the sink or in the bathtub. She didn't want to get undressed so she decided on the small sink. Her head could barely fit let alone her hair but she refused to acquiesce to reason. She squeezed and contoured in the porcelain bowl until her hair got washed. With a tiny towel wrapped around her neck she returned to bed to roll or braid. Again the dampness of the floor made her pause as well as the fact that she could have sworn she saw the tub full of water. This time she stopped and observed the rug. It was soaking wet now. The compression of her steps sunk down into the floorboards. She leaped into bed trying to avoid touching it all together. Once she wiped the excess water from her hair and feet she was back to the business at hand of looking presentable for the stage. Once she started the rolling process all moisture investigative probing ended. She was tired and just wanted and needed rest.

It was just as she was about to doze off though, when she saw it, him, them. A priest - all dressed in brown with a holy collar walked or rather materialized into the room. It would have been startling enough had it been through the hotel door or window but it was instead through the opposite adjourning wall. At first formless, then they seemed to melt and appear as if solid through the sheet rock. Clark held herself steady. It sent a chill down her spine and her eyes magnified twice their normal size. He came over recognizing that she could see him. He must have sensed that she was frightened for he sat at the far end of her bed and simply smiled. Clark could not move any of her muscles. Her face was a frozen cast and her body was cemented into the covers. She mentally screamed but nothing was audible. It spoke too and then reached out its hand towards her. She couldn't even move to shrink away from him. Then out of her periphery there through the wall came more visitors. Another man dressed all in black, in a suit that looked to be the fashion a decade ago. He carried a large white parasol that had a fluffy ruffled apron at its trim. Underneath the beautifully crafted umbrella was a woman, a girl, maybe a teenager. She was dressed in white matching the frilly covering over her head. The man in brown recognized them from the reflection off of Clark's pupils. He turned and joined the line of now at least six or seven people, beings, apparitions - ghosts. Then they marched somberly and silently, thank goodness, across the room and then vaporized into the sheet rock wall facing the street. Leaving Clark so frightened that she fainted on her pillow.

Early that next morning with just a tad more anxiety than anything else, Clark approached the main desk. The counter was empty. It was not, by any stretch of the imagination, a busy place. It was *any inn U.S.A.* and two people of East Indian decent were behind the counter. The smell of curry was about. Clark wasn't quite sure where it was originating from but rather than seek out its origin, she focused her attention on the pictures of the motel's past. There were several black and white and sepia tone photographs of it at its inception in the fifties, which could have been a hundred years ago as far as Clark was concerned. She was young and though familiar with the past, it didn't hold much significance to her. The aged images looked just that, aged and therefore ancient.

"Cani 'elp yu?" the man spoke and the woman hovered round for Clark's answer.

"Ah…I….ah…I…hum…I…" Clark couldn't fault them for glancing at each other as if there was something wrong with her.

Unfortunately, due to her fretful sleep, her rollers fell out leaving her hair standing on end – again. And, meanwhile, outside she could see her manager practically breaking his arm to get her to join them in the van. He kept tapping his watch, bulging his eyes out as if to say get your butt over here pronto. Clark could also see that everyone else hadn't exited their rooms as yet, so she still had at least five minutes more before she would be permanently placed on his bitch list. Arnie was gay and handsome and most proud of being catty and capable of holding a grudge for-ev-er. He would give her the cold shoulder for the remainder of the trip, of that she was sure. Clark really didn't want that to happen because it came with less and less opportunity to be rehired. Actors had to play nice with their road managers else they wouldn't be on the road for long.

"I was over there last night and…" she began, finally, pointing out the room that she and *weirdo* were in.

"Ch'es…" the man spoke again.

He and the woman were very patient with Clark and simply stuck their faces out towards her to continue. Clark cleared her throat knowing that the next words from her mouth were going to be either the most bizarre thing they ever heard or something that would give them cause the throw her out.

"Well…I…I was wondering…" long pause, "…This is going to sound strange…" she thought she'd at least warn them of what was coming next.

"Ch'es. Ch'es," the woman spoke this time, "Was 'verything al-rright?"

The woman seemed to think that there was something wrong with the room. Clark thought, 'There was something wrong with the room, all right.'

"No, no, nothing like that…I mean, yes, everything was fine. It's just that…I mean…Did anyone ever, I'm just curious, mind you, not that there was anything wrong, it's just that, I'm just saying, just curious now, but…did anyone ever drown in that room?" Clark took a small step back away from the counter.

She felt like she needed to give them room to breath. Yet, to her surprise, the couple merely looked at each other inquisitively, as if they were seriously contemplating her question.

"Well, let me 'tink," the woman spoke and leaned her head in her hand and lifted her eyes towards the ceiling.

"We are not the original owners, you know, but…" the man said, "I do believe that someone did die in that room."

He rattled something off in Hindu to the woman. The woman nodded her head up and down in recognition of his statements.

"Ch'es. Ch'es. They did say that it was a girl. Ch'es a girl died in the tub. She drowned. Suicide," the woman said.

All they saw was Clark's back as she bolted out of the door, fleeing towards the van. She didn't stop until she was wedged into one of the seats with a seat belt fastened around her little body. She was really, and truly ready to leave. Arnie raised an eyebrow and stared but didn't say a word. He was used to dramatic actresses and knew that Clark was just one of many. Clark was shaken by all that she had witnessed and felt sure that she couldn't contain it all. She needed someone to talk to about it but who? It's not every day that you see a dead drowned girl with her priests, etc., walking with her to God only knows where. Clark stared out of the window the whole ride as the tour went back towards Tennessee. She had a lot on her mind and looked forward to now seeing Peter and being at home.

"We need to talk," Peter told her over the phone at their last rest stop.

Clark now had thoughts of Peter's cryptic statement together with her ghost stories to make the trip seem like a drug-induced hallucination. Her friend, Thelma, beautiful Southern Belle, kept asking her if she wanted a drink. Clark kept answering, "Heavily." Thelma was used to her father and uncle who made their own hooch in their yards. Thelma would say that if you drank it, and lit a match, you could actually blow yourself up. Clark wished beyond reason that she had a little of that kind of action.

"When will you be home?" Peter asked tersely.

Clark didn't like his tone at all. He seemed as if he was making an ultimatum.

"You know that this is my profession, my job," Clark yelled, sensitive and aching to yell and scream some more at the audacity of him asking her to stay home rather than go out on anymore tours.

"I don't know if I can take another few months of you not being here," Peter told her, all this over a pay phone on her quarter.

Clark was not the type of person who could take the whole do this or else scenario. She felt like she was back at home, five-years old with her mother telling her what to do all the time. She was now less than enthusiastic about going home. She didn't want to walk into a fight. She wanted to run home to him with outstretched arms having him listen to the wild time that she had on the road. If no one else wanted to hear about her brush with the dearly departed, she knew that he would at the very least listen to it with an open mind. With this latest development however, she wasn't sure.

"What are you saying?" she asked him.

Meanwhile she was thinking that he better retract his latest comments with a string of apologies. None came.

"I'm just saying that I'm not happy with the way things are," he told her.

Clark couldn't believe that he was bringing all this up while she was surrounded by Mack trucks and rat infested toilets. The phone itself was sticky from the many grimy hands that had held it. Clark thought about the drown girl and wondered if even she might have been one who handled the receiver. She was concerned about her mental state at this point because every thought made her return back to that girl and what led her to killing herself. Clark had her own thoughts of suicide at those times when things were not going her way where she just couldn't imagine a future on the horizon. Only to realize that at her funeral it would be too late for anyone to repair the damage that they had made her suffer. She knew that they would all be regretful and mournful but would she have given them any opportunity to redeem themselves. She had always liked the make up part of any argument, where gifts were given in remembrance of a friendship prior to the fight. She just thought the whole idea of suicide wasn't exactly expedient. If the purpose was to get back at loved ones then outliving them would seem a smidgen more effective. Only in life can one drive another insane, case in point, what Peter was doing to her. It took extreme effort for Clark to listen without retort, response, or anger. Though she was so flipping mad that her entire body grew hot with every word, threat, utterance he spoke. 'Who does he think he is?' she thought.

CHAPTER SEVENTEEN

*T*he Parables of the Mustard Seed and the Yeast ¹⁸Then Jesus asked, "What is the kingdom of God like? What shall I compare it to? ¹⁹It is like a mustard seed, which a man took and planted in his garden. It grew and became a tree, and the birds of the air perched in its branches."

²⁰Again he asked, "What shall I compare the kingdom of God to? ²¹It is like yeast that a woman took and mixed into a large amount of flour until it worked all through the dough."

The Narrow Door

²²Then Jesus went through the towns and villages, teaching as he made his way to Jerusalem. ²³Someone asked him, "Lord, are only a few people going to be saved?"

He said to them, ²⁴"Make every effort to enter through the narrow door, because many, I tell you, will try to enter and will not be able to. ²⁵Once the owner of the house gets up and closes the door, you will stand outside knocking and pleading, 'Sir, open the door for us.'
"But he will answer, 'I don't know you or where you come from.'

²⁶"Then you will say, 'We ate and drank with you, and you taught in our streets.'

²⁷"But he will reply, 'I don't know you or where you come

from. Away from me, all you evildoers!'

[28] "There will be weeping there, and gnashing of teeth, when you see Abraham, Isaac and Jacob and all the prophets in the kingdom of God, but you yourselves thrown out. [29]People will come from east and west and north and south, and will take their places at the feast in the kingdom of God. [30]Indeed there are those who are last who will be first, and first who will be last." Passage Luke 13:

Bernie thought, 'What in the world is he talkin' 'bout?' All he knew was that there was something very irksome about those words. He thought about that particular issue together with the near fatal mistake of saying what he thought out loud in front of his wife.

"So now you know more than Jesss-us, Mr. Bernard Jeremiah Kennedy, Jr.?" said Lillie watchful of the next remark to escape Bernard's wayward lips.

"I...uh...uh, what?" when in trouble confuse the issue, Bernie decided.

"'Uh, uh, what?' You're the one bring up the fact of what, Jesus, our Lord and Savior, blessed Lamb of God, Messiah say..." Lillie went on obviously just getting warmed up.

Bernie didn't rightly know where to look and felt that he was too close to Lillie's back hand.

"...Holy trinity, the blood, the blood, the blood, the blood..." she cried.

"Honey, now, honey.   I didn't mean anything t'all by...Honey..." Bernie truly tried to console her.

"…the One who was slain…" she whimpered and fiercely hugged herself.

Bernie wanted to pull over and reason with her.

"…the One slain for our sin, our iniquities, the chastisement of our peace was upon HIM…" she sobbed.

"Jesus," Bernie sighed.

"HOW DARE YOU USE THE LORD'S NAME IN VAIN!" Lillie shouted.

The car swerved right and skidded left as Bernie tried to maintain his ten and two o'clock position on the wheel.

"I was talkin' 'bout Preacher John not Jesus, honey," Bernie spoke ever so sweetly to her.

"Preacher John? Preacher John? He was quoting the word of God! The precious bread of life! The awesome revelation for mankind! The truth!" Lillie shouted.

Silence.

Bernie didn't know what to say as they approached their house and Lillie tore out of the car before it had come to a complete stop. He didn't know what to say as she threw his plate of spare ribs at him and tossed piping hot buttered biscuits at his head.

"Thanks, dear," Bernie timidly told her.

He ate like a man at his last meal, slowly with trepidation. He would sleep on the couch for sure. He would receive the silent treatment for a week or so, for sure. He would duck and weave whenever he saw something sharp in her hands for a while, to be sure. Lillie wasn't a violent woman ordinarily. She was, in fact, a kind gentle creature, but if she had quarrel with anyone, it was most probably deserving.

Bernie was none too thrilled that next morning either. Between the sore, aching back and positively unyielding neck, he couldn't stand correctly and to move his head from side to side would require vice grips. There was a loose floorboard that he'd been meaning to fix for years, which he now believed Lillie arose early just to walk back and forth across at his expense. It'd squeak and he'd peep out at her with a squinted eye wanting to catch her grinning at his misfortune. However, she was either too much of a lady or far too advanced in her cleverness to get caught. Bernie couldn't discern the truth, with such an extreme lack of sleep, and a stiffness that made him feel like a piece of wood. He knew deep in his heart that he was affirmatively not trying to besmirch the name of the Lord and savior. On the contrary, he knew that Jesus obviously knew exactly what he was talking about, being the son of God and all, but he was certain Preacher John hadn't a clue. What with the "…earthly portholes and passageways between heaven and earth…" and the "…legal authority to transcend from heaven…" and such, Bernie thought it all absolute, 'Nonsense,' as far as he was concerned. 'Sounds more like science fiction,' he thought. 'Hell, I could make up something like that too and get the pastor's paid for that matter,' he surmised, 'I'll take it right out of Star Trek and no one would be the wiser.' That was all he really wanted to say to Lillie but he should have known to tiptoe, and above all tread lightly, and for Christ's sake be completely respectful around Jesus, or else.

Once Bernie had a moment to really think about Preacher John's sermon, he realized that all he was talking about was faith. Bernie just didn't like his approach is all and wanted Lillie to explain it to him in plain English. 'But, Lillie was like some kind of attack dog fiercely defending *the* defender,' Bernie thought and had to laugh. Sure, he could smile now that he was safely at work surrounded by armed guards. Lillie had no power there save in his head and she tormented him there relentlessly all darn day. That is, interspersed with his current thoughts of Judge Binghamton's recent behavior. For one, Judge Binghamton had practically snapped his head off when he was delayed in bringing in the jury. The attorneys had demanded a closed courtroom for a few questionable questions. Then the jury was brought in afterwards. Bernie wanted to tell his Honor that some of them had to go to the bathroom but Judge Binghamton wasn't concerned about people having to "go" in their seats. He had been there and done that already with the now infamous, Mr. Raymond Brown. The only thing that Judge Binghamton was concerned about was eradicating himself from this particular court case. Everybody knew it too. At best he was short tempered, bitter and cold, at worst he was down right mean and capable of ruining careers.

"I didn't ask you for no damn explanation," he mumbled to Bernie as the jury was being seated.

Bernie knew better than to respond. Had he done so, there would definitely have been a fight. And for Bernie, in the mood he was in, it would be a physical one. Bernie had to laugh inwardly imagining two relatively old men, one in a robe, throwing jabs at one another in front of a packed courtroom. Bernie sighed, and let it all go, fully recognizing that neither of them was really upset with the other. It was that loony trial that had them both on edge. Bernie looked across at *damn scary*, the defendant, with his new suit on. It was a solid shade of emerald green with pink piping along the corners. He looked like a broken Christmas gift especially as he sat with his team of attorneys all in their charcoal grey and navy blues. However, no one really looked at the defendant long enough to have any opinion let alone one that would illicit a response from him. He still seemed menacing though clad in the bright colors. His lawyers hadn't managed to tone down the evil that emanated from the man at all, if that's what they were shooting for. It was Bernie's job to keep watch on him and everyone else, so he glanced over from time to time but never long enough for it to ever be misconstrued as outright staring.

Andrew Harrison, III, Esquire was busy preparing to question yet another witness.

"Your Honor, I call Mrs. Anita de Martini to the stand," he said.

A stunningly beautiful, island woman clothed in a vibrant yellow skirt suit strutted up front as if on a runway.

"Do you swear to tell the truth the whole truth and nothing but the truth so help you God?" the little trainee asked.

He had practiced that line over and over again so that he no longer had to write it on his palm in order to recite it. He grinned in admiration at himself and barely waited for Mrs. de Martini's sultry, "Yeeeesssss."

"You may be seated," he abruptly told her.

Mrs. de Martini quickly sat and crossed her legs as if she wanted everyone within miles to see them. They were absolute perfection. The muscle tone shaped them in such a way as to lead every man's eyes sloping down each curve and turn. She twined one around the other and then the toe rested round the ankle of the same leg forming an intriguing mystery. Her body was agile and nimble, breasts perky, pushing her dress top to the full extent of the darts. The very essence of the woman screamed sensuality.

"State your full name for the record, Mrs. de Martini," Harrison said shyly fanning himself as he approached her.

"Ah, Mrs…a…der Mar-teen-y," she uttered in unmistakably incomplete, sloppy, irksome English.

One could hear a pin drop. She looked as though she came straight off a yacht from some exotic land; but unfortunately, it was definitely by way of Queens. Her squeaky accent actually assaulted everyone's eardrums in court that day but none more so than Judge Binghamton, who gestured away from her every time her lips parted. Suddenly the beautiful silhouette that her gorgeous figure created began to look clutched and hunched.

"Could ya' 'ear mey, hunny?" Mrs. de Martini asked the stenographer.

The stenographer didn't even lift her eyes in her direction.

"Could 'ya or whut?" she asked again, indignantly.

Judge Binghamton jumped and shifted in his seat. He was the closest to her and that was assuredly about to become everybody's problem.

"She heard you fine, Mrs. de Martini," Judge Binghamton said sternly, then cut his eye at Harrison as if he would actually *cut* him.

"Ah, Mrs. de Martini…" Harrison began before he was ready on account of not wanting to be prematurely dead.

"Ann-ni-tah," Mrs. de Martini interrupted.

"Ah, Anita…" Harrison continued.

She smiled and looked lovely once again. As long as her

mouth was closed, she could pull off a strikingly beautiful picture.

"…You gave a statement to the police, did you not?" Harrison asked.

"Did I not, whut?" Mrs. de Martini asked.

"Did you or didn't you give a statement to the police?" Harrison rephrased.

"Whot polize? I know quite a few of 'em? Which ones and for whut raison?" Mrs. de Martini asked.

The jury actually laughed because it did seem like a fair enough question. Judge Binghamton rolled an even wickeder stare over at Harrison.

"On the night of July 11th 1975, did you give a statement to the police about what you had witnessed that night regarding my client?" Harrison asked her pointing to the defendant.

"May-bee," Mrs. de Martini responded coyly.

Bernie wasn't certain but he could have sworn that Judge Binghamton was about to cry.

"Mrs. de Martini…" Harrison began.

"Annnnnnnnnnnnnnnnnn-ni-tah," Mrs. de Martini cut him off again.

"Anita, what did you tell the police that night when you allegedly said that you observed my client?" Harrison asked hoping beyond reason that she would just answer the question.

"I'm not sure-r. Could ya' repress mey memory?" Mrs. de Martini asked.

Bernie almost lost it when he heard her say repress. Harrison started to correct her, thought better of it and just pulled out the police report. He couldn't understand why Mrs. de Martini was acting like she was on American Bandstand instead of a witness stand. Judge Binghamton reached across his bench and opened up a bottle of Bayer Aspirin. He took out two pills that didn't resemble the brand at all and plopped them into his mouth. They seemed to immediately calm him but it was like the wearing of a ship before the squall. His eyes grew glassy and he began to look a little too languid for Bernie's taste.

"Exhibit 12 A!" Harrison shouted, then simply read from the report, "Quote, 'I saw him pick up a bottle and just start swinging at him, at that man. It was awful.'"

Mrs. de Martini looked at Harrison as if she didn't know what he was talking about.

"Mrs. de Martini….Ah…Mrs. de Martini?…" asked Harrison looking directly at her, trying to get her attention.

However, now Mrs. de Martini was turned otherwise, elsewhere. She was actually eyeing *damn scary* as if she was trying to get to know him better. Harrison as well as everyone else in the courtroom turned to see exactly what had her so enamored. When they all realized that it was the defendant, they looked otherwise elsewhere too in order to avoid being caught in his gaze. Bernie thought it was a rather disturbing display to say the least, what with her dress hitched to her waist leaving nothing to the imagination and him suited up in his psychedelic threads.

"…Mrs. de Martini! Mrs. de Martini...!" Harrison shouted.

"An-ni-ta," Judge Binghamton practically sang to her, suspiciously tranquil.

Her head snapped around at attention.

"Yes. Yes, I did say something like 'dat," Mrs. de Martini told Harrison, "but…"

"But, what, Mrs. de Martini? But what?" Harrison practically begged.

Everyone in the courtroom leaned forward in her direction in anticipation.

"But he look different now," she said as if she wouldn't mind having him over for dinner.

"Different?" Harrison said enjoying what he perceived to be coming next.

"I object," said prosecuting Attorney, Michael Solomon springing from his chair.

"You object to what?" waved Judge Binghamton in a yawn.

Bernie studied Judge Binghamton then the content of the Bayer bottle on his bench.

"I…I…" stuttered Solomon.

"But, what, Mrs. de Martini?" Harrison continued this time smiling over his shoulder at Solomon.

"But he looked…I don't know…well…" she went on squinting at him to get a better look.

"He looked like what, Mrs. de Martini, Anita, what, what?" Harrison kept at her to continue.

"He's badgering the witness, your Honor," shouted Solomon from his table.

Judge Binghamton simply waved Solomon away again as if he was a pesky fly.

"He looked what, An-ni-ta? Please tell the court for the record what you saw," Harrison said ever so sweetly.

"I don't know, he looked…meaner, I guess," she said and winked at *damn scary*.

That was not the answer Harrison was looking for. Witness after witness, it was becoming quite clear to him if for no one else that his client was indeed guilty. He felt a rather sinking feeling in the pit of his stomach. Suddenly he needed air, fresh air. He wanted to turn tail and run out of the courtroom. Judge Binghamton simply stared over at him from the podium. As far as he was concerned he could care less how this trial went so long as it went. His friends were all out golfing; meanwhile he was stuck with the likes of dregs and drones of a/k/a Jimmy's life. Each person that got up on the witness stand was a character, the likes of which he never wanted to see again.

"You may step down," Judge Binghamton informed Mrs. de Martini.

Bernie took her outstretched hand and led her out of the box. She winked at him in a way that made him blush. It wasn't until he lifted his head that he observed Harrison glaring at him. Harrison obviously wasn't finished with this particular witness. He wanted to prove that she didn't see his client at all that night, what with it being so dark underneath the bridge. Judge Binghamton wasn't deliberately trying to ruin his case, but he wasn't trying to help it either. Harrison's client, however, was looking at him. He had a look on his face that said he wasn't getting the fairest of trials. When Harrison walked back to his table, *damn scary* leaned into him and cursed at him or at least that's what it looked like to Bernie. Harrison kept waving at him to calm down. He didn't want Judge Binghamton to get wind of the fact that his client wasn't anything but the picture of a solid citizen. Everyone in the courtroom knew, however, that the defendant was trying his hardest to look that way but was failing miserably. Bernie thought that it was only a matter of time before he'd lose all patience with Harrison and launch out swinging. Bernie was preparing himself for that inevitability. Harrison, however, managed to sooth the beast and they both sat back in their seats quietly for a breather. It had been a tense hour with Mrs. de Martini on the stand. They both believed that she would be the one to say that *damn scary* was innocent or that it was in fact too dark to see him clearly but that was just not the case and at least one person in that courtroom knew the truth.

CHAPTER EIGHTEEN

It would be the first of many, many firsts, Peter, right beside her, hand in hand, smiling in a way that touched her soul. This moment actually made an imprint there in her heart as big as a sweaty palm against a glass. Patsy Mae screaming with delight saying, "That's my baby right there! That's my ba-by!" Hugs that scooped her up, toes scraping the floor, breath spent and a laughter that hurt her gut. It had been a while, but Patsy Mae finally acknowledged Peter with a firm form of respect and he also toward her. Their battle field had been any and every subject yet the place of neutrality for both of them was the kitchen. Peter had been a sous-chef at some of the finest restaurants in Manhattan, The Carlisle, The Four Seasons and Oceana, to name a few. Clark and he ate well now that he found his passion could be used as a tool for pay. And Patsy Mae could and often did stir up sheer masterpieces of cuisine. Soul food, she could do in her sleep, but Italian, French and even some Central American dishes with authenticity and as tasty as if they were made in those respective countries was her God given talent. She was often told that she should sell her food, possibly opening a restaurant of her own. She'd shrug her shoulders and say, "This stuff?" making light of what others perceived to be edible miracles. Clark and her sisters would imagine their lives different working side by side with Patsy Mae as she came up with inspiring delicacies only to have her smile and say, "Some day. Some day."

They were all sitting and some standing around watching Clark's latest creation of sorts, her Aqua Fresh toothpaste commercial. She was a solid twenty-five playing a very young fifteen. Clark had one of those faces, blessed by God passed on from generations that seemed to stay fixed in time. Clark, of course, didn't see the goodness in it for a long while wondering when adulthood would finally kick in. There she was looking even younger than the real teenagers, "Smiling all the way to the bank," her brother Marlin told her. None of her family had a clue to how much she'd make, for that matter neither did she. There was a three hundred and fifty dollar session fee that one acquired for simply shooting the commercial. Everyone knew that that was not where the real money was to be made. She would now receive something called residuals. The whole family drooled over the word, re-si-duals. Clark explained.

"Every time you see this commercial, I'm supposed to get some kind of a check for it," she said not fully sure of the specifics but seeming more of an authority than anyone else in the room.

"How they know every time I see the commercial?" Miss Beatrice asked with the straightest of expressions.

Everyone looked over to see Patsy Mae's response seeing as Miss Beatrice was her oldest, and dearest of friends. Patsy Mae politely ignored her.

"Well…well…they…" Clark merely began to answer.

"They have people who's job it is to count, that's how," said Marlin with a strong sense of reason.

Clark knew that he was right about that too once she remembered what other seasoned actors told her about collecting money in the business.

"You're right, there's a thirteen week cycle. I get paid the most money at the beginning of the cycle then the pay goes further and further down," Clark saw the frowns on her family faces, "It's still a whole lot of money though."

"Yeah, no doubt," her sister chimed in also with great authority.

The actual commercial was down right comical. Aqua Fresh had decided to switch their packaging to a pump instead of a tube and Clark was the daughter who didn't know what this new invention was, asking her mother, a lovely actress, whether it was a rocket. Clark would discover later in life that women saw her holding the pump one way and men saw it a whole other way. She'd laugh about that in the future but presently, it was serious acting for which she would be handsomely rewarded.

"You look sexy," Peter whispered in her ear.

She couldn't help but blush and fall for him all over again. Gone were the days of him fighting her over her time spent abroad in pursuit of her career. Now that she had a commercial running and money coming in, she could stay put for a while. She didn't have to take any old job. She had a choice now of being a little more selective than in the past.

"I still don't know how they gonna' know when and if I see yor' 'mercial on television. That just don't make sense to me. Do they have something attached to my house?" Miss Beatrice contemplated.

Marlin rolled his eyes to the ceiling thinking, 'There's something attached to your house alright.' Once again Patsy Mae ignored her but this time with emphasis. She leapt from her bed and shooed everyone into the kitchen. It was time to eat something now that everyone had showed their support for her daughter, Clark. Patsy Mae smothered the essence out of some pork chops and fried corn and green bell peppers where they melted and blended wonderfully in one's mouth. Peter went on and on about what kind of seasoning she used to the point where everyone else wondered if he and Patsy Mae had some sort of secret code.

"Cumin?" he asked.

"Close, Caraway," Patsy Mae grinned.
Peter nodded acknowledging his mistake with squeals of delight at the difference in flavor.

"Dill?" Peter questioned nibbling a small amount on the tip of his tongue.

"Close again. You do know your spices," Patsy Mae teased. She loved the fact that he was so attentive to her meal.

"Well, what is it?" Peter asked again.

"Ani…" Patsy Mae started.

"Anise. Of course," Peter shook his head acknowledging the subtle distinction.

Peter looked over at Clark who had the happiest smile ever seen on her face. She felt so full of joy that she imaged her heart bursting.

Unfortunately, like summer it didn't last long. Their relationship was just one year away from being completely over forever. Neither thought hard of marriage or being together forever. They hadn't a clue about being a wedded couple and would each live a life always wondering what if they'd done it. She smiled back at Peter and caught Patsy Mae staring over at her also smiling. It was a good day, one that meant more than Clark really realized. She had done something that most people in the world only dreamt of doing. Like Patsy Mae though, she thought nothing of her talent. It was just something that made her happy for the moment but even she didn't see herself doing it forever. She could do anything she desired which took less effort than most, this fact made her blasé about her accomplishments. That very commercial came with a 5:00 a.m. call time after a night of doing an Equity showcase at Amos Theater. No matter, she arose excited. The actual taping took a total of one hour and ten minutes. The producer thanked her for her professionalism and said that that was one of the faster takes they'd ever done. Clark remembered much later what took place. In truth, she was too tired to have enjoyed any of it then. She would tell no one for many, many years that she had slept walked through the entire thing with her mind and body on autopilot. She couldn't have enjoyed the experience with her head longing for the strongest aspirin known to man. With her manager, Shelly Donovan, calling her every half hour until 12:00 midnight to see if she was prepared, it was impossible for her to feel well rested.

The interruptions weren't the main factor but rather the igniting of self-doubting thoughts that swelled her head like circling vultures. Her mind galloped a pace faster than her heart, which plowed like thunder in her chest. She was suddenly scared. That next morning, show time, she was a nervous wilting wreck with dark circles under her eyes to boot. She had to convince the fairly reluctant make-up artist that with proper coverage and shadow she could pull off the look of a fifteen year old.

"I don't know," the make-up artist told Clark, "...but, I'll try."

The make-up artist was not as confident as Clark would have preferred. Clark glared up at her in the mirror and prayed, not that she knew to whom, but she said please, higher power, please make me look young enough to please these producers of this commercial. She didn't know that the make-up artist was pulling her leg a little. That's how exhausted she was.

CHAPTER NINETEEN

In truth, things couldn't have been better. It was tantamount to a family reunion. Sure, he was now a ward of the State at Riker's Penitentiary but with three squares and enough streetwise credit to afford him cocktails in his cell; he really couldn't complain about a thing. His father was three cells down, armed robbery, three counts, four known kills, extortion, a slew of alleged aggravated rapes and an assortment of misdemeanors. He wasn't going anyplace for three consecutive life times. Yes, his father was overjoyed that now all three of his sons would be with him for breakfast, lunch and dinner. His babies' mommas seemed almost jealous when they got the news. It had become the family legacy to opt for prison rather than four years of higher learning. It was considered a badge of honor to get busted, get out and roam the streets a bigger criminal than when one entered the joint. *Damn scary* or Busta or Clinton James Thomas, as his lawyers called him, only had two regrets, one, that he didn't get to cop a feel from Mrs. de Martini and two, he hated the color orange.

Jimmy entered his room one sunny afternoon, thinking there was a fire in the corner. No, it was just Busta clad in his cellblock jumpsuit. Jimmy was so sensitive to colors that he nearly left on account of over saturation. He really and truly didn't recognize him and not just because Mr. Thomas was on the toilet taking a dump. Judging from the size of it, Jimmy felt blessed that his sense of smell hadn't increased along with his sense of sight. In fact, he couldn't smell anything. Looking at him now, he recalled that in life he never liked Busta. Busta was an opportunistic criminal, the family business obviously. Not that all criminals aren't predisposed to the highest bidder but Busta took this premise to new heights. He was a deviant to the deviant. Most killers wouldn't kill for the hell of it unless they were psychotic. Alas, Busta wasn't crazy per se but shrewd. He knew that if he had a reputation of doing the jobs that no one else would, then he would be hired a lot more often than all the rest. Before his demise, Jimmy was considered not worth the effort of a kill. The word on the street was that he, Jimmy, mainly kept to himself and would eventually make good on all his outstanding debts. That description was practically like calling him a solid citizen.

Jimmy just stared at his killer. He had nowhere else to be currently. His ladylove, Clark, was at some club singing, so there he was with his old pal, Busta, except he didn't really know what he wanted to do with him. He kept his distance and rested, so to speak, on the ceiling. As he peered down at Busta, it gave him great pause. He looked so helpless sitting there making scrunched faces as he did his business. One thing Jimmy did know for sure, he wanted to scare the hell out of him, if such a thing was possible. He knew many had tried and failed but he had something more special than the rest. He was the wind. He was a god. He could if he tried real hard, enter Busta's body and make it do things that Busta wouldn't normally attempt. Maybe he might kill him. He paused. That idea fascinated him. In fact, it thrilled him. The more he thought about it the more he liked it. It would be a stunning death. He would attack him in his sleep as he had done many times to Peter, Clark's other half. Only this time, he wouldn't be playing around. He would do it for real. He would torture this son of a bitch tortured soul and make him beg to be dead. That's what he'd do to poor old, uneducated, murderous, Busta. He hadn't done anything like it before. He hadn't even killed anyone in real life but how hard could it be? His very own death was easy, quick even. He had passed from body to spirit in less than an hour. Heck, he didn't even know that he was actually dead for several days. He still tried to speak to those he had known in life like Raymond and the guys from the bar. The fact that no one answered back didn't even occur to him. It was the same in life with their conversations, as it were, resembling two simultaneous monologues, both adrift in self centered thoughts.

Jimmy contemplated his options there in Busta's cell for several weeks. Again, he had no place else to be. Occasionally he'd take an excursion out to the scene of the crime underneath the Van Wyck Expressway. He'd stand frozen in disbelief that he was no longer among the living. He so enjoyed life. Even with all its drama and harshness, he had no real worries, basically living from pleasure to pleasure. Though it had been several years now, he could still feel his presence there as if he had never left. The crime was shown to him in his mind eyes. He had it uneasily replayed from beginning to ending. There he was stuck in his own horror film for the soul whereby he was murdered over and over again, his blood spitting out and dripping to the sidewalk amid dirty, broken bottles and crushed beer cans, cigarette butts and puke. Even the countless rainstorms hadn't diminished the images that plagued him. It had only wiped away what was on the surface, what is observed by the naked eye. However, for those fortunate or in his case unfortunate enough to see beyond the grave, every detail was still there flashing brightly, disturbingly forever. His sole problem of being in this deceased state was remembering life. It clung to him like a relentless forming scab that's too soft and tender to remove as it covers a raw sore. When he could take no more of this tormenting memory he was once again in Busta's cell, three solid concrete walls and one with iron bars extending from floor to ceiling, bolted into reinforced steel plates. Once again Busta's jumpsuit startled him but he pressed on. He was going to kill him but he still didn't know how. He hadn't managed the technique of moving objects. However with something similar to a breath he could create a smidgen of wind when he became angry enough.

Busta was lying on his bunk. He didn't have a roommate anymore. No one wanted to share with him not even his own brothers because, simply put, he had never played fair a day in his life. That very same day, his latest cellmate, Otis Bullock, a three hundred and sixty-five pound man of iron, threatened to rip him into a million pieces with his bare hands if he continued to touch his highly coveted Playboy magazine summer edition 1985. Busta would, for lack of better words, use it and leave residue of his usage in between several sheets, thereby making it impossible for poor Otis to open said pages when he wanted to then use it himself.

"Yo, keep your damn hands off my stuff! I ain't playin' wit' yu," Otis would say laying down the law that promised brutality following.

"O', you crazi," Busta would respond waving at him all the while.

"Oh, I'm crazy now. What 'bout this?" Otis would say trying to pull two pages apart.

"No bodi' touch yo' stuff, mainn'," Busta would say as if it were utterly ridiculous to think that the men at Rikers had any desire to see a bunch of beautiful, full-bosomed naked women, "O', go on 'bout your business, mainn'."

"Oh, I'm gonna' go on 'bout my business all right. I'm gonna' go on 'bout the business of kicking your lying ass," Otis had stormed.

Otis' thick arms went around Busta's neck within the blinking of an eye. Before he knew what hit him, Busta was gasping for air, frantically squirming to get from underneath towering Otis Bullock. Neither one heard the cheering and bet wagering from their neighboring inmates, nor the alarms being sounded for an emergency lockdown. Nine guards pulled Otis off of a very lucky Busta. Otis and the paraphernalia in question were both eradicated and confiscated for further investigation. This material was never seen again and neither was Otis who was thrown in a cell underneath the prison for several months to think about his behavior. Otis could see Busta smiling as he was being dragged from the cell. He thought all right; he thought about how he needed another couple of minutes to finish off the dirty little weasel named Busta once and for all.

Jimmy witnessed it all with such indifference. Oddly the only thing that intrigued him was the fact that as Busta was being expelled to the other side by Otis, Jimmy could sense Busta's life slipping away. Suddenly, Busta's spirit rose a few feet from his body and Jimmy saw it hanging there hovering over. This happening gave Jimmy an idea. He wondered if he could somehow push that very same spirit out of Busta's body. He vowed to give it a little try that night while Busta was at his weakest. With that he waited until Busta did his bedtime routine, very little washing up, very little brushing of teeth, absolutely no prayers, to the toilet with very little wiping up then off to bed. It was a toss up as to who seemed scarier, Busta or the ghost of Jimmy. Busta was fast asleep in less than two minutes and Jimmy was fast at work immediately standing on his chest. He figured that was as good a spot as any but without a body it was hard to press upon Busta's rough leathery flesh. Busta didn't even stir though Jimmy stood there for four straight hours.

Finally, Jimmy had to accept the fact that it was impossible for him to accomplish this feat. So, he sat down and mulled over other options. As he sat, Busta began to breathe in a little more heavily giving Jimmy some encouragement. Jimmy began to gather up all of his hatred for Busta into the center of his being and forced it all downwards into Busta's ribcage. Busta wheezed for breath this time, coughing on every inhale. Jimmy felt a flutter of excitement at this new occurrence. The more Busta choked the harder Jimmy began to push. Although Jimmy was just an image, he was in a seated position, butt on Busta's chest forcing himself through Busta's body. Busta felt as if the weight of the world was upon him as he struggled to break free from this invisible uninvited anchor. He could feel the air escaping from his body and began to swell with lightheadedness. The sudden dizziness scared him the more and he opened his eyes and tried to sit upright but this unseen force of a ton of bricks kept at him. It penned him to his bunk and demanded his very life. Busta tossed and turned, struggled and churned but he was no match for the dead, determined Jimmy. Jimmy was a giant exploiting his strength over the rather weak and helpless puny human, Busta. Perhaps if Busta was a physically stronger man, if he'd opted for more exercise and less booze and women. Maybe if he took a vitamin now and again or drank eight to ten glasses of water or jogged a mile a day or two, then he would have had the energy to combat the likes of Jimmy. Alas, Busta was a lazy, lowly sinner with one foot in the grave since birth. Though hardly thirty-five, he was a poor specimen of a man, skinny and flabby at the same time. He was probably age sixty on the inside, broke down, hypertensive and slack. Jimmy could actually feel Busta's spirit slipping out of his caucus. The sheer joy of that compelled Jimmy to push down even harder and poor Busta to forfeit the fight. For, Busta too could feel this slipping away sensation, and rather than wrestle with it any longer, he gave in to it. He thought, "So, this is what dying is like." And with that thought, he took his last breath.

CHAPTER TWENTY

Her presence made him glow and transform into his favorite mythical figure - again.   He felt it appropriate to look virile and as a capable man should. It was for her pleasure. Although, she couldn't even see him, it was an image that he believed she saw in him when he was alive. Though, he seldom came upstairs. He seldom showed his face, said hello or did anything to endear himself to the Green family in any memorable way. In truth, they hardly knew what he looked like when Mrs. Beatrice made the announcement that he had died. The kids were only shocked because Jimmy should have been someone to whom they'd more than a passing acquaintance. After all, he lived in their house. Still Jimmy assumed himself to be a strong, handsome warrior type in the light of Clark's eyes. Unlike with poor old Busta, where he was the devil himself come to call. Jimmy saw him too, Busta, there on the other side, beyond the cloak of death, looking curiously stunned. His recognition of Jimmy came in short stops and starts as if his new vision needed time to adjust. He was a bluest vapor, and bodily pale and shriveled. Jimmy marveled at his handy work. He was a true craftsman. Busta stood near his loose flesh and mourned like a baby. This too was marvelous to Jimmy especially since it was so easy for him to do. Busta was hardly any effort, which is what got him into thinking about what he could do to Clark. Now that he had Busta somewhat trailing behind him with questions, maybe he could make something happen where he'd really have what he wanted beside him - Clark.

It was just as perfect a plan as any he had ever had. He'd simply push her out of her body. He swelled at the thought of it. Now, with this simple act, they could be together forever. She had removed herself from her pesky family and now even Peter was out of the picture thanks to him. He had wiggled his way in between them so often that they assumed it was a failed relationship. Each had taken their complaints to others and had whined incessantly about the pitfalls of love. Their friends had ill advisedly told them to seek greener pastures and such. Neither Peter nor Clark knew from longevity and life time commitments. They were young, ultimately foolish and inexperienced. They assumed that they had fallen out of love. Jimmy laughed at their stupidity adoring the fact that it worked in his favor. Even he knew that love was a choice. He had chosen not to do it so often, especially with those who bore his children.

He plopped down on her chest as soon as she stretched out in bed that night. He could feel right off that she was uneasy about something but that would soon be all behind her along with everything else she held so dear. He loved her almond colored body and though he couldn't touch it he imaged all kinds of things he would do with it if he could. It was like his playground and he knew every, single inch. He imagined her breath sweet and every inhale had to mean that she could sense his presence and yearned to be entwined together with him. He went to work quickly even before she was completely asleep, pressing with all his energy and with severe urgency just until she coughed.

He liked that because it told him that he was making progress. Like Busta, it was just a matter of time before her life would be ebbing away and gathered together with his for all eternity. Immediately her heart felt tight and stained. She tried her hardest to breathe more deeply thinking that she needed to calm herself down. She had already opened her eyes and could feel that she was essentially losing consciousness. Jimmy laughed at the idea that she was actually trying to will herself back from certain death. Her struggle made him more aggressive. His pressing became vigilant and ultimately violent. With his imagined hand, he struck her across the face and pulled at her hair. Smacking her about the face got him so hot and excited that he plunged his imagined penis inside of her thinking that with each stroke he pushed her further and further out of her body. Clark tried to stand up, sit up, anything to stop her heart from feeling like it was about to stand still. She gasped and fought to remain alert. She kept thinking, 'Am I dying? Am I dying?' Jimmy could see her spirit now being stretched and pulled from its home. This made him extremely hopeful and even more zealous. He pushed and pushed some more this time with determined, powerful, preternatural strength. He was about to have his bride, his love and the possibility of that realization sent an electrified current through him so commanding that he could scarcely stay centered on his objective. At that lapsed moment, while he was in the haze of anticipated expectation, the phone rang and Clark sprung up to answer it. As she leaped from her intended deathbed, she could see what appeared to be the same image she'd seen before of Adonis straddling her body. It was a peculiar second but she knew what she had just witnessed. She had been seeing spirits now practically her entire life but witnessing Jimmy again gave her great concern. It gave Jimmy great concern too that she was still walking around in her body. He pouted and pushed pass her to taunt and to haunt her. She picked up the receiver just as a cold, damp chilly wind knocked into her.

"Hey, Clark…" a voice said.

There was no answer from Clark. She was looking around the room for ghosts, scared beyond reason and frozen with fear.

"…Hey, Clark, you there?" the voice asked again.

Again, nothing from Clark.

"…Hey, Clark, it's me, Larry. It's about your sister," Larry said and Clark finally awoke.

"What?" Clark muttered.

"It's your sister…" Larry said.

Clark was in her car and at Brooklyn Hospital in twenty minutes flat. She lived on the Upper East Side of Manhattan and raced downtown as if she had a siren atop her Honda Accord. It stayed in fifth gear even around corners.

When she entered the hospital, Gloria Johnson, Tara's best friend, greeted her at the door.

"Where you been?" she shouted, tears welling up in her eyes.

"What?" Clark asked bewildered.

"She's sick! She's really sick," she told Clark.

"Where's she now?" Clark asked and Gloria pointed to the double doors marked Emergency Personnel Only, exclamation point.

Clark raced in that direction only to find the doors unyielding to her pushing. Gloria came over and pulled her away thinking that they both might be thrown out.

"Clark, where have you been? I've been calling you all night," Gloria chided at her.

"I've been home," Clark said defensively, "I must not have heard the phone or something. I don't know," Clark said puzzled.

Gloria glared at her as if she didn't believe her.

"Yeah, well, I've been calling practically every half hour and it just went to your machine," said Gloria in a huff.

Clark sighed in desperation hoping that Gloria would simply stop talking.

"I don't understand why people just let the machine answer their phones anyhow. It's rude. It's just plain rude to do that to someone when they're trying to tell you that they sister almost died…" she cried.

"What?!" Clark shouted.

Gloria leaned into her for a hug and Clark reluctantly gave her one still hearing the public spanking ringing in her ears.

"Can we go see her?" Clark asked and Gloria sobbed and nodded at the same time.

They simply needed Visitor passes. Clark obtained two from the front desk and together they entered through the double doors and down a long corridor. Clark saw the tag at the bottom of the bed first which read Green, Tara. It was appropriately stated because that's exactly how her sister's face looked, a discolored shade of green. She had several machines attached to her extending from her nose and mouth, her left arm and even a few about her chest. Her hair had sweated into an afro and she appeared to have lost five to ten pounds in a matter of hours. As they turned towards her she was filling a waste paper basket with about a pound of black phlegm. She looked terrible.

"Hi," Clark said trying not to weep like a baby.

She and Gloria had to wait for Tara to expel more goop before words could be uttered. Clark almost immediately grabbed a box of tissue and started to help her. Gloria was reluctant and stood firmly by the curtain steadily trying to duck behind it so she wouldn't have to witness any of this. It took the entire box to wipe up the mucus covering her sister's face. The dreaded asthma plague had almost taken her sister clean out. It's remains meant nothing to Clark. She threw them in the trash. She was happy that it was leaving without taking her sister with it.

"Is she going to be okay, doc?" Clark asked as Dr. Shapiro walked over and started poking and prodding Tara's chest as she laid there completely exhausted.

He was checking vitals and the amount of mucus still within her lungs. He touched her back and she choked up some more. He adjusted her drip and she coughed out a big chunk. Clark tried not to appear in any way startled by the enormous, sludgy bits of matter. Tara seemed to be made of the stuff. Once Dr. Shapiro disappeared off to another patient, Tara began writing down instructions for both Clark and Gloria. They were to help Larry, who was apparently at her co-op, in cleaning the sheets, blankets, carpet, dishes, clothes, curtains, in other words, anything that may have contributed to triggering this little episode. Clark had her own idea of what placed her sister in the hospital but she needed more proof. So, off she went the Tara's apartment without Gloria. Gloria decided that she'd had a long day already, and that the kids needed dinner, etc, etc.

When she entered her sister's place, there was Larry resting rather comfortably on the sofa. His back to the cushions, feet raised up draped over the armrests, he looked asleep until Clark walked in. There were several bags of dirty clothes sorted and waiting at the door, the kitchen smelled of pine and ammonia as well as the bathroom. By all accounts it appeared as if Larry was doing a bang up job. That is until Clark took a closer look in the kitchen to see dishes piled in the sink and oven, a ring around the large Jacuzzi tub, a closet full of clothes that had yet to be cleaned.

"Hey," Larry mumbled.

"Hey, yourself," Clark said to him sighing at all that had to be done, "I'm reporting for duty."

"How she doin'?" Larry asked.

"Okay, I guess," Clark replied.

She never liked saying too much to her sister's boyfriend. He had a tendency to take things the wrong way. So, she'd tread very lightly in all matters.

"I'll go put a load in," Clark told him, grabbing hold of the laundry bag and planning to drag it to the washer and drier in the building's basement.

"Wait, wait, I'll help you with that," Larry sprung from the couch and into action.

Clark really and truly wanted him to stay put. She wanted to reflect on what happened to her that morning and not have to be preoccupied with a bunch of small talk. With Larry, there was never anything particularly interesting in his conversation. She yielded though and allowed him to escort her to the basement where they heaved the clothes into the washer and started the cycle.

"You know when you called last night you didn't tell me about Tara," Clark said.

"Yeah, why?" Larry asked.

"Well, wasn't she sick then?" Clark asked.

Larry looked a little stunned by the question.

"I mean, for her to be this sick now, it must have started earlier, right?" Clark asked.

"Yeah, well she wasn't feeling well and I was taking care of her," Larry said almost to himself.

"You were taking care of her?" Clark asked.

"Yeah, I was taking care of her," Larry repeated.

"So, at that point she was really sick?" Clark asked probing for the truth.

"Look, I know how she gets and I knew how to deal with it," Larry said defensively.

It was two days later when Clark found out that Larry was instructed to call the family and tell them about the severity of Tara's illness. Gloria made it clear to him that everyone was to be notified while she held Tara's hand in the hospital. Meanwhile, Larry decided that he wasn't going to do that. He decided that he'd report this little occurrence in a way that showed him in the best light. He'd tell the family later and make sure to mention that he was the hero throughout. That's why Clark never got the messages because there weren't any to be had. Gloria would call Larry and say, "Where's Clark?" Larry would reply, "I don't know. I just called her."

When Tara was feeling better and when the threat of death was a memory, Clark would tell her in no uncertain terms that Larry was the trigger. He was trying to kill her. She would convey that Larry had a possession obsession that would not be denied. He was trying to make Tara his prisoner and trying to keep her from her family. Clark was so angry with Larry for months after, that every opportunity to besmirch his name was taken with extreme responsiveness. Still, it would be years later that Clark would come to know that both she and her sister were in danger of losing their lives that night for similar reasons.

Chapter Twenty-One

B illy Earl and Patsy Mae sat up right in bed as the television announcer told them that Clinton James Thomas, the convicted killer of James P. DuBois, was mysteriously found dead in his cell that very morning. He also claimed that an investigation was under way to determine the cause of death. He further claimed that they had a suspect in custody but that nothing was conclusive. Billy Earl kept his mouth open throughout the rest of the announcements wondering if what he just heard was his imagination or actual fact. He was actually confused.

"I heard it too," Patsy Mae said confirming his sanity.

"Well, I'll be damned," he said.

"Yeah," Patsy Mae uttered, also stunned.

"Mysterious, they said," he said.

"Yeah, mysterious," she repeated.

"I wonder what that mean," he said.

"Yeah, I wonder what that mean," she repeated.

"Don't make sense really," Billy Earl told her.

"Noh, it don't really make sense at all," Patsy Mae told him.

"You think...nohhh...maybe..." he thought out loud.

"What? What?" Patsy Mae said in a panic.

"You think *he* did it?" Billy Earl hesitantly asked.

"He who?" asked Patsy Mae as if she didn't want to be sure.

"He, him, that's who," said Billy Earl sure that she did in fact know who he meant.

They both contemplated that theory a while, long faces, their brows in a quandary. Patsy Mae pulled the blankets up to cover her body as if Jimmy's ghost was in the room with them listening.

"I wouldn't be at all surprised," said Patsy Mae eyeballing everything in the room with suspicion.

"He could be clever now, that Jimmy," Billy Earl informed her.

"How so?" she asked.

"Well, when it came to sumthin' he wanted, he could find all kinds of ways of gettin' it, you know. Memba' a time when some girl told a lie on him..." he shook his head in remembrance, "...well, he didn't rest until he paid her back."

"Paid her back? How so," Patsy Mae asked now clutching the covers.

"Now, I don't know how true it was and all...but...the word is he found sumthin' real dirty on her..." he said.

"Like what?" she asked.

"...like, I don't know, like she was messin' around behind her husband's back, you know...Sumthin' like that. I'm not sure if it was the husband or the boyfriend, but it was someone in her life, you know..." he said with a head nod.

"Okay," she said for him to go on.

"Well," he paused for effect, "...that son'a bitch, Jimmy...well...he befriended the husband..." he smirked.

"Nohhh," Patsy Mae exclaimed knowing where this story was heading.

"Yeah!" Billy Earl told her, "And, you know what happened then..."

"Goodness, that's devious," Patsy Mae agreed knowing what Billy Earl was going to say.

She and Billy Earl had known each other for more than thirty years and were married for most of that time. She had been with him longer than she had with her first husband, Mann Green, Jr. They knew each other well.

"Yeap. He took that poor son'a bitch husband right to where she was, naked and in the arms of some other poor son'a bitch."

"How'd he get him over there?" Patsy Mae asked.

"Jimmy was a funny man, you know. Word is they say that he told him to come and see sum' hoes that'll do anythin' for a buck."

"Nohh, he didn't," Patsy Mae laughed nervously.

"Yeap. Man didn't know that it would be his own wife. Word is, they just stood there staring through the window for fifteen minutes before the man recognized her. Now, I don't know if this is true but…word is, Jimmy held down the wife, while the man punched her in the face."

"Now, you know I don't like that kind of talk, Billy Earl," Patsy Mae said sternly.

"I know. I know. I'm just repeating what I was told. I don't really know if any of this is true but with Jimmy you never know. That man was capable of anything," Billy Earl said.

"I know. That's why I didn't want him in this house, Billy Earl," Patsy Mae said smoothly, rehashing and further confirming that particular fact.

Billy Earl realized that he had said too much.

"I know, honey. I know. I'm not saying that I would do sumthin' like that or nothin'," Billy Earl tried.

"You bet on your life that you won't. It would be the last thing you ever did. Rest assured that my foot would be so far up yo' behind that you going to need rectal surgery to take it out.

Mark my words."

"Sure you right, honey. Sure you right," Billy Earl laughed but not too heartily.

Bernie had also heard the news of *damn scary's* mysterious departure. He was going to miss the guy in a certain way. He didn't know him well but he did have an acquaintance with him. Out of respect for the dead, he decided to think of him by his proper name. He wondered if Mr. Clinton had a family who would miss him, any children, brothers or sisters. Bernie believed that everyone was capable of having at least one person miss them when they were gone. Though, he wondered constantly about this premise when it came to his very own wife, Lillie. Would she miss him? She had smiled a little too sprightly, for his taste, when he took out additional insurance at the prodding of his new insurance agent, Ms. Kelly Nelson, who informed him that it was only two dollars more per month to increase the death payment by fifty thousand dollars. Bernie hesitated signing the renewal form when he casually observed Lillie grinning from ear to ear.

"Baby, what you waitin' for?" Lillie asked him a bit too cheerfully.

"I could ask you that same question," he responded with a jerk of his head.

Then there was the way she helped him pack before he set sail each morning. He felt as if he was being pushed out of the house. He'd awake to see the cooler packed high to over flowing with Budweisers, wrapped baloney and cheese sandwiches and a couple of Snicker's bar, miniatures, his favorites.

"Baby, what you staring at?" she'd ask him as he bent over to count the beer cans.

"How many you got in there?" he'd ask with one eye steady on her.

"What's wrong now?" she asked, hand on hip ready for a fight.

"Nothing. Nothing…but how much do you think I can drink? I am driving, you know," he'd explain.

"You are not dri-vin'. You're on the boat in the middle of the wata'," she'd inform him.

"Still, you tryin' to get me drunk out there in the middle of the wata'?" he'd ask pointedly as if to catch her in a lie.

"Man, you crazy. You know that," she said turning, waving, and walking away "Drink, don't drink, I don't give a damn."

Bernie watched her go back into their bedroom continuing to reflect on his mental stability.

"I've never heard such utter nonsense in all my born days…What in the world…They gonna' haul you out of here one day in a straight jacket, truly, honest to Gawd…Lord Jesus, help my husband…because when they come, I'm gonna' sign that paperwork without them asking permission…honest to Gawd," she went on.

Though she certainly professed otherwise, he was still unsure of her true motives. He'd take one or two beers out of the cooler to be sure. Ten was enough for one day but maybe Lillie knew that twelve or so would kill him. He couldn't be too cautious. So, to be on the safe side, he just brought what he could comfortably carry. His boat was docked in the backyard. So, he didn't have far to go. Bayside, Queens was just one of the most beautiful of places he could ever have imagined living in, but with five children, he was never able to make use of the bay area water way. He'd look out the back window staring at it daily, longing to be engaged in it other than the spray carried by the wind. Though for many years he couldn't afford to comfortably feed his family and support his dreams. Now, that he was finally retired, his children grown, well, life was just as sweet as those miniature Snickers he loved so much.

Now he sat, Budweiser in hand, pondering the events of Jimmy's trial on his Prosport, laughing spontaneously from time to time out in the open air. Everything about that trial had him in stitches from the Judge, Binghamton, who needed a prescription of painkillers to get through it, to the assorted witnesses, who lied, flirted and even peed on the stand. It was just a memory now as he pulled on his Zebco and set it taut on the rod against the stern. It was always one thing after another with that case and looking back Bernie realized that it was only fitting that his killer would have died in such a baffling manner too. Funny enough, it was never a matter of the victim. He was very much just a spectator in the courtroom along with everybody else. His friends, so called, representing him well by basically saying that they couldn't trust him as far as they could throw him. What really stood out though was the incredible effort it took and how many people were involved in bringing his perpetrator to justice. As far as Bernie was concerned, the trial just went on and on and on. Bernie guesstimated that between the lawyers, associates, assistants, stenographer, clerks, Judges and all, Jimmy's case had cost the taxpayers a whopping three million dollars. That total would include Mr. Busta Clinton's vacation at Riker's too, that is, until he was removed on a stretcher. Bernie wondered if his tombstone would read Killer or Clinton or Busta or, his favorite, *damn scary*. He laughed a lot on that one. Half the day in fact he tilted his head back and hollered mightily then giggled until his side hurt. It wasn't until he had his second to last beer that he started to tear up at the thought that Busta was only human. He thought about the fact that he may have simply made a mistake that was irreversible. Only one tear fell before he watched the sun setting over the Manhattan skyline thinking how beautiful the whole world seemed. He just couldn't help thinking that maybe it was just because Busta had finally met his maker on the other side. There was one less killer on the street and although it may have been just one error in the miserable man's life, it was his choice to make and no one else's.

CHAPTER TWENTY-TWO

S he wasn't necessarily trying to be cynical. She just earnestly wanted to know how many times she had to say the chant before she could go to bed. After the horrible audition she had that day, she was seriously tired.

"It's an exclusive," Shelly told her.

'Yeah right,' Clark thought as she entered Ogilvy and Mather and was greeted by at least half of Manhattan's finest young twenty-something actresses. No one looked unique, all had brown skin, all were five feet by five inches more or less, all were slim more or less and since talent had nothing to do with it, all would be at the mercy of someone's suggestive tastes.

"Nam myo ho rengay kyo Nam myo ho rengay kyo Nam myo ho rengay kyo…"

Was it one hundred times? Didn't someone say that just after one day of chanting they were given a Mercedes by a complete stranger? Or was it a Pinto? No, it was definitely some type of luxury vehicle. Clark really wished she had been paying attention to that part of her new education. She could use a new ride. Hers was old and rusted. She was just about to take the poor thing to Maaco. She was still on the fence about whether to keep it in its original *American Express* blue or to change it to something completely different like orange. Why couldn't someone just give her a brand new one like she heard one of Lisa's friend's say? Mrs. Lisa E. Warren now, and marriage really suited her, marrying someone with loads of cash made her practically sparkle. Clark believed wholeheartedly that Lisa was on a secret mission to prove the old woman wrong who had so early in life predicted a dreary future for her. From that day forward, Lisa went swiftly from man to man in an all out mission to not just have any old husband but to have the best of the bunch, and so far, no children. Now, she was acting as Clark's good friend turned spiritual guide, the one who just days ago struggled to teach her the blessed chant.

"Nam myo ho rengay kyo Nam myo ho rengay kyo Nam myo ho rengay kyo…"

She felt as though she didn't have a choice but to listen to Lisa's instructions because at this point she sincerely believed that she was losing her mind. That was mainly due to the fact that she hadn't gotten that much sleep of late no matter what time she went to bed. It was becoming more and more frustrating to go on an audition when she could barely keep her eyes open. Her very latest audition went well until she exited the agent's office and ran smack dab into a glass partition. She didn't see it at all and rode home on the I.R.T. number six train wondering why fellow actors laughed at her misery and why the agency had a virtual lawsuit waiting to happen constructed in the first place. She needed to take her mind off of the events of her day. It was too embarrassing. And now she would have the difficult task of calling Shelly, and telling her how the audition went. Clark was surprised she hadn't heard from her yet, ever eager to keep an eye on potential money.

"Nam myo ho rengay kyo Nam myo ho rengay kyo Nam myo ho rengay kyo…."

The over the counter sleeping pills seemed to have worked the first night she took them but now they were like candy with a bad after taste. She knew in her heart that there was more to it than simply a lack of rest. Lately she was waking up with more unexplained scratch marks all over her body. She didn't know what to make of it. If it was stress related she couldn't detect where from on her person. She felt fine but to be on the safe side, she practically asked everyone she knew what they thought. Lisa always seemed to be so up beat so she decided to ask her what kept her sane.

"No kidding?" Clark remarked generally shocked that Lisa hadn't said the Bible.

"Yeap, I really, really think it's the reason I met my Charles and the reason he bought me this here house, not to mention my new job down at Prada," Lisa said matter-of-factly.

Clark was impressed.

"So, what do I have to do?" she asked Lisa enthusiastically.

Clark thought, 'So, I chant this stuff, whatever it means, get a whole bunch of nice stuff and live happily ever after. It's really a no-brainer.'

"When can I start?" she asked Lisa.

"Why don't you come over to our next meeting," Lisa suggested.

"Sure, thing, where is it?" Clark asked also enthusiastically.

"My house. It'll just be me and, of course, Charles, my husband, and our spiritual group. Just a few people," Lisa informed her.

"Just a few people, huh?" asked Clark suddenly less enthusiastic.

"There are six of us in all," Lisa reassured her.

Clark honestly wanted to start this religion, honestly she did, but she wasn't quite sure if she wanted to do it in front of a whole group of people. She was hoping that she could just kind of do it in the privacy of her own apartment and, viola, she's in the club. She didn't want to be stared at as if she had two heads while she was pouring out her heart to a bunch of strangers.

"I don't know...I..." Clark mumbled.

"So, you'll come, right? You'll really enjoy it. I promise," Lisa told her.

"I don't know...I...I just...I don't know," Clark kept on.

"You don't know what?" Lisa asked.

"Are these real close friends of yours? I don't want to feel out of place," Clark said concerned.

"You worry too much. There's no reason to be afraid in any way. It'll be fine," Lisa reassured her some more.

Once the meeting got going, not one person other than Lisa paid Clark a lick of attention. She settled back and tried to blend in. For her it was like watching a reality show, where apparently everyone was a star, and used to being followed around and gawked at. She was their audience, so to speak, in this particular episode of their lives. And, as such, they couldn't be bothered to stop and assist her along her spiritual path. They were too busy taking care of their own. Clark wanted to ask questions but that was quite impossible. So, she settled down in the lotus pose, like everyone else, legs crossed in front of her, hands stretched on either knee, relatively comfortable. Then she closed her eyes like everyone else. She was trying to remember the names of everyone in the room that Lisa and Charles had literally thrown in her direction as they entered the enormous den. He and Lisa had spared no expense in their decoration. Lisa told her that Charles had chucked all of their old combined furniture and bought everything new from Ethan Allen. Clark told them that she loved the smell of the mahogany wood maple finishes. Then after the mantra was chanted one hundred plus rounds, it was time for the cool down. Everyone remained in a circle and began speaking about their past two weeks with this magical Nam myo ho rengay kyo.

"Since I've been a Buddhist my entire life has changed," began Erica, " I just can't believe it, really. It's like my eyes are finally opened and I can see for the first time," she said.

"How so?" asked Charles.

"Well, in the beginning I was depressed a lot, and I didn't hardly want to get out of bed and I didn't want to go to work or anything else…well…but now it's like my whole life has turned around," she said.

"How…I mean, what's changed exactly?" Charles repeated.

"Well, see this bracelet here," Erica said waving an arm around the circle, an arm filled with diamonds, "Well, my boyfriend just gave this to me the first night I started chantin'," she said.

Everyone's eyes lit up including Clark's. Everyone in the circle started owing and awing as they stared at all the glitter Erica was presenting with glee.

"Nice, Erica. Very nice," Charles told her. Then he turned his attention to the next person in line, "What about you, Ryan? So, now I hear you're up and working again," Charles said.

"Man, I started chanting and chanting like crazy and before I knew it, someone gave me a brand new tool box filled with brand new tools. Each and every one of them was something that I needed too. You know I do construction and I always need a little this and that on the job and sometimes I didn't have what I needed to complete the job and before I knew it I couldn't finish some of the stuff I started. Sorry, Lisa," he said in Lisa's general direction.

Lisa smiled back at him as if she was finally at peace with whatever they were referring to.

"Well, now, now I'm just thankful because this was someone that I didn't even know hardly and they just knew what I did and knew how hard I was makin' out and coincidently had these tools in the attic or something and came across them one day," he said with a shrug, "I think it wasn't a coincidence but that it's me chanting and praying, you know."

Clark overheard Lisa discreetly telling Ryan that she had made a few phone calls on his behalf.

"You're so right, brother, because I've had similar things happen to me, just like that. I'm sure we all have, right?" Charles asked the group at large.

Clark wondered what in the world these people were talking about. It really and truly didn't make sense. Therefore when everyone nodded yes to Charles, she did not. Earlier in the evening she was thinking about whether or not chanting was of any value, as well as the fact that things such as these never ever in a million years happened that way for her. In fact, she was thinking that just the opposite happens to her. She always has to fight and work and then work and fight some more to get practically everything she ever has in life. However, she was willing to give it a try because what she was doing wasn't apparently working either. So, that night she chanted one hundred and thirty-six times some more.

If the world could hear him, it would have sounded like an earthquake he was laughing so loud. Within himself, it was thunderous and raucous. He didn't know what she was doing at first nor did he care save the fact that he couldn't continue what he had purposed to do if she was going to sing all darn night long. Not only was it irksome and annoying but it was also a terrific bore. He liked her better when she had company or when she was bathing or showering or even watching television. At least then there was motion, activity. Now she sat with her legs in a twist trying to meditate on god knows what. He'd crash into her several times to create a rise out of her but nothing. To his dismay, she continued that annoying racket half the night. He couldn't wait for her to be done. Then he'd do his usual routine of lying with her then pushing with all his might upon her chest.

Like clock work, at three o'clock Clark awoke with a start. Groggy still, she had the oddest sensation that she was not alone. Once again, she was literally pinned down to her bed, struggling for breath. It was faint but she felt as if someone or something had its hands around her neck. She tried her hardest to see what it was but could only make out a grayest glow above her head. It smelled horrific too, a kin to day old moldy garbage that had been in the sun too long. Again, she tried to see it by closing her eyes shut then whipping them open as she had done many times before in order to catch a glimpse of this same eerie figure. Unfortunately for her, this technique worked again, for there he was looking down upon her frightened, fatigued face.

'She's a stubborn little bitch,' Jimmy thought. With Busta, he hardly exerted any energy at all. It was quite a different story with Clark. She practically fought him back. For the life of him, or the death of him, he couldn't figure with what weapon she possessed. He hit her, marked her body up with the wisps of his spirit, yelled into her ears where if she could hear him, she'd be deaf by now. Frankly, his patience was growing thin. He longed to have her all to himself and sadly this possibility was dimming. He had to discover what, if anything, was keeping her alive and therefore perhaps work on that first. Maybe, he thought with a glimmer of hope, if he killed off her precious family then he could finally have her weakened and fittingly at his disposal.

CHAPTER TWENTY-THREE

There she was shriveled up in all her glory. She used to be hell on wheels but now her prune shaped sunken, leather face belied that yesteryear image. Long gone were the days when she was the matriarchal tyrant who'd lord her dominance like a scythe whacking away at a sheaf of wheat. Now, she had a chill that threatened to kill her. Auntie Clarice Wallace brought in a quilted blanket and tucked her frail arms and toes underneath, cocooning her tightly inside. She whispered now instead of her frightening growl that used to send worry down her family's back. Patsy Mae never much cared for her mother-in-law and thought of her dying as simply the way the world worked. When informed that Clark and Tara would go to pay her a visit all the way down in Richmond, Virginia, they were met with curious stares and seemingly uninterested shrugs.

"If that's what you'll want to do. I can't stop ya'," she told them.

"Would you like us to tell her you said hello?" asked Tara innocently.

"Did I say that I want you to tell that woman anything? Now, I didn't say anything like that? If she wants to say something to me, she should have said it a long time ago. I don't have anything at all to say to that…woman…you hear me!" shouted Patsy Mae.

She would have slammed her door behind as she stomped into her room but Billy Earl had yet to fix it properly on its hinges. So, she shoved her side chair instead. Its legs scratched across her wood floor as it bounced up then settled back down. Both Clark and Tara wanted to laugh but held very serious faces until Patsy Mae was seated on her bed and her back was facing them. Then they gave each other the tightest of closed mouth grins.

"In fact, if she has any gotdamn thing that she wants to say to me, tell her that I'm dead, okay? Just remember that, I'm no longer living and therefore don't have to hear a gotdamn thing that comes out of her gotdamn lying mouth. You two hear me!?" she shouted.

At that, they couldn't contain their laughter and simply giggled right there in front of her. Patsy Mae joined in too after a few more huffs and bitter bickering. It was a fact that the mentioning of their grandmother's name made Patsy Mae's blood run cold. If it weren't for her children and their marvelous way of drawing her out of a state of depression, she would have remained there for hours fussing. Apparently, at their father's funeral, Mann Green, Jr., Grandma Olivia, his mother, accused Patsy Mae, his wife of killing him. The fact of the matter was that all of his meals were of the liquid variety and Patsy Mae was forced to support him and their family with her two jobs of nursing the elderly and cleaning other people's houses. Her son was an innocent little lamb until big bad Patsy Mae led him astray. It was never mentioned but Patsy Mae was completely ostracized from that side of the family from that day forward, not that she minded. Sure, everyone was civil but if they could legally kill one another, the entire family would have been slaughtered especially Grandma Olivia Green.

The story goes that she was the only colored member of her family, everyone else was practically white. She took after her Black mother whilst each of her three siblings took after their Canadian French father, Sir Preston Grenier. Her brothers and sisters not only looked Caucasian but they acted that way too according to the times and married that way as well. Olivia hadn't seen them or heard from them since they were kids and certainly not since their parents both died tragically in an accidental fire. Sir Grenier, married, Isabel Forrest, a stunningly beautiful brown skinned woman of African and Cherokee Indian decent. He didn't care that there wasn't a town in Virginia that would openly support their union. He went out and built his wife a town of their own. It was a few miles outside of Prince George sitting on the one hundred and three acres that he had inherited from his father. There was a court house, a school, several riding arenas, horse stables, a grocery and even a church. His love for Isabel would have garnished her an entire city if Sir Grenier had lived long enough to acquire more property. After all that they had been through to marry, then raise four children, it was devastating to have it all go up in smoke. Grandma Olivia's eyes would tear up at the mentioning of her parents. Then she'd immediately curse her brother and sisters who abandoned her to grow up homeless, family-less and by all accounts penniless in a town that thought nothing of her at all though it bore her name.

She grew up hard after that, laboring away in cotton fields and doing laundry on the side as if she was born a slave. She grew up resentful too and with a chip on her shoulder the size of the State. Then her husband, Mann Connor Peterson, insisted that she change her maiden name to Green, claiming that no one in his family could pronounce it the way she did by rolling her tongue around the r. She couldn't understand why it mattered when she would be known as Mrs. Peterson anyway. They argued briefly before she simply conceded to his wishes. He was the only man that she had ever been with, had ever kissed, had ever asked for her hand in marriage. She felt obligated to him for taking a chance on someone who had nothing but a meager savings and no family to speak of. Mann told her that he had family enough for the both of them. She wouldn't be disappointed by that statement, and received more than she bargained for. It was painfully clear that her husband, Mann, was a mamma's boy and everything Mamma wanted, Mamma got. It annoyed Olivia to no end that every holiday was spent underneath his mother. When Olivia's children were born, they became Mamma's children outright. It was understood by the entire Peterson family that she had very little if any rights to her own flesh and blood. She wondered what family was supposed to mean when all it ever brought was sorrow.

As all things come to pass, eventually Mamma died and to Olivia's shock and surprise, she became the new head of the Peterson's enormous family matrix. Now, everything she wanted, she got. Everything she said - went. It was a beautiful thing. And with practically no formal education to speak of, she led the family in the only way she knew how - hard. She was miserable and therefore everyone else would be miserable too. Marriages were conducted like small business transactions. It didn't much matter if there was genuine love and caring. If the intended groom didn't cut the muster, meaning if his family was dirt poor, they didn't get into the Peterson clan. Many family members ran away on account of this point but most stayed and endured thinking that they didn't have a choice but to obey their elder. Mann Peterson had no say in the goings on of the hierarchy either. He ran the family grocery store and that was his only domain. When asked why he didn't stand up to Olivia, he'd say that he didn't like to argue. The truth is his Mamma hadn't prepared him well for overcoming excessively domineering women. He was agonizingly out of his league in the presence of crafty, outspoken members of the opposite sex. Olivia had him so well wrapped around her finger that soon after Mamma died, she changed her name back to Grenier, though everyone still pronounced it Green. She didn't have to officially change it. She simply announced to the family that no one was to call her Mrs. Peterson ever again. Mann was hurt by this latest development but, of course, acquiesced to her demands. What else could he do? He didn't exactly have a backbone. Olivia didn't make the connection that as she had hated Mamma for the harshness of her reign and rule, so too did her family towards her. She would die lacking that epiphany.

Little did Clark and Tara know, they were visiting the worn out version of Olivia. She had mellowed to a mere grunt of her original bark.

"See, I didn't know at the time what they were really asking me. They liars those people. They lie, you know," she said barely audible with her face turning away lost in thoughts of the past.

Clark and Tara leaned real close to the side of her bed and tried to listen without breathing too loudly.

"My name was Grenier...hell the whole town's name was Grenier..." her accent was flawlessly French.

It was the first time either Tara or Clark heard her speak in her original language. It was grand and perfect. Clark smiled at the thought of what life must have been like for her growing up being both French and American. Her eyes sparkled and danced thinking that it was probably one long unending gala ball.

"They called themselves censes, or census, huh, government something or other," she huffed, "Damn liars each and every one of them. That's what I'd call 'em...damn liars..." she trailed off again as if she could see their faces somewhere in the very room she was lying in.

Auntie Clarice brought her some tea and placed it on the nightstand beside her bed. She fluffed her pillows and brushed her hair back from her face with her hand.

"They ask me my name, you know. I didn't think anything of it at the time..." she coughed to a small choke.

Auntie Clarice lifted up her thin body and patted her gently on the back. Meanwhile, both Tara and Clark were breathless at the telling of Grandma Olivia's story. No one spoke of the past in their family except in spurts and they couldn't wait to hear the rest of this tail. They were starving for answers of their past. They didn't even have baby pictures. Grandma Olivia was their father's mother. They didn't even know him at all except in flashes of a memory that could be equal to the last television show they watched. He was there in the house until they were seven and nine respectively. Then he was there in a grave having passed away from something that ate a gigantic hole in his liver. Auntie Clarice sewed dresses for them to wear to the funeral made up from old off-white curtains that hung on their living room window. The dresses were dyed pink because Grandma Olivia didn't want her grand babies wearing black. It was bad luck she said to anyone and everyone who would listen.

"Your father was right there in the room with me when they knocked on the door," she said smiling at Tara and Clark, seeing his face within theirs.

They smiled back trying desperately to recall what he looked like, then imagining what he looked like as a boy.

"They came right in...right up into my kitchen, they did...sat right down. Smiled at me even," she half grinned, "It was the devil come to call. That's what it was pure and simple, the devil."

She leaned back on her bed as if she was done with the telling of the story.

Clark shifted her eyes toward Tara, who then turned to Auntie Clarice. Auntie Clarice waved at them both for patience. She had heard this story many, many times and knew that this was just recess. Then Grandma Olivia popped back up.

"All they did was ask me my name and how many child'ren me and Mann have. That's all..." she chewed as if she had something in her mouth, "I told 'em Green, you know. Just like that, I say, Green. I was thinking that maybe they couldn't pronounce Grenier like everybody else in town, you know. How was I supposed to know what the census do..." she placed her head on her pillow and closed her eyes.

Tara and Clark shrugged at Auntie Clarice for answers but before she could speak, Grandma Olivia was up again.

"Those liars took my 'eritance from me. Those liars. They stole it away from me just like that. See, they were looking for the Greniers. They didn't say that but that's what they were looking for. See, it was about land," she coughed to a choke.

Auntie Clarice reached over and handed her her tea. She took one small sip and then threw her head back onto the pillow, tired from all this overexertion. They all watched her for several moments thinking that she was going to spring up again but this time she did not. They waited a lengthy couple of minutes to be sure. Then just as they were tiptoeing out of the room and about to exit, she spoke once more.

"You...you..." she said looking vaguely toward the door.

Clark pointed at herself while moving in Grandma Olivia's direction.

"Me?" she asked.

"You...you...get married, okay?" Grandma Olivia said staring off beside Clark as if someone else was standing there along side.

"Promise me?" she demanded.

"Okay. O-kay..." said Clark curiously.

Then Clark looked around in wonder. As Grandma Olivia lowered herself once more Clark wanted to ask what on earth she was talking about and why not say what she just said to Tara as well, the older sibling. Why me, was all she could think about.

Before Clark got the chance to ask, Auntie Clarice ushered them out of Grandma Olivia's room and into the kitchen for peach cobbler and black coffee. Once there, Auntie Clarice further explained the land situation and how some fairly shrewd businessmen ripped off quite a few blacks of their land and property in those days. She also told them that there was a rumor circulating that her grandparent's death might not have been the accident that the local sheriff reported it to be but a sure fire way of separating the Grenier family from their wealth. Unfortunately, for Grandma Olivia Green, she seemed to bear the brunt of the suffering with just the answering of a simple question. Grandma Olivia's hatred of her husband for having changed her name, her absentee brothers and sisters, her parents dying, and then the loss of her fortune; all were attributing factors in making her heart as solid as a rock. There was a dust that settled over her entire family with her at the helm, old and moldy like rotted bread. It was coarse and immoveable, as rigid as reinforced steel. Auntie Clarice admitted to her nieces that she had felt it as a child and that's why she was one of the first to run away from home. In fact, she took off with the first man who proposed. It wasn't a matter of love but of transportation. Her husband, Mark Wallace, would soon learn that Clarice merely tolerated him but really and truly adored and cherished the fact that he had his own engineering business and more importantly a car. Years later and as soon as Mark Wallace died of a massive heart attack, a ninety-seven year old ailing Grandma Olivia moved in with her. She didn't have anywhere else to go. Most of the family vowed never again to have anything to do with her. By then she had alienated everyone who was ever close to her. It was forever said that even her own husband, Mann, had to die to get away from her.

CHAPTER TWENTY-FOUR

He was short, squat, generally languid, a glutton who had a fairly uneven temper, and some called him moody as well. However, Antonio Sanchez-Walker, although fat, small in stature and at age forty-five, a relatively young warden, was not to be taken lightly and never for a fool. Actually, it would be considered sheer stupidity to assume that he was incapable of handling himself. He had a full head of curly black hair and a bushy mustache that he would twirl with his forefinger and thumb from time to time, deep in thought as if no one was awaiting an answer or decision from him. He spoke with a thick Dominican accent. Everyone knew to listen real close to what he was saying rather than interrupt. He never repeated himself, ever. He wasn't a patient man at all and would bark and flair-up at any seemingly insignificant, trite word or challenge. It was his nature to be ill at ease and thoroughly distrusting of everyone. He was a veteran, shell shocked, some called him. Even before the Persian Gulf War he had killed many men while on international preoperative missions and was, therefore, unafraid of killing or of death. Many believed he welcomed the latter. His daily carton of Marlboro's together with his consumption of no less than six full greasy meals gave credence to this notion. With or without guards in his office, with or without his .38 attached to his belt; inmates sat obediently across from the man who held their futures in the palms of his stubby hands.

He'd turn his back on them as he gazed through the window at the seagulls mingling with the dirty City pigeons. Not that anyone knew this but he liked the way the sunlight speckled underneath their tiny feet and lightly blinded him with its reflection off the river. He couldn't smell it for the doubled plaited glass but the look of the water so reminded him of the San Cristóbal Province where he grew up and the Nigua River and the sands of the Najayo Beach that it made him smile just thinking about it. He was a long way from home and further still from the idealistic little boy he used to be growing up there believing that life in America was an exquisite dream. After forty-five years he realized now how pathetic and flimsy was the delicate picture he held of his future back then. The things he had seen and done would forever desecrate that perfect image into something yellowed and stained. He had befriended army buddies instantly, needing desperately to trust them with his life by day only to see them blown apart by early afternoon, blood and guts fussed into their very tanks and the earth. It was then his job to collect those soldered remains, sort them and then carry them ironically to the nearest medical unit. How naïve he was; war, up until him fighting in one, was a movie in Technicolor. Killing was something he'd executed as a sharpshooter at a safe distance of being completely impersonal. How was he supposed to know that grown men cried as they died; some shrieking and wailing in excruciating pain, with ghastly screeches that permanently scarred one's eardrums? He'd like to believe as he held his revolver to the butt of some nameless man's head, that that man was his mortal enemy. However, as he watched their eyes look towards Heaven, he knew instinctively that they too were little boys once with dreams of a better life, a rich life, full of possibilities too. It was the most human sensation he had ever felt in his life as he pulled back on the trigger letting the metal inside burst out and shatter their skull. However, that cessation of life was at the darkened end of the spectrum where heartache, sickness and fatal disease reside, where one feels alive in moments of crippling fear. How dare he take from these men what hope was left within their souls? This haunted him, so he drank and numbed their pleas for mercy that seemed to echo from the grave. This weighed him down as if he had to now drag their torn bodies around with him for all eternity. It was little comfort to note that they'd simply turn the tables and place their enormous weapons at his head instead, if given the chance. Now life held so little meaning in the dregs of his prison where anything and everything filthy and ungodly could overwhelm. Where was that child in him that dreamed of becoming a big shot in the States?

Otis Bullock sat patiently awaiting his fate. Sure, he didn't do it but that didn't mean much in a place where everyone cried innocence. Usually such a statement was followed by, "Yeah, yeah, right, right, sure, sure…." Bullock didn't have a leg to stand on. He could have killed him by blinking but to have his hands around the guy's neck the very night he died, well, that was just pure dumb luck, which was the only kind of luck Otis possessed. He had looked forward to getting out of there around retirement age but now even that seemed far fetched and unrealistic. Now he'd be on cloud nine if he got out before he died. Optimism was no match for cynicism and regret. What landed him in jail took exactly twenty-three minutes and thirty-nine seconds, that's what the prosecution said in their closing statement. He just couldn't reconcile how something that small could take so long to fix. As he made himself at ease in one of the two visitor's chairs in Sanchez-Walker's office, he thought long and hard about that imbalance. What else was he doing? Besides, the incarcerated were obsessed with their criminal careers. They had endless amounts of time to mull over every minute detail, every poor choice and decision. Most left prison knowing more about criminal law than an entire troop of judicial professionals. He looked up at Sanchez-Walker's thick back and wondered what else the Warden could do to him. He had lived in solitary confinement for years on and off on account of a temper that needed pitchers full of Ritalin with an OxyContin chaser. He had worked every intolerable chore the correction facility was capable of drumming up. Now, his been there done that attitude drowned out fear and replaced it with trance-like complacency. He was a little curious though, because Warden Sanchez-Walker had a reputation for being insane. Everybody knew that he could and would kill a man with his bare hands. His military record honoring him for bravery had been secretly copied and passed around the yard. To those who read it, it sounded like a ghost story. The fact that he was rewarded for his cruelty and crimes against humanity, made it downright gripping as well as disturbing. Warden Sanchez-Walker would have been considered the most feared prisoner at Riker's were it not for the fact of him running the place.

"So, Bullock…what's going on?" asked Sanchez-Walker still with his back to Otis.

Otis sighed audibly but didn't say a word. He was still chewing on the idea of turning ninety-five behind bars. Then he too stared out of the window mentally chronicling his youth.

"So, nothing to say, huh, Otis?" asked Sanchez-Walker.

He liked Otis. He really did. Were it not for him being a prisoner in his jail, they might have even become good friends. Alas, that was not going to happen. He turned to see Otis shrugging and placing his chin to his chest. He looked like an over grown hound in a dog house.

"You didn't do anything, right?" Sanchez-Walker patronized, "You're innoc..."

"That's right!" shouted Otis but not too loudly, "...damn right I'm innocent."

"I see," said Sanchez-Walker strutting back behind his desk and plopping down into his high leather back swivel chair. He rocked there for several moments as if Otis wasn't there. Otis knew this technique of silent rebellion having done it himself, and simply waited with his eyes fixed on birds forming figure eights against the clouds. He could wait it out all day with Warden Sanchez-Walker. It was more comfortable in his office than in his cell. Besides, sitting around doing nothing was his life. It was that very thing that ultimately got him arrested.

One foolish evening he and his buddies decided to rob K & L Liquors, nothing better to do, and in need of pocket change. He was the look out, sitting in the running, gas-guzzling Buick Regal, in the dimly lit driveway of the convenience store while TJ and Willie entered to take care of the heist. The whole thing didn't take much thought. They had smoked a dime bag of weed before concocting the charade and as the prosecution said, twenty-three minutes and thirty-nine seconds later, the twenty-nine year old store clerk was bleeding to death behind the cash register. Otis didn't even know that Willie had shot someone until three days later when the cops showed up at his front door. Even then he was puzzled when they asked him had he known that Willie was packing.   Otis sat stunned throughout the interrogation. The Police believed he was slow and spoke to him like he was five years old. He simply melted in the chair wondering what on earth was happening. Incarceration had allowed him time to ponder that segment of his life for many, many years, basically serving time for being born stupid. Willie committed suicide long before the trial by taking that very .22 and placing it in his teeth. His father, the owner of the weapon, found his body that evening. It's safe to say that at the time, neither TJ nor Otis knew that Willie was nuts, not the laughable kind but the type that would have landed him in Bellevue. They always just assumed he was funny and buck wild. However, anyone who could shoot themselves in the mouth without opening it up first was perhaps clinically crazy. It was important information, the kind Otis wished he had had beforehand. He sat there wishing that things could have happened in reverse so he'd have seen who he befriended and ended the relationship right after the introduction.

At that thought, Otis smiled.

"Hope you're not thinking about your future, Otis," Sanchez-Walker mentioned as he observed Otis.

Otis slouched further down in his seat fanning his tongue across his front teeth.

"You don't have to worry about that anymore, not with this latest episode," Sanchez-Walker smiled.

"You know what, Warden…" Otis began.

"What, Otis?" he asked.

"You're right," Otis said with great resolve.

At that Sanchez-Walker swiped the smug look he had off his face. He really liked Otis. Other men, lesser men, would have fought him and screamed for justice. Not Otis, he wanted to talk things through, real easy like. Sanchez-Walker was tempted to invite him to lunch. Alas, that wasn't going to happen either.

"How so?" Sanchez-Walker asked, now politely sitting up and listening.

"You're right, I don't have a future here...because..." Otis began then stopped.

"Because, what?" the Warden asked.

"Because the fact is you probably know good and well that lying Busta was very much alive when your soldiers pulled me off of him...and..." he paused.

Sanchez-Walker had a smile across his face broad and shiny.

"...well, let's just say that the facts won't mean much right now for poor old unlucky, Otis, right?" Otis succinctly concluded.

Sanchez-Walker stepped around his desk and leaned on it and into Otis.

"Listen, I like you Otis, I really, really do...but...I can't have my inmates killing each...excuse me, trying to kill each other, now can I?" he blinked.

Otis didn't pay him much mind after that. He'd be serving a few more years for this crime too same as the one he already was. He wondered if he would have some satisfaction in all of this if he actually was the catalyst that led to these two men's deaths, rather than someone tantamount to a bystander. He didn't think himself completely innocent just not the one at the center of the mess, sort of like on the outskirts, a suburb of the main city, as it were.

"...Now as for your future, which I told you not to worry about...Now, you do what you're told. Play nice and all, we'll see what we can do about privileges and such..." said the Warden with the greatest of ease, "...but as for seeing daylight outside of these grounds...that's not likely."

None of the particulars mattered to either man. They had each resolved that truth was like any other opinion, no power save if it had some force behind it. Warden Sanchez-Walker was going to spin this situation to make his inmates behave same as he had allowed his military records to accidentally leak through the prison gossip mill. He liked Otis, he really did, but alas, Otis was just another cog in the wheel. The only thing Warden Sanchez-Walker was trained to do was to kill a man, and in this case he didn't have to lift a finger.

CHAPTER TWENTY-FIVE

'She died in her sleep, whatever that means,' thought Clark. Auntie Clarice called that morning just before the crack of dawn to tell Clark what had happened. She repeated three times that she wanted Clark to tell Tara and the rest of the family. Clark assured her that everyone would know before breakfast. Clark could hear the mournful sound of anguish coming off of her. Having buried her brother, her husband and now her mother, it was only fitting that Auntie Clarice would seem like she was weeping oceans. She informed Clark about the arrangements. Apparently, they were already set. Grandma Olivia would be buried in the Peterson family plot but not next to her husband. He was resting in peace beside his mother, naturally. The only thing Auntie Clarice had to do was buy flowers and a tombstone. Grandma Olivia had a few insurance policies, not much money, but enough to purchase a few things that would garner a respectable funeral.

"How are you doing?" Clark asked her.

"Fine. Fine. Just fine," solemnly spoke Auntie Clarice.

Silence.

"I walked into her room this morning for no reason at all. It's as if I knew something wasn't right, you know. I just walked in and knew. She was very, very still and I knew. I don't really know why but I knew…" Auntie Clarice said.

"Yeah…" was all Clark could say back.

"So, it'll probably be this Saturday. I have to hear from the funeral home what times they have available," she said.

"Yeah."

"So, if you and Tara can't make it because you were just here and all, that's all right. It's up to you though. She knew that you two loved her…and…and she loved you too," Auntie Clarice told her.

"Yeah. Yeah. I know…we do…" replied Clark wanting to say that they *did* know but not wanting to make the distinction of Grandma Olivia being referred to in the past tense.

Then she thought about how her mother would react upon hearing the news of Grandma Olivia.

"Huh hum," Patsy Mae said as if hearing the weather report.

"I don't think we'll be going to the funeral," Clark mentioned.

"Huh hum," Patsy Mae grunted.

"Auntie Clarice sounded really upset," Clark said.

"Yeah, she was always one of the nice ones. We used to hang out like sisters back then before… before…" Patsy Mae did not continue her thought.

Clark knew what she meant by before, before her father died and before Grandma Olivia kicked Patsy Mae out of the family.

"…I never had any problem with her. Never," Patsy Mae said, referring to Auntie Clarice.

Earlier that morning, Grandma Olivia saw Jimmy gleaming larger than life over Clark's shoulder. He was as frightening as a living shadow could be, just following behind Clark as if he were a part of her. Grandma Olivia at first thought he was attached to her granddaughter somehow and that's why she hesitantly told her to be on guard the best way she knew how. She knew that a man provided covering for a woman and therefore told Clark to get married. She felt as if she had done her duty seeing as she was still head of the family and still had an obligation as such.   Somehow though, as her two grandchildren left the room, she knew that he, this thing from hell, was not altogether pleased with her little comment. He remained behind, simply sitting at the foot of her bed at first ever so comfortably watching her. Grandma Olivia had seen the devil before and he didn't scare her none at all. In some ways, she was ready for him. She even tried to sit up and allow him to do his worse to a strengthened body. However, she didn't have the energy to follow through with that pretence. Who was she kidding? She was weak, tired and ready, more than anything else, ready to go. She had lived a long life of disappointment. This grim reaper didn't seem gruesome at all but welcome. She wasn't stupid. She knew that her entire family, kids and all, hadn't any desire to have her around anymore. She was an old woman now, way pass her prime. 'Maybe someday,' she thought, 'they'd know how much I loved them, how much I really cared.' She would have done anything for them and felt satisfied with what she had already accomplished. She began as an orphan who had managed to raise four of her own children and seventeen grandchildren. All were healthy and seemingly happy too, except for her precious baby boy, Mann, who died on account of marrying the wicked woman, Patsy Mae. 'Who names their child Patsy Mae?' she thought and grimaced. She was glad though, glad that he was now finally at peace. Yes, she was quite proud of herself and although everything hadn't turned out the way she'd hoped, she still felt like a success.

Just then he moved. In a flash he was up by her head,

hovering over, just staring down at her. He looked gentler than she imaged death would. She was used to seeing these characters depicted in movies whose faces were skeletal and cracked. This thing looked almost human, like a white cloud. She didn't fear it at all. Then she considered that that might be its intention, to lure her into a false sense of security then take her by surprise. She figured that was fair. This whole experience almost seemed as normal as breathing. She looked up at it and spoke.

"Well?" she simply asked, wondering what was taking it so long.

She always believed that death came swiftly, charging forward and knocking one off their feet before they knew what hit them. This thing just waited and watched. She didn't want some long drawn out spectacularly lengthy episode. She could hear Clarice, her daughter, calling out to her.

"Mom, you all right?" she asked.

"Y...yes...goodnight..." Olivia told her succinctly in a whisper.

She thought about saying good-bye instead but she just didn't want to seem morbid. She would miss her, she decided. She would miss Richmond too. She always liked the way it smelled with all its trees and fresh air, all of its modern conveniences too. It was a big city to her small town upbringing. She would miss her other children too but there was something special about Clarice. She was her first born and there was always something special about the first pregnancy. During that time, she remembered thinking that life was not the misery it had been after all. That lasted nine months before it was replaced by her constant lack of enthusiasm again. After that, came actual motherhood and she couldn't say that she necessarily enjoyed all of that largely due in part to Mamma Peterson, her husband's mother. Her little baby girl, Clarice, stayed at Mamma Peterson's house much more than she stayed home. Mamma Peterson insisted she keep the child while Olivia recovered from the demands of childbirth. It was as if Mamma Peterson was the doctor who snatched Clarice from Olivia's broken womb. After the blatant kidnapping, Olivia was inconsolable for months, not that anyone cared. Mann kept telling her to go out and enjoy her life, her freedom, but try as she might, she couldn't make him understand that she had had enough emancipation. She was freed from her parents when they died and freed from her siblings when they ran off across the color line. Contrary to her family's desires to separate her from her new-born; Olivia wanted to feel connected and to create a bond. For her, being alone hadn't rendered liberty but dissatisfaction and emptiness. They couldn't see why having a child of her own meant the world to her. For them, children were hired help that they didn't have to pay. For her, children were her way of rewriting history, giving her daughter everything that she missed and lacked, showering her with a sense of belonging and the security of a loving family. For nine months she treasured her unborn child carrying her with the anticipation of finally having the family she so desperately longed for. It was a cruel joke played on her that she would suffer with labor pains only to then just suffer. Mamma Peterson told everyone that the only thing Olivia was suffering from was post partum depression. Said it was only natural. Mamma Peterson loved little children and since she was too old to have anymore, she took everybody else's as her own. Olivia inquired about this principle ever so gently once.

"Do you ever see your son?" she asked a fellow sister-in-law.

"It's easier this way," she told Olivia then turned and walked away.

If the wimpy young mother felt otherwise, Olivia would never be allowed to hear it from her lips. Olivia realized that her fate was sealed when she wedded Mann Peterson and that was that.

Jimmy looked at Olivia and began to see something that was surprising to him, happiness. It startled him this happiness. He thought it was the oddest thing to see on someone's face who was about to die. He curiously stared.

"Well?" she asked him again.

That made him smile, the fact that she wanted him to do what he was just about to do. It also made him hesitant too. For he never did anything that another wanted him to. He was in control. He would kill her when he was good and ready to and not a moment before. 'Who does she think she is?' he thought, 'She's not running this show.' Again she smiled in his direction looking totally at peace. It made him smile too as if it was contagious. He didn't like that feeling at all. This transference smile also made him glow even brighter. He couldn't control the sensation that started from the center of his being and worked its way outward. He felt like an unwilling light bulb. It infused him, this energy that over took his previous devious state of being. Suddenly he wanted her gone in the worst way. She was actually forcing him to do something that he loathed, be at peace, smiling for no reason whatsoever. And the more she smiled the more he brightened. It was thoroughly frustrating and humiliating for him. The sheer weakness of it, the weary calmness was down right unsettling. He wondered if old people had some kind of power to warm others up whether they wanted to be or not. It was troublesome. He liked being on edge. Chaos was a welcome friend. Tragedy was his life with joy coming in at peaks and valleys. This thing with her really began to irritate him. Now he looked down at her and wanted to immediately choke the life out of her. He knew that it wouldn't be too difficult. She was practically dead already. The very fact that she could see him was a clear indication of that fact. Alas, she saw him all right.

"You comin'for ta' carry me home, right…" in a raspy voice, she sang.

She was ready. Actually he was too. He didn't want to do it though while she was staring up at him. Ironically, he found that to be creepy. However, he knew that he could get over that feeling. He was already dead and in a few moments she would know how the other half lived.

"Swing low sweet char..ri…ot…ot…comin' fo' ta' car…" she whispered gruffly.

He decided to do this one differently. Seeing as she was ready and all. He thought that he'd simply be the little angel she believed she was seeing. 'Crazy lady,' he thought. Then he imagined himself a beautiful child of light and his shape took on the characteristic of a white dove. He pressed himself upon her upper body.

"Oh, sweet Jesus…sweet…sweet…Je….us…" her heart quickened a pace.

She held her eyes tight against the image before her. It was so beautiful and how did God know that she adored birds.

However, as she stared into the darkness of her room, she could see something else, something beside it, shadowing it. It was - she was just making it out - it was - something ominous and foreboding. She could feel it too. It was wicked. It made her insides churn. Her face went pale. Though Jimmy was trying to fool her, she was able to see him now for what he really was.

"Ahh…" she screamed but her breath had already slowed way down.

Now, she was frightened, scared. She was no longer as sure as before, now thinking that this thing wanted to take her straight to hell.

"No…" she screamed faintly.

She didn't wish to go there and began thinking of all the things that might have led her down in that direction instead of up in the other.

"Oh…Je…sus…" she said willing it all to be different.

She was asking for forgiveness with her heart and mind because her voice had escaped her. Again her breathing went soft and this time she could feel the moments between inhalation winding down. These intervals became gigantic, enormously painstaking and harder still to avoid.

"Oh…Je…sus," she sang the song of the accused.

Then beyond this thing that had now blackened and turned to something akin to solid matter, shone a light. It was a pinpoint at first, just a small pocket flashlight spray that went from Olivia's eyes straight to her heart. It was calling out to her. It had a voice and a presence that reminded her of someone she had known before, but she couldn't see a face or a body. Again, her breathing slowed down further still and the time between breaths became extremely tedious. She could see that the light behind this fiendish thing was actually calling her name. It sounded so sweet and pleasant too. She smiled and the dove above her just vanished. It was replaced with Jimmy in all his splendor. He was terrifying too, but she as once before wasn't scared. Now when she looked up, she could clearly make out the faces within the bright light directly in front of her and just beyond him. Then all at once, she knew what was happening. She knew that he was already dead and had been looking forward to her demise. She knew that he was assisting her to this end for the most hateful and depraved reason, that, he was in love with her granddaughter, Clark, and wanted her to live in hell with him. All of this came to her as if suddenly everything in the world came into focus.

The mask had been lifted and she was seeing creation, and all in life that truly mattered. It was her family there in the distinctness of that room. She could feel them and just knew them though they were without form. At this point Jimmy was leaning into her. Yet, she could laugh at him now, and did. She could tell that when she laughed, he became more frustrated and pounded even harder. He couldn't hurt her though and yet she thought that maybe there was something, a little speck of him that possibly may have led her in this deathly direction. She wondered if she would be facing this heavenly light had he not entered her room that day trailing her granddaughter like a stalker. Unfortunately, that secret was never revealed to her, the cause of her now intended fate. She might never discover why, she simply would be no more. It happened quickly and yet for her time swelled and lingered allowing her to meld into it as if she were orchestrating every second out of her own spirit. The light grew wider and all of life expanded and let her into its most wonderful intimacies. Then the overwhelming love that she felt for her family consumed and ultimately engulfed her.

CHAPTER TWENTY-SIX

S he had heard of love at first sight but had never, ever once experienced it. She tried as hard as she could not to look directly at him. If she had, she knew she'd have fallen in. His eyes were black onyx orbs that masked an ocean behind them. She felt like she had been arrested by them, they captivated her so. He was trim all over, even his hair made an even line as it gently cascaded down to his beautifully shaped shoulder blades, with skin that should have been the definition of delicious and a physic that made her heart stop ticking. She was defeated by a sensation that drove her into the distinct, undeniable belief that they were destined to meet, someone lost in her past, familiar even, and safe. His very existence was irresistible. She wanted to reach out and touch him - everywhere. She knew him though they had never met. Yet it wasn't just pure animalistic, primal attraction. It was something more unfathomable and visceral. He reminded her of a marvelously brilliantly unfolding sunset. He looked up and smiled. That's when Clark realized that her lips had been permanently glued to her teeth for fifteen minutes as she sat across from him simply staring. Now his curious gaze made her stop and rethink this activity. After all, she wasn't coming to see him but his live-in girlfriend.

"She'll be right out," he spoke.

Clark trembled inside.

"She has someone in session," he spoke again.

Clark could barely say, okay. She nodded diagonally. He

was looking right at her and this action made her feel wonderfully indecent. He chuckled at her pain and continued reading his newspaper. She looked out of the window at the Bedford Stuyvesant architecture, away from the man whom she would marry if he but asked. Besides she had this appointment set a month in advance. She didn't want to jeopardize it in any way, like by slinging the woman's boyfriend down and having her way with him right there in the woman's foyer. She just couldn't help herself though; there was something about him that honestly disturbed her system.

His girlfriend, whom she had never met either, was a Yoruba Priestess named Enomwoyi. She had heard from a fairly reliable source in these matters, Arlene, that, quote, "She tell you sum thing that make you thannnnk," end quote. Clark ran into Arlene at a regional Equity showcase she was doing at Amos Theater. Arlene came screaming backstage telling everyone she saw that she was a personal friend of Clark's. Clark didn't have the heart to tell her that they were in East Harlem not Broadway. Arlene sat patiently as Clark changed from Actress Number 2 of the chorus into her street clothes. Arlene didn't mind. She was so excited to see the many lit mirrors and the other cast members signing autographs and prancing around high on after show adrenaline. Clark was excited too because she had some serious questions for Arlene and was happy to have run into her. She figured that someone like Arlene could help her with what was happening to her at night. She'd been awakened every night with sweat dripping down her skin and literally something that looked like cut marks between her thighs. She desperately wanted to tell someone who'd understand the things she'd been seeing because now her visions of the dead had become daily occurrences.   Long gone were the times of occasionally witnessing these beings while asleep, now she saw them wide awake as well. She was passing an abandoned church one day on her way to an audition. It was one hundred plus degrees in the shade. She had an hour to kill, so she took her time walking. When she crossed the entryway, a cold, frigid wind blew her down to the ground. This burst of air had a face and a tail. She fell into a puddle of dried mud. It got all over the crisply ironed white shirt she was wearing. So she took the bus back home to change and then had to run to her audition in order to make it on time. She was ten minutes late, which, to a casting director, translates to her not really wanting the job. She was just at a loss for words. How could she tell anybody, particularly a stranger, that she was being haunted? The coincidence of seeing Arlene was sincerely welcome.

The door opened and a strikingly handsome woman in her mid-fifties entered into the little foyer where Clark and her gorgeous new friend were seated.

"I am Priestess Enomwoyi," she said emphasizing the 'nom' in her name.

Clark didn't know whether to shake hands or bow or simply say hello. How should one properly greet a Priestess?

"And you are?" she asked Clark.

"Oh…oh…uh…" Clark stammered.

"Clark Green. She's Clark Green," the unbelievably beautiful man said.

"Yes, Yes. I'm Clark," Clark finally uttered.

Suddenly, she didn't want to proceed any further, so she

awkwardly stared at the gorgeous man.

"This is Paulo, my man," Priestess Enomwoyi told Clark, emphasizing 'my' and 'man.'

Clark immediately put her head down in shame wondering what in the world was wrong with her. She had just insulted the woman whose house she came to for help. Even so, the very gracious Priestess Enomwoyi led Clark through her entrance way farther into the house where her office was located. Compared to the rest of the massive brownstone, it was a small crawl space beside a dreadfully lived in kitchen and hallway. There were dirty dishes in the sink piled high enough to touch the cabinets above. Everywhere else was messy too. Yet, all in all, it was comfortable. Clark saw pictures everywhere of children, hers most likely. They looked just like her. As Clark followed Priestess Enomwoyi, she could hear them playing upstairs.

"Mommy's, working! Keep it down!" yelled Priestess Enomwoyi up a flight of stairs.

After that Clark couldn't hear anything but her heart beat.

"That's an interesting name, E-no-mi-ni…" Clark told her.

"E-nom-wo-yi. Enomwoyi, thank you," she nodded, "It's Benin meaning one who has grace and charm."

Clark thought that Priestess Enomwoyi bore her name well. She seemed to guide across the floor and carry herself as if supported by servants. She radiated dominance like she was born a queen. She could see why Paulo was attracted to her even though the difference in their ages was more than twenty-five years. Priestess Enomwoyi was striking. Her skin was a shiny caramel coloring, her hair was dreadlocked smelling of roses, and swung down to the back of her thighs. It was thick and had to be heavy but Priestess Enomwoyi held her head up high despite its weight.

"Sit, please," she told Clark and Clark obeyed.

Suddenly she felt uneasy.

"What can I do for you today?" Priestess Enomwoyi asked also sitting in an high leather back chair.

She looked regal as Clark watched the reflection of the sun bend the light into a crown over her head.

"What?" Clark asked distracted by this poised woman who sat facing her.

"What-can-I-do-for-you, Clark?" Priestess Enomwoyi asked again cracking a small smile at her guest.

"I...well...I..." Clark stuttered.

"You need assistance with things that are not of this world, right?" Priestess Enomwoyi asked and leaned into a very surprised Clark.

Clark started to ask how she knew then quickly remembered that that's what Priestess Enomwoyi did for a living and the reason she came to see her in the first place. So, she simply nodded yes.

"Let me begin by asking you why? That is to say what has been going on in your life?" Priestess Enomwoyi leaned back into her chair and knotted her hands together in a fold.

"Well, I...well...it's just that when I wake up there's these strange marks all over my body especially...esp..." Clark pointed to her private area.

"I see," Priestess Enomwoyi nodded that she understood, "Anything else?" she asked.

Clark wanted to say, 'Isn't that enough?'

"I mean do you see anything there in your sleep?" Priestess

Enomwoyi pointedly asked.

"Well…now that you mention it, there's something over me sometimes. Sometimes it's in my apartment with me too. I can feel it," Clark told her now feeling a bit more comfortable.

Priestess Enomwoyi sat up and started pulling things out of her desk drawer and placing them on top. First, was a purple velvet bag of stones and then a set of Tarot cards. Clark really and truly didn't want her to read these things the way she'd seen people do at carnivals. She became disappointed with the prospect of someone entertaining her with hocus pocus tricks. Then Priestess Enomwoyi pushed these things aside and then pulled out a single sheet of paper and a lead pencil.

"I'd like you to draw it for me," Priestess Enomwoyi told her.

"Draw? What?" Clark asked.

"I'd like to see what you see," Priestess Enomwoyi told her.

Clark hesitantly took the pencil and turned the paper towards her.

"Right now?" Clark innocently asked.

Priestess Enomwoyi smiled and nodded yes. Clark thought herself a terrible artist. She couldn't even sign her name legibly let alone do a rendering of something she sees when she's half asleep. Yet she took a deep breath and thought about her visions of this thing that hovered overhead, whose presence was always in her apartment. It would be like drawing smoke. How does one draw smoke? Priestess Enomwoyi studied Clark's twisted face.

"Try," she told her.

Clark began to sketch on the blank page. She muttered inwardly of what a grand waste of time it was to draw smoke but she was in no position to protest. In fact, she was scared out of her wits and most times slept with one eye open. She couldn't bring herself to reveal that little bit of information with the high priestess. So, she did the best she could from memory and turned the paper around on the desk for Priestess Enomwoyi to see. Priestess Enomwoyi took it and brought it towards her, examining the, for lack of a better word, picture. Clark had shaded some parts and made long curvy strokes around the page to indicate that the thing floated. She hadn't any artistry training whatever, so the image looked like a two year old had done it. Clark wanted to laugh at how bizarre it was to have Priestess Enomwoyi take the thing seriously and she did. Priestess Enomwoyi stared at it then focused on thin air in order to see it in her minds-eye. Then she'd take another glance and do the same thing several times more. Each time she did this, Clark would sit up in her chair hoping that Priestess Enomwoyi had some answers.

"Well…what do you see?" Clark finally asked her, anxious to have something that would make her rest easier.

"Well…is right," Priestess Enomwoyi said and looked at the paper a few more times.

Clark was now on edge with the way Priestess Enomwoyi said 'well.' It was filled with innuendo and meaning. It was pregnant with thought. Clark began to swell with worry especially when Priestess Enomwoyi's attention then shifted suddenly to her. Now, she stared at Clark, examined her as if she were reading her mind. Clark shifted in her seat and tried to look elsewhere but it was impossible. It was the grin that Priestess Enomwoyi was wearing. It made her lips tilt to one side as if her entire face was melting. It was ominous and foreboding, altogether wicked. Clark didn't like it one bit and truly wanted to bolt right out of there. She longed for Paulo to barge in on them. She knew she wasn't making sense but was feeling desperate for escape. She believed that these people who consorted with the dead were weird and that she didn't belong anywhere near them. She decided that she didn't want to delve any further into the occult. She wanted to leave. She couldn't believe that she let Arlene talk her into going to see what basically boiled down to a dime store psychic. Plus she was paying a mere two hundred dollars for the privilege. Finally, Priestess Enomwoyi faced Clark and spoke. And she simply said, "His name is…Jimmy."

CHAPTER TWENTY-SEVEN

Clark stumbled out of Priestess Enomwoyi's house, barely able to see straight in front of her for the cloud of confusion in her head. She took the train home with her mind on automatic pilot. Her whole system was out of order. Her stomach hurt, her back was achy, and her hair was standing on end. Even her eyelids throbbed. She kept thinking, 'What on earth was she talking about - Jimmy?' She was searching the thin recesses of her troubled mind trying to remember just who this Jimmy person could be and was hesitant to delve into why he would be with her. First things first, who is he? She wiped the dust off her high school year book, Performing Arts for Theater, thumbed through it and couldn't find a single Jim, James, Jimmy, not one male's name beginning with the letter J. Then she went to her college yearbook, but there was no need. She didn't really know anyone there at all. She spent most of her time honing her craft and seldom had a moment to enjoy anyone else's company. She didn't even recognize the book let alone the people within. She only knew the people who were directly related to her discipline and everyone else was just that, everyone else. She hated the fact that she didn't have a clue because admittedly she went through four years of college with her head down.

She had stripped down to her underwear at the door of her apartment and rolled into bed as is. She'd usually take off make-up and such, or shower off the day but nothing could make her feel better at this point except sleep. No sooner did her head hit the pillow did the name Jimmy do more than just swim in her thoughts. She realized that she only knew of one who bore that name. Recognizing that, she leapt from her bed and immediately phoned her mother.

"Ma, hi, it's me," Clark said in jagged speech.

"Hey, baby," Patsy Mae replied.

Silence.

"Clark, that you?" Patsy Mae queried, knowing her daughter well and that something was bothering her.

"Yeah…yeah…Hey, Ma…ah…" suddenly Clark didn't know where to begin.

"You okay?" Patsy Mae asked.

"Yeah…Yeah…I just called to see how you were doing," Clark told her knowing full well that Patsy Mae knew better.

"I'm fine. Just fine. I was just sitting here deciding what I'm gonna' fix for that man tonight. I don't really feel like nothing myself but knowing him, he's gonna' come in here starvin' as usual," she laughed.

Clark laughed too remembering how sometimes he'd eat his dinner standing over the stove and how Patsy Mae would ask him if he had any common sense.

"You think he'd get full every once and a while, but no, he could eat all day long and not gain a single pound. He's still just as thin as he was when we first met. Honestly, I've never seen anything like it," Patsy Mae went on.

"Yeah," Clark said.

"Clark?" Patsy Mae asked.

"Yeah, Ma?" Clark replied.

"Why'd you call, ser-ious-ly?" Patsy Mae asked wanting to

get to the heart of the matter.

"Well…it's just that… well…" Clark paused, thinking.

"Come on, tell it," Patsy Mae told her.

"Well…it's just that I've had a problem lately with something," Clark began.

"Something? Something, like what? You pregnant? Is it Peter's?" Patsy Mae asked.

"No, no, nothing like that. Nothing like that," Clark corrected her.

"Well?" Patsy Mae asked, "What then?"

"You're going to think I'm crazy," Clark warned her.

"I'm not gonna' think anything, but you're making me nervous. Tell me what's going on with you right now," Patsy Mae ordered as mother's can with authority and love mixed.

"I think that I'm being haunted, haunted by Jimmy's ghost," Clark blurted.

"What?" Patsy Mae said more in shock than anything else.

Clark nodded yes as if Patsy Mae could see her do so. Then they each allowed Clark's words to sink into their spirits. Patsy Mae was not a novice in these matters having grown up in the South, she had seen all kinds of things of this nature before she could walk.

"I see," she said.

Clark once again nodded gripping the phone with sweaty hands hoping she didn't have to say too much more. She already felt bad enough. She didn't want her mother to treat her as if she was losing her mind.

"What color was he?" Patsy Mae asked.

Clark paused before saying, "White."

"I see," she said.

Then they both mulled this over for a good two minutes before either said a word. Clark wanted to sink into the floor because she was really beginning to feel very, very frightened. She kept thinking that she was going to have to deal with this thing alone because only she and Priestess Enomwoyi at two hundred dollars per session would even believe it.

"I see. I see," Patsy Mae repeated.

Clark's heart was deflating in her chest as she waited and wondered what her mother's reaction would be.

"Now, I know what you think it is you're seeing. I understand that, I do, but...the man's dead. He can't hurt you now. He dead," Patsy Mae said with as much love and comforting as Clark had expected from her.

It wasn't exactly what she wanted to hear but she had to admit to herself that she was probably expecting too much. What does one say to another who claims they've seen a ghost?

"Now, Mann Jr., your father, did visit me once, you know. I've told ya'll about that. That was a long, long time ago, before I even met Billy Earl. Your father was a gentle man, you see. He wouldn't hurt a fly though he did eventually kill himself with that there wine, you know. Anyway, I was lying in bed, you know, asleep, and there he was; he just came into my room. He was smiling too. Boy, he had a handsome smile. He say, *"Take care of my kids. I know that you will do real well,"* That was it. That was all he say. He was real gentle, you know. Never could even raise his voice too loudly. Well, with a mother like Grandma Olivia who could...anyway, you know what I mean..." Patsy Mae said trailing off in remembrance.

"Yeah," Clark replied.

"Listen, baby, I was a married lady, then I was a widow. My

husband came to say good-bye and that was that. Now, I know that there are things out there beyond living and all, but ghosts, is just our fears made to seem real. That's all that is, honey. You living there all by yourself now without Peter and maybe things is just getting the best of ya'," she told Clark.

Clark took a deep breath, realizing that she definitely wasn't going to get what she was after from her mother, well meaning though she was.

"…Now, if you decide that you want to come back home and live with your mamma, now that would be nice. Your room is still here. You know that you always have a home to come home to. Anytime," Patsy Mae said warmly.

Clark couldn't resist thinking that living with Patsy Mae would put a serious cramp in her style. She'd move in as a twenty-eight year old adult but by the time Patsy Mae gave her a curfew and chores, she'd be reduced to a twelve year old once more.

"Well…" Clark said mulling over that possibility.

"Well, I know. I know. You want your freedom. I get that but some of this may just be loneliness. You ever think of that?" Patsy Mae asked.

Clark wasn't about to argue with her mother. How could she tell her that she was not lonely and that the things that she was going through were real? It was impossible.

"Baby, like I said, you can always come home, okay," Patsy Mae reiterated.

"Yes, I know, Ma. Thanks," Clark told her, "I love you."

"I love you too," Patsy Mae said with an air kiss, "Now, let me hit this kitchen before you know who comes in here looking in my mouth. That man makes me live in the A& P the way he eat. Honest to God. I've never seen anything like it. You would think that at this age he'd be done with eating all together but no. It looks like he's just getting started again. Remind me of Marlin when he was ten years old. Honestly. He's gonna' eat what I fix him though. I'm not going crazy."

Clark laughed, "Yeah, okay then," pause, "I'll call you tomorrow."

"Okay. Love you, honey and remember what I said, okay? You can always come back home," she told her and then hung up the phone.

Clark let the receiver slip down, steadily repeating her mother's words, 'You can always come back home,' 'You can always come back home.' She realized that as much as that statement was true in the natural, one can always pack and move back in with their parents, however, there is a price, especially if one has had a small taste of independence. She decided that she would have to really and truly think about that as an option. As much as she loved her mother, one overwhelming realization kept popping into her head, she didn't want to live with her anymore. She couldn't believe that Patsy Mae would even want her to. After all, her mother spent a great deal of her time gently pushing her children lovingly out of her door. She raised them to be self-reliant and capable. Clark didn't want to disappoint her by now running back home with her tail between her legs. She didn't want to be that type of daughter who couldn't make it in the real world. So many years ago when she told her that she was going to school for acting, Patsy Mae advised her to learn how to type. That was her assessment of acting as a profession. Needless to say, she didn't have much faith in it. Though she hadn't even realized how much her statements hurt her daughter. She couldn't return home now. No one would believe it was for protection. No, Clark needed to figure this problem out on her own. If for no other reason than that she just couldn't accept the fact that her mother's career choice for her life might have been right. Alas, playing it safe was obviously not in the cards for her.

CHAPTER TWENTY-EIGHT

"HELP! HELP!" Bernie yelled scrambling to maintain his balance. There was a fishing boat not more than a quarter of a mile away. "You okay over there?" the man in the boat shouted back.

"HELP! HELP!" Bernie yelled again, "Can you give me a hand?"

The man quickly scurried over to assist him, steadily maintaining his beer in one hand, and greasy, fried chicken leg in the other. He pulled up his anchor and slowly motored alongside Bernie's ProSport. Once there, he anchored again and tied a knot from his boat onto Bernie's.

"Hot damn!" the man said once he boarded Bernie's boat and was able to see what Bernie was struggling with, dropping his poultry, "Hot damn! Look at that thing!" he yelled reaching out to take hold of the rod within Bernie's slipping hands.

His Budweiser went rolling and spilling down the side of Bernie's deck.

"Thank you! Hold her steady! Come on now!" Bernie yelled giving instructions to both his new friend and the fish.

"It's a whale out there, damn! I can barely hold her," the man said.

Bernie turned all the way round in order to grip the fishing rod with both elbows and placed it firmly between his knees.

"I'm holding her as best as I can. Why don't you reach over and try to scoop her up with that thing," Bernie nodded in the direction of a fraying net.

"You sure you can hold her by yourself? I don't want to let go unless you're sure, now," the man said.

Bernie went down onto his knees practically lying down on the deck floor, trying as hard as he could not let go of his big catch.

"I think I can manage! Go on!" Bernie told him all the while straining to maintain his balance.

"You sure now 'cause we can just keep on tryin' pull this bastard in. We can do it, you and me 'gether, you know. I won't let go unless you are one hundred percent sure," the man said also straining to retain his tight grip.

"Well..." Bernie started wanting desperately to wipe the sweat trickling down his forehead, "Better go now before I run out of steam. Go on now."

With that reassurance, the man let go of the rod and leapt over to the net. He lifted it up and realized that it was a bit tangled.

"Damn thing!" he bellowed twisting it up and down trying to loosen the knots.

"Come on now! I'm not sure how long I can hold her!" Bernie screamed.

"I'm tryin'. I'm tryin'! This darn thing, it don't want to mind me," the man told him all the while struggling to get the net to straighten out.

"Just put it in the water! Go on now! I – don't – know – how – long... Go on!" Bernie shouted.

The stranger took the net and slammed it hard against his thigh and the net fell perfectly loose at his side. He then ran to the side of the boat, net in hand and scooped it into the water.

"Well I'll be damned! Well I'll be damned!" he exclaimed.

"What? What?" Bernie yelled in a panic.

"That's the biggest thing I've ever seen," the stranger said steadily leaning over the boat and reaching for the fish that was zigzagging through the water faster than he could follow.

"Can you get it?" Bernie asked, hopeful, "Can you get it?"

"As God is my witness, I'm sure as hell gonna' try. Just you hold on now. Don't let go. No matter what happens, don't you let go," the stranger said and leaned further over the edge of the boat.

Just then, a westerly current blew the boat making it rock. To its passengers, it seemed as if it were moving forward. Bernie's new friend was knocked off balance.

"Oh Jes-us!" the stranger exclaimed.

"What? What?" Bernie asked in dread.

"Do what I said. Don't let go!" the stranger yelled back from his position of straddling the boat one leg outside, one on the inside.

Nothing deterred him from his quest, not the cold water whipping against his face, the intermittent notion that sharks might be about, nothing. However, he went so far over the edge that when Bernie finally turned to check on him, it looked as if he'd fallen over.

"Hey! Hey!" Bernie shouted.

"Don't let go, damn it! Don't let that thing go!" the stranger shouted right back.

"Okay! Okay! You just don't fall in the water," Bernie advised him with a bit of a strained chuckle.

They both started laughing nervously through the wind and the arduous task. It was good to do so to remind them both why they loved fishing.

"This ain't no porgy, I tell you that," the stranger said

shouting over the edge.

"What the heck is it?" Bernie shouted.

"Can't say – yet," the stranger said while angling his body with his front towards the boat and leaning back into the water in order to get a better grip.

The net just touched the fish once and the stranger almost slipped right out beside it.

"I'm gonna' get you! It's on now! You're not smarter than me. No, you're not," he yelled at the determined fish.

The stranger leaned in closer to the water.

"It look like a whale!" the stranger screamed.

"What? What?" Bernie screamed back.

"Don't let go! I said, don't – let – go!" he shouted while fanning the net out into the water in a sweeping moment, "Oh...oh...oh...!" steadily scooping the net under the fish. Then finally, "Got ya'," he proudly said.

With that he held the net with the enormous fish in it and used all his weight to pull it up from the water. The fish shimmied and jumped trying to break free. It leaped up and tried to force itself from its entanglement, but Bernie and the stranger were even more determined. Bernie placed the rod down to the deck floor and completely stretched out down upon it. Meanwhile, his friend slowly and painstakingly continued to hold on to the fish while hoisting himself up and back onto the boat. He hollered in pain as he inched his leg over. Then with every last bit of energy he pulled the fish and his body up and onto the boat.

Bernie, the stranger and the fish lay on the deck floor for several minutes each at varying degrees of trying to catch their breath. Then Bernie turned around.

"We get 'em?" he asked, eyes still adjusting.

His question was answered as he faced the stranger, who was, like him, trying to stand. Their mouths hung wide open as they stared and stared in utter amazement at what they saw. It was more than they could have ever imagined.

"That a shark?" Bernie queried keeping his distance.

"Nah, that there's…" the stranger started walking around the flopping mass before them.

"Well I'll be," Bernie stood agog.

"I saw those fins and thought that it was, but nah' that ain't no shark. Not at all….Let me think now. I know what that is," the stranger told him scratching his head and still breathing heavily.

"Well I'll be," Bernie kept on, "We need a picture of that thing. I bet we could win some kind of award for that. Hell, that thing could feed a small country."

They both laughed. It was a hardy laugh this time now that the job had been done. They were quite proud of themselves and continued to look at their enormous prize.

"I believe…I believe that that's a Fin…a Blue Fin…" the stranger said.

"Well I'll be," Bernie continued in shock.

Then, as the fish slowed its struggling, they began to circle it, really examining every inch of it. Neither of them wanted to admit it but they were afraid to have done so while it was clearly still alive and looking very much like a shark.

"God, how much you think that thing weighs?" Bernie asked.

"I'll send you my doctor's bill for my back," the stranger grinned.

They laughed.

"It felt like a ton," the stranger told him.

"Who you telling? I couldn't hold her no longer. Another minute, I'd have to let her go. Just like that back out to sea. Let one of those real fishermen catch her," Bernie said seriously.

"That's it!" the stranger exclaimed.

"What?" asked Bernie.

"That's where I've seen something like this before. Up there in Long Island, like way over there in Montauk, you know. That there's where I've seen those. I didn't even know you could catch something like this over here. Man, she's beautiful!" he said.

"Ain't she though," Bernie agreed.

Bernie and the stranger quickly started up their engines and took a ride over to a weighing station filled with the excitement of kids on their birthday. They were startled to find out that they were the proud owners of a Blue Fin weighing nine hundred and seventy-five pounds, a record apparently. They were told that their big fish wasn't known to swim in those waters and that they were truly in the right place at the right time. Bernie's grin stretched his face out of proportion in the standard Polaroid taken to commemorate the really, really big catch. His lips didn't go back to their normal position on his face until he returned home.

"If you think you're bringing that there thing into this house and putting it on my table, you are out of your cotton pickin' mind," Lillie told him turning on her heels and slamming the back screen door in his face.

"But, Lil," Bernie tried.

"But Lil nothing," she said audibly from within the kitchen

banging pots about on the counter.

The stranger was poised by the boat ready to extricate the mammoth creature from the deck and place it on Bernie's table.

"You ready?" he innocently asked Bernie.

Bernie turned and eyed him immediately recognizing then that the stranger most probably did not have a wife.

"Well...ah...Maybe we should bring it into the shed instead," Bernie advised him trying to sound like he was still in control.

Bernie brought a handcart over to the boat and together they hoisted the fish onto it.

"Oh boy, oh boy, this is gonna' taste real good with some turnip greens and some sweet potata's, right?" the stranger asked.

"Yeah, turnips," Bernie muttered underneath his breath.

He could still, though try not to as he might, hear Lillie tossing the kitchen utensils.

"Thank you for invitin' me fishing with you," the stranger said.

They laughed.

"It is funny, isn't it? Actually, though, if it weren't for you, I never would have gotten this thing. Thank you for your help," Bernie sincerely told him.

"T'was nothin' really. Nothin' was biting for me. That's why I was having lunch when I heard you calling out," the stranger said, "By the way, name's Earl, Billy Earl," he reached over to shake Bernie's hand.

"Name's Bernard. Call me Bernie," Bernie told him.

Then they stood for yet another hour looking in awe at the Blue Fin. They could have stared at it all night long.

CHAPTER TWENTY-NINE

"Hi," he said smiling brightly. Clark tried her best not to stare at the man as he fanned his hand open to allow Arlene and her entry into Priestess Enomwoyi's hallway. Yet she stared and she stared. It was as though she couldn't stop staring. At one point she thought there might be something wrong with her she was staring so fixedly. It dawned on her, though, ever so surprisingly that he might indeed be staring back. In fact, he seemed practically enamored, intrigued even, although, she couldn't be absolutely sure.

"Enomwoyi and the others are in the living room," he said virtually twinkling like a star.

'The others?' thought Clark with Arlene in toe. Clark was so glad she brought Arlene along. She wanted and needed a friend to lean on at this, for lack of a better word, event, and Priestess Enomwoyi only invited people she knew, those who dealt in the occult, to this *egungun*, a celebration in honor of ancestors and deities. Arlene was once a client of Priestess Enomwoyi's when she was having a rough patch in her marriage. Plus, Arlene begged to come. Neither had ever been to something like this before. They were excited and spent hours getting ready. The only thing they were told was to wear all white. Clark only had one white cotton skirt and one white t-shirt, which clung to her small frame and made her already curvy figure look even more so. She also only possessed a single white hat; it was a floppy summer linen that made her look like a movie star. Paulo really,

really stared. She could feel his eyes all over her even when he was in the next room.

"Would you like something to drink?" he asked her having walked all the way across the room filled with most probably other thirsty people.

Clark shook her head saying no while Arlene indignantly waited for him to acknowledge her.

"I'd like something…!" she yelled at his back.

Two minutes later he was back in front of them with two glasses of grape juice. He reached over and handed them each a drink, all the while leaning ever so slightly closer to Clark. She smiled when she took hers; happy that he hadn't listened to her when she said she didn't want any. Arlene, however, snatched hers out of his hand and eyed him with gall. Then, Paulo walked away and made sure that his eyes were never far from Clark. At times, she even felt uneasy by his gawking as if he was groping her with his thoughts. Her discomfort, she realized, was mainly due to the fact that she didn't want Priestess Enomwoyi to think that there was anything going on between them. Yet, the mutual attraction was undeniable. It was like an affliction.

The ritual began subtly with just the slightest hum of drumming from five conga players positioned against the far living room wall. Clark hadn't really noticed them at all until their music filled the tiny room and seemed to push every other sound outside. At one point Priestess Enomwoyi opened the front and back door to allow whatever she suspected was present a chance to leave. Then she slammed the doors tightly shut. She proceeded in making sure that every single window was also thusly closed and locked. It was an obsession with her. She pushed them down with one hand then forced them even more secure with the full extent of her body weight. Although everyone was talking, the only thing Clark could hear now was the click of the window latches and the drumming. It had satiated all of her, mind, body and soul.

"You hear that?" Clark asked Arlene in a whisper.

"What? What?" Arlene answered surveying everything in every direction.

Clark couldn't explain what seemed to have overtaken her senses so she remained silent and just watched and waited as the room began to amass with what she could only describe as floating people. Yet they were not actually people at all, for they were definitely no longer among the living. One by one, they entered or rather descended, each with a distinct likeness to humanity about them as if they had never left.

One female spirit wore a headdress of bright multi-colored fabric, which began a swirl at the crown of her head and circled down around her entire missing body. She was stunningly beautiful and austere, definitely the leader of the bunch. Her companions marched behind humbly and obediently almost reverently. Priestess Enomwoyi stood at the entryway of the living room with her hand open, welcoming, her body in an ushering posture. She was greeting her guests, the ghosts; souls that she seemed very, very familiar with. Clark's eyes went wide just before her mouth formed into a scream. Priestess Enomwoyi peered over in her direction and with a glance squelched the sound from her lips. Clark felt parallelized as she watched Priestess Enomwoyi's eyes penetrate into her own.

Then gently Clark could feel her body giving way to Priestess Enomwoyi's calmness. Instinctively she knew that she wasn't meant any harm and eventually as if by suggestion, her thoughts turned elsewhere. Clark turned and faced the drummers. While the ghostly guests glided ever so regally into the room and went directly over to the empty chairs that were obviously designated specifically for them. The seats were upholstered with thick silk fabrics of gold, emerald green, deep purple and the darkest shades of blues. Their wooden frames were sanded down smoothly and refinished by someone skilled in making them look brand new. These beings filled the seats, and waited patiently as Priestess Enomwoyi, who had gathered together ornate vases, beaded jewelry and fresh cut wild flowers, and placed separate bundles of these items at what used to be her guests' feet. Clark caught a glimpse of this out of the corner of her eye and immediately nudged Arlene.

"Huh?" Arlene uttered to Clark without facing her or turning away from the musicians.

That was about the time when Clark realized that she was the only one witnessing what was going on with Priestess Enomwoyi. She alone saw the ghostly guests waving and smiling thanks to Priestess Enomwoyi for her gifts. She alone saw Priestess Enomwoyi go into the kitchen and return with a great big pitcher. In front of each guest she poured a tall glass of water and placed Irises inside, together with baby's breath, shavings from tree branches, and tiny twigs. This all struck Clark as odd how Priestess Enomwoyi paid such particular attention to this endeavor. Especially since, among other things, her guests couldn't smell, taste or feel anything. That's when Priestess Enomwoyi poured some of the flowered favored concoction out a little at a time right in front of their chairs. With that done, Priestess Enomwoyi then bowed down to the floor in what only could be described as worship. She also chanted and sang something that sounded like a spell. Her body shook and twisted unnaturally. She started foaming at the mouth and batting her eyes in a flutter. Clark was too terrified to move. That's when she noticed the statues on the inlayed walled shelves behind each chair. The statues were made of cedar, having strange carvings upon them representing people or animals or a combination thereof. Some figures looked like lions and others like tigers, others bears. Clark scanned each one and then looked at the beings directly below in the corresponding seats. The resemblance was uncanny. She shivered. Priestess Enomwoyi shivered too but in a manic display of wild dancing and singing, in shrieks and shrills. Her voice was raw and hollow, now without a hint of familiarity to that of her own. She lay upon the floor convulsing and squirming around feverishly, then nothing. Nothing moved at all.

All eyes were on her as she simply coughed once then sat up right trance-like; her back so straight it hardly looked humanly possible to perfect that position. Then, without so much as a push off, her entire body slid across the living room floor never once changing from her seated rigid pose. She giggled like a school girl as everyone stood with mouth agape watching and waiting for her next trick. Sensing their anticipation, she slid again but this time purposely towards the drummers, who leaned into her and started whacking upon the skins more feverously in her honor. Clark glanced over and again saw the seated guests now minus the elder, nodding their heads in approval. Some waved their handkerchiefs and titled their heads grinning at one another acknowledging a tribute made just for them. Then Priestess Enomwoyi slid again but this time her body bumped right into Clark's feet. Now everyone began to stare directly at her as Priestess Enomwoyi glared up into her eyes. Clark couldn't be absolutely sure but she kind of got the impression that Priestess Enomwoyi was no longer pleased with her and now neither were her ghostly guests.

There was an intimidation factor about them that left Clark feeling weak and vulnerable. It startled her how utterly panicky she became with each preternatural eye drilling imaginary holes into her flesh. They hissed and somewhat barked at her as if she were a filthy mess of rags. She couldn't understand what turn of events had left them in such fowl humor. Clark didn't know where to look or who to turn to. Arlene, who was normally so well versed in these matters, had already left her going over to the drummers as if she were networking for her next party, leaving Clark at a standstill; perplexed and terrified. That's when the ghostly visitors all at once took off in flight from their seats as if they knew that they had her now. Then they swarmed a vicious circle right around her. They taunted her, snarling, launching towards her face and swooping down around the mid-section of her body. Clark tried to duck away from them and cried frightfully while they all out attacked her. She could hear them too, their thoughts began to swirl in her head. They were telling her to get out, that she wasn't welcome among them. 'Not welcome among you,' she mentally repeated, 'Isn't it the other way around,' she thought while searching the room for someone or something to come and help her. There she was flailing her arms about trying to strike at them, trying to shoo them away. It was like trying to hit a shadow. And no one paid her any mind. Mainly because there wasn't a soul who could appreciate what she was going through or what she was up against. She figured that everyone must have thought she was possessed. Clark could feel them too. The energy coming off of them felt like slaps and scratches against her skin. They were actually taking turns, each shifting round ready to take the next whack at her. She was utterly defenseless. Slowly with each wilt that appeared on her arms and legs, she grew more and more angry, not fully understanding why Priestess Enomwoyi would use these dramatic tactics. 'Is all this really necessary,' she wondered, 'It's just flirting.' She didn't have to sick her sacra sancta demons from hell on her. Suddenly, Clark fell to the floor when one of them rammed itself directly into her mid-section. She scrambled to get back up patting herself down as dust flung to her white clothing. Then she stumbled backward as she was still relentlessly being forced into a corner. It was becoming clear that she was in this strange woman's house; one who was possibly capable of making her disappear. She'd die of a heart attack and no one would know that it was brought on by evil spirits, and magic spells. Her back quite literally against the wall, she quickly decided that she was far too young to die, least not at the hands of jealous, crazy Priestess Enomwoyi. So, she mustered whatever courage she could gather and ran. She sprinted as fast as she could through the crowd toward the front door. It was difficult because everyone had dispersed and were now congregating in the center of the room. She realized that in her panic, she had pushed a few out of her way. She apologized along the way but it was an inaudible mumble from someone flashing by. She was almost home free rounding the hallway into the foyer but as soon as her foot touched the welcome mat, Priestess Enomwoyi had reached for her sleeve. Clark shrieked. Everyone could hear her blood curdling scream as she felt Priestess Enomwoyi's cold touch.

"Child, where you goin'?" Priestess Enomwoyi asked her.

Clark didn't turn around. Her body wouldn't let her. Though, she could tell by the mellow tone in her voice that Priestess Enomwoyi was herself once again. Even so, that was hardly proof that all was well. Slowly, ever so slowly, Clark allowed her eyes to meet hers. Yet she kept one foot facing the entrance. To her surprise, Priestess Enomwoyi seemed warm and gentle. That was Clark's initial thought, but at closer observation, there was something just below the surface of her demeanor, something unsettling. Clark didn't trust her.

"I don't know who you think you are but that was totally un-called for!" shouted Clark, backing away from Priestess Enomwoyi ever so slightly.

"What you talk, sister?" Priestess Enomwoyi inquired defensively.

"You know good and well what I mean!" Clark again shouted this time with her hands upon her hips and her eyes glistening with rage.

"You don't know what you're saying," Priestess Enomwoyi told her condescendingly, "There are things of this world that you are not able to understand, only the *chosen* know."

Clark hated the way the word chosen came out of her mouth as if she were saying the ones that are better than everybody else.

"I don't care who you are, no one treats me like that and

thinks they're going to get away with it! To hell with you and your roaming eye boyfriend and this crazy party and…..." Clark's ranting abruptly came to a halt upon seeing a shift in Priestess Enomwoyi's expression.

"What does Paulo have to do with this?" Priestess Enomwoyi pointedly asked.

Clark was mortified, utterly so, and she could do nothing to shield herself from Priestess Enomwoyi's scathing stare. In retrospect, Clark knew that what she saw on Priestess Enomwoyi's face a few moments earlier was mild amusement; now that look was replaced with simmering hatred.

"You're leaving, right?" Priestess Enomwoyi asked as if it were a warning.

"Ye…ah…" Clark mouthed trying to sound tougher than she felt, "…Yeah, I'm leaving."

Clark tried to collect herself, her pride mostly, having Priestess Enomwoyi now fully aware that something might be going on with her and Paulo.

"Honey, t'wasn't you they were after…not yet…anyway…" Priestess Enomwoyi told Clark as she withdrew into the kitchen.

Clark could say nothing. She thought, 'Now I'm being haunted by a whole band of ghosts together with Priestess Enomwoyi, who apparently could conjure them at will.' Her body shook in a sudden fever. She tumbled back in revulsion at the sheer horror of it all unsure what pit of hell she managed to fall into and, more importantly, how was she going to crawl out. She leaned against the wall for support knowing that although made of reinforced wooden beams and sheetrock, it couldn't hold her up from what she was suffering. She grew faint as the entire room swayed beneath her. As she was about to collapse, a cold breeze shot pass her face and just for a split second she swore she felt hands sliding against her cheeks, or was it lips.

"You all right?" someone approached her as she was sliding down the wall unable any longer to stay firmly footed.

"Uhaaa…" she shrieked turning sharply to find a bewildered Paulo standing right beside her with his handsome forehead scrunched and a curious grin upon his face.

"You all right?" Paulo repeated for emphasis.

Clark wished that it were as simple as how she was physically. She did have a headache but that was hardly all there was to it. 'What remedy is there for dead people throwing you out of a room?' she thought.

"Yes. Yes," she lied to Paulo hoping he'd retreat back to the party, function, séance, whatever.

In fact, all she wanted to do was go home and preferably with some kind of dignity else without looking like she'd been given the boot. She knew that everyone had heard, if not everything, at least the part where Priestess Enomwoyi told her to leave.

Then Paulo did the strangest thing, he took her hand in his and led her back into the living room. Though reluctant and fearful of Priestess Enomwoyi's scorn, Clark couldn't resist Paulo. Her eyes were transfixed on his shiny black locks that fell in a wave from the tip of his head, and gently cascaded down around his smooth cheek bones. Clark wanted to pull at them while slobbering wet kisses all over his gorgeous face. She thought that it would be infinitely more titillating if he was naked from teeth to toes and she was straddled across him likewise. Who was she kidding? She was helpless at his every request. It was his penetrating eyes that did her in. Else that's what she kept telling herself. He looked like one of those Jesus paintings where the eyes follow the viewer around the room. She would have followed him anywhere and the touch of his hand upon hers practically made her entire body drizzle. They entered together arm in arm, Clark timidly two steps tightly shadowed behind. She immediately looked toward the thrones and found that the guests, ghosts, whatever, were no longer seated upon their perches; and neither was Priestess Enomwoyi gazing adorningly at them. Priestess Enomwoyi was upright now, center stage so to speak, being showered with praise and awe from everyone present, all save Clark. Clark just stood at a distance watching her. While Priestess Enomwoyi stood prominently, a goddess now, a symbol of all that was possible in life and the miracles and secrets possessed herewith and hereafter. Clark was hesitant to join in. After all, she was no longer welcome. Besides, she didn't think the theatrics of Priestess Enomwoyi all that interesting. So, she went about the business of finding, Arlene. With her in tow, they'd make haste towards the nearest exit. Paulo had the warmest most electrified fingers. They sent a genuine pulse from his body through hers making her feel as if she were being reborn. She knew that he enjoyed her too. His adoration of her seemed all encompassing. Clark got a sense about him that he didn't do anything halfway.

Then Clark felt a chill, worst than the ghostly guests, coming directly from across the room. It was short, sugary sweet and unequivocally to the point, "Let go of Paulo's hand or I will cut your skinny ass up."

Clark swore that she could actually hear Priestess Enomwoyi

saying just that. She had already willed herself to release Paulo's grasp, but it was obviously not fast enough for Priestess Enomwoyi. She wasn't sure if Priestess Enomwoyi said anything but the voice in her head was so strong that it could have very well been the tip of a blade.

"I hope all that didn't make you want to run away," Priestess Enomwoyi said appearing before her as if coming out of nowhere.

Her words came out gently but there was a biting coldness to them that gripped Clark at the throat. Clark managed to snort out a half laugh steadily heading towards Arlene, who was currently getting her groove on with some guy in an off-white jogging suit.

"I thought you were on your way out," Priestess Enomwoyi said to Clark sounding severe.

Clark stood still, feeling exposed and alarmed. She wondered what Priestess Enomwoyi and her little unearthly friends had in store for her in the future. She wondered why they attacked her. She mostly wondered how she could extract that information from Priestess Enomwoyi without ever having to ask her or to ever see her again. For all her indecision, she just continued to stare blankly looking more and more dumbfounded. It was by no means a legitimate plan of action. Coupled with all of the emotion she was experiencing, her feelings were hurt too. All of this ghost business had made her raw and as sensitive and jumpy as if needles were being poked at her from all sides.

"I am," she uttered, unappreciative of Priestess Enomwoyi's venomous tone, "I came with Arlene, remember?"

Before exiting, she turned to Paulo for answers, yet he remained placid with his permanently sexy smile, which wasn't at all learned but a rare gem from ancient times when chivalry still existed. Again, Clark caught herself staring at him or was it Priestess Enomwoyi staring at her?

"Okay," Clark chirped again but this time it was the 'see you around - never' kind.

She had to practically wrench Arlene's arm from around her muscularly terrycloth clad dance partner. Arlene didn't let the fact that she was happily married stop her from waving and cooing something awful at him as she was forcibly unraveled from his embrace.

"Whaaat?" she growled at Clark.

Clark humorously threatened to call Juan, Arlene's husband, and tell him all about Arlene's diminutive affair. They laughed about the incident incessantly on the ride home. Arlene repeatedly reminded Clark, "Ah ain't deaaaaaad." Clark laughed but every time Arlene said the word dead, she thought she might faint.

CHAPTER THIRTY

D r. Saunders reluctantly pricked her arm.

"Ouch," she yelped, "Easy…easy."

He glared at her, lingering longer than he wanted to in order to still appear professional towards his patient but he in reality had grown weary. It had been an excruciatingly long day. Plus, his wife forgot to pack his lunch and he could, unfortunately, still taste the cold, bland, mayonnaise intensive, shrimp salad sandwich, Bella, his assistant, gave to him out of her "secret stash" of leftovers. He could feel his patient's eyes as if she were leaning over his shoulder. So, he turned farther away from her and held her chart up between them like a shield. It was customary to make sounds of discovery while reviewing a patient's chart and he knew that she knew that he knew that. So, for her sake, he grunted, though timidly.

"What? What?" she said suddenly startled.

"Miss Green…" he said trailing off when he saw the absolute panic on her eyes.

"What? What is it? Do I have something?" she asked him.

"Well…" Dr. Saunders started, paused, then swiveled his chair closer to his thoroughly narcotic guest.

He sighed several times. It wasn't necessarily her fault. He mostly blamed it on his inability to sufficiently breakdown dairy products. He was sure that his face was yellow and swollen and that his breath most probably stank to high heaven.

"Listen, Miss Green, Clark…" he swallowed.

Clark took a deep breath not knowing what the heck was

coming next. If the look on her doctor's face told the story, he was about to give her the estimable time she had left to live.

"Look, we've done a test for diabetes, anemia, sickle cell, malaria, TB, leukemia, and cancer, to name a few. Your platelets are fine. Liver looks good, healthy, and pink. We've even done one for AIDS as well as for pregnancy. By the way, you're not expecting," he said with a grin.

Clark didn't laugh. She would have needed air in her lungs in order to do so. At the mere mentioning of AIDS, she was too busy counting past lovers, trying to remember whether any of them wore rubbers. Suddenly her whole small life was flashing before her eyes. She saw her spotty career, her failed relationships, her living on a shoestring budget. The only reason she could afford Dr. Saunders was because she was temporarily working at Long Island College Hospital. During her brief employment stint there, she got everything medical at a discounted rate. So, she used this opportunity in her life to get everything checked out from teeth to feet. Saunders knew that and she knew that he knew that.

"The thing is…" he sighed.

Clark lowered her head and tried to contain the panic welling up inside her like a geyser.

"…well…the thing is…all your tests are, well, are negative…" he said reaching into her chart and pulling out her lab results.

One at a time he held them up in the overhead, making every effort to show Clark that he had efficiently covered every possible angle. He liked Clark as a patient despite the discounted, practically free service on account of her connection with LICH, but the truth was, he didn't want to see her in his office ever again.

"...Look, you're healthy. Get out of here. Hang out with your friends. Go to a movie," he told her with a wink.

Clark sighed with relief though she didn't immediately believe him. She sat wondering what other test he could run, what other symptom she should have told him about. She was at a lost. Everything that came to mind led her back to Priestess Enomwoyi's party, séance, whatever. 'What in the hell is going on with me,' she thought and tears began to surge to the surface of her cracked face, and she really and truly didn't want him to see her cry. That would be the living end for her. She knew that he was being patient with her out of professional courtesy. Her boss was his tee off partner on the green at Trump's Course in Briarcliff Manor. The unofficial golf club of LICH, it was like a fraternity - brothers for life. He knew that she knew that and that he was giving her the red carpet treatment but that her VIP status was about to come to a sudden brisk halt.

"Well..." she sighed, though not so much from relief of what he said, but with more questions; questions that she sincerely wished Dr. Richard Saunders could answer.

Oh, how she would have loved to have this whole nightmare behind her. She was drained having literally run from pillar to post trying to discover why she felt like she was dying. She had all the typical ailments that went along with this theory too, shortness of breath, heart palpitations, restlessness and an extreme case of fatigue, and to round it all off, she was seeing things that weren't there. She had told Dr. Saunders most of the list, except for that last part.

"Well, is right. You're as healthy as a healthy twenty-eight-year old should be. There's nothing I can do for you that Mother

Nature hasn't blessed you with already. You're fine," he said spinning back around in his chair and speedily rolling towards the door.

"That's it?" she asked knowing she wasn't quite finished but that he definitely, positively and emphatically was.

Dr. Saunders shrugged. He was aware that her inquiry was filled with disappointment but what else could he say or do?

"Listen," he stood ever tilting toward the exit, "You need to do whatever you need to in order to make yourself feel better. I see it all the time, there's nothing medically wrong but stress can lead to major physical problems," he offered the practically frozen Clark.

She did hear him and she did want to believe every word; that went without saying. More than anything else in the world, she wanted to take Dr. Saunders at his word.

On the way home that's all she thought about, '…do whatever you need to in order to make yourself feel better…' She picked up twelve candy bars along the way, thinking that they would be a good start. She was going to sit in front of whatever was on TV and eat until her stomach ached. She had an overwhelming urge to call Paulo over, thinking, 'that would make me feel better too.' Alas, he was with his woman, Priestess Enomwoyi, most probably discussing what took place at their party, séance, what-ev-er.

CHAPTER THIRTY-ONE

She had bought them at a local Pathmark along the way. She was just there picking up some ground beef and depositing her Government check into her future. That's what she called her savings account. It only earned a half of a percent but she didn't care about such things. With a whole five hundred dollars and seventeen cents just sitting there with nothing pressing for it to pay, handle, or rescue; it was like a hair weave she never ever had to take out or redo. It was all hers too, free and clear, to do with whatever her little heart desired. Sometimes she'd pretend that she'd go strolling into Saks Fifth Avenue and buy anything she wanted. She passed by the store once in a while visiting the City and was too intimidated to even walk inside. She felt as if people were staring at her like she didn't belong. That's how she felt anyhow in her Half Price bargain clothing. Other times she'd daydream about taking herself and all of her six children to Red Lobster for dinner. They all went there together once with a friend of hers named, Oscar Preston. He was the man who sold her two Encyclopedia Britannica's, at cost, with a ten dollar per month payment plan. She bought letters T and H. She didn't listen to her children or the nice Mr. Preston when they said they preferred A and B first so they could eventually have the full alphabet one day. She put her foot down as sole breadwinner in the household. She had something else in mind. She wanted to look up the two words that all of her pregnancy doctors repeatedly suggested she should do. However, she never took their suggestions seriously because she was too proud to ask them what they meant. Now, given the chance, she wanted to thoroughly familiarize herself with the terms tube-tying and hysterectomy. Mr. Preston offered them dinner after spending several hours trying to explain the whole concept of having some form of reference material in the home. At first Mr. Preston told her that he didn't want anything in return but that was merely his way of trying to act like he was a gentleman, while secretly anticipating that they would soon become lovers.

She placed the bouquet on the cement slab. She had exactly eight minutes to say her usual tearful good-byes. Eight minutes before she'd have to run for the next bus, so she could get back home in time to pick up Jimmeesha from daycare. They swore they'd teach her her ABC's. She was so proud of that. After all, this was her special baby. The sun was perpetually shining whilst she was having her. It was more than she ever wanted, more than she thought she deserved. Plus, she looked exactly like him. She was eleven pounds at birth and her skin was a bright shade of red, just like his, with a full head of curly wavy hair, just like his. So unlike any of her other children, she could barely comb through theirs and most times didn't even bother. No, Jimmeesha was definitely his child through and through. She touched the head-stone, perhaps she padded it a little too. Somehow, she believed that he could feel it when she did this, and that he even liked it. She slid her hand gently across as if it was his very shoulder. When she breathed in she could still taste the sweetness of his cologne, Musk oil. His strong, masculine body would be drenched in it during their encounters.

Jimmy appeared at the top of his head-stone, aggravated, uncertain why of all the people to come call, why this one in particular persisted on. He hated, no, reviled the fact that she called and he came. There was something linking him to his old self and apparently, he couldn't shake it off because it was welded to his core. Naturally, he had made several frustrating attempts. He knew that eventually he'd have to kill her to make her stop. 'What's her name again,' he pondered. He knew what he used to call her but for the life of him, or death of him, he just couldn't remember what her real name was. He used to call her *bulldog*, but that definitely wasn't God given. He called her that because that's what she reminded him of. Their first meeting will forever be burned in his memory. They were at an exclusive local *Swap Meat*, so called. He saw her initially from behind. She was completely nude, bent over servicing one of his good friend's, Raymond Brown, who was directly in front of her, also butt naked. The way she had him going, Raymond couldn't even see straight while the dog was attacking him. At least that's what she looked like to Jimmy, like a *bulldog*. Her skin was rough and coarse and hairy all over except atop her head, which had splotches of hair here and there – mostly scalp peeking through. Then roaming his eyes downward, he counted no less than four stomachs; all rolled tightly round her middle, with discolored stretch marks running throughout the rolls. Then there was the cellulite hanging down from each of her thighs. They looked like two filled pants pockets swinging and bouncing about as she moved. That's the part that from a safe distance appeared to be dog's ears, that is, in that position. What smattering of hair she did possess reminded him of a dirty, old, worn brush; one that needed to be thrown out but had become useful at serving other purposes – like for polishing shoes and scrubbing toilet rims. Once she was finished with Raymond, who literally fell to the floor much like an accidental slip, she turned around and began eying Jimmy. Jimmy stared at her all the while trying not to laugh. It was moments later when he realized that his restraint was, in fact, gone, that he openly howled at her. She was, bar none, the most terrifyingly, ugliest woman he had ever seen in his life. Everyone in the room heard him say, "Dammmmmnnnnnnnn!"

From the front, for starters, her eyes were unevenly about her face. That was the first thing he had noticed about her. One sagged to the side and the other sagged in the middle. They also jetted out of her head, almost as if just a small string held them in their sockets. Then there was the mouth and the breasts, all three hanging down in opposite degrees and locals, apparently in an all out race toward the floor. She was frightful but that didn't stop her from flashing a snaggletooth smile while moving in the distinct direction of poor old Jimmy. He had the shakes he was laughing so hard. All he could see was Raymond stretched out on the carpeting behind her and her crawling on her hands and knees towards him, breasts and flesh dragging below. Jimmy too, was completely naked. He had just done Jacqueline or Christine, somebody with big arms, and three lines of coke. So *bulldog* really made him giggle when she approached. No one noticed them, as they were all into their own mid-evening corralling. The party would be over soon though, as most had to be home in time to either cook for their husbands, or else feed their wives a whooping lie about why they're late coming home from work. Jimmy didn't know what *bulldog* had on her itty-bitty mind and truly had no intentions of finding out. He was high, satisfied and comfortable. If someone attractive came his way, he might have mustered something up but not for *bulldog*. Besides, he was as limp as a wet fart and didn't want her anywhere near his manhood. So as out of it as he was, he felt the express need to straighten up because she was almost upon him. Then before he knew it, she was right there at his feet. He could feel her squishy mounds of skin resting on his bare legs. In the visceral state he was in, he believed he could feel his flesh crawling, mainly trying to escape from her clutches. This was no longer a laughing matter. If he had any strength, he'd have hurled her into the hi-fi but it was playing one of his favorite songs. Thelma Houston sang, *"Don't leave me this way. I can't survive. I can't stay alive. So, don't leave me this way…"* Then of all vile things, *bulldog* lunged at him. Before he knew what was happening, his entire being was smacked hard into the back of the well-worn sofa. She came at him with such force that he nearly passed out. Then, also without warning, she reached down and swallowed him whole. Not that he had ever experienced it, but it was as if a jellyfish had swallowed his penis and began gnawing on it. His first inclination was to knock her head off, off him and off of her own body. However, there was something about the way she went about her business that all at once took his mind off of everything else. He was her complete and utter prisoner. Every single bit of tension within him, even what he could and couldn't recognize, literally melted away. Even the coke, which normally left him alert and pensive, was now in *bulldog's* aggregate control. He looked down upon her sparsely covered head thinking that surely ten other women were helping her. Before he knew what he was doing, he began to moan louder than he would have had he had any power over his bodily functions, his erection growing to abnormal size. He quickly became her rag doll, a condition he was loath to be in. What could he do? He felt like he was being eaten alive and he simply loved it! He didn't want it to end. It was excruciatingly pleasurable. Then, also without his consent, he came inside of her hot, wet mouth. The organism lasted a good ten minutes long. During which time, he actually roared.

Needless to say, such unbridled passion was categorically uncharacteristic of him. He was never one to loss his cool, especially not over a woman, and positively not over one who looked like something that could guard one's home. Almost immediately afterwards, he felt more than a little bit – embarrassed. How could he not be? She assaulted him; him the big strong man, helpless in her grasp. So, he smacked her head and knocked her down to the floor. What else could he do? It was disgraceful, her making him look weak like that. *Bulldog* simply lay there wiping what he unwillingly gave to her now mixed with blood from her lips. Then she turned and smiled once more at him. Both knew that she clearly had the upper hand. Both knew that he would see her again even if his life depended on it. Yet and still, he couldn't look at her. She now reminded him of his vulnerability. He especially didn't want anyone else to see how much he enjoyed himself. So, he glanced past her. There was his buddy, Raymond, still in repose muttering and whimpering joyfully on his back. That disgusted him too. He wanted to do the same but just couldn't give her that satisfaction.

Debra, which was *bulldog's* real name, reached over and fluffed the flowers so they'd look a little fuller. Yet at five dollars a bunch, there was no hope. Besides their skimpiness, they had been compressed betwixt her bosom the entire bus trip over. Debra was deathly afraid of being underground. So, she'd ride the bus from Queens into Brooklyn, though it would take two hours longer and three bus transfers. Alas, her meager floral arrangement didn't have the impact she originally had hoped. Though dearly departed, she knew that souls still frequented the earth. She believed that he would come and appreciate all that she'd done to beautify his resting place regardless. She could feel it within her that he was present and that he still remembered her, maybe he even loved her. She'd think about that fact the whole ride back home. She loved him from the first time they had gotten together there in Jacqueline's basement. Those times they'd have in that basement warmed her heart. She reminisced upon them fondly. In her mind, those parties were where she went to be loved. She had had sex many times before but those were unwelcome occurrences. At Jacqueline's, she was in charge. She could pick and choose with whom and when and how much. At first she'd sit in a corner watching, feeling unattractive and isolated. Jacqueline, her ex-social worker, told her that there was nothing but acceptance at her little get-togethers. As far as Debra was concerned, Jacqueline was absolutely right. Not one man rejected Debra there. Sure Jimmy would call her names behind her back but he'd keep watch for her whenever he came around, which was often. She knew that he was always waiting for her to come his way each time too. He'd even push aside other girls to insure he'd be free for her. She knew that in his own insecure way, that he loved her.

Somewhere deep inside, he loved her.

Without any provocation, Debra unexpectedly fell to the ground as if someone had pushed her. She swiftly jerked her head around from side to side to see who it was, but no one was there. Yet and still she could have sworn she felt something or someone shove her, of that she was sure. Before she could adjust herself and stand back up, a heavy weight of some sort began pressing down upon her chest. It startled her more than anything else. 'Heart attack?' she asked herself, '…that pig feet sandwich I just ate…?' She couldn't be sure but she was out of breath and now clutching her chest. She tried massaging it in order to relieve the pain. Her sternum burned as if her whole body was on fire. 'What the hel…' she moaned, thinking that she was going to expire on the spot. In the back of her mind she could see all six of her children crying hysterically over her dead lifeless body. 'What in the worl…' she garroted. Now the pain was elevating, better yet, moving from the chest area to around her neck. If she wasn't mistaken, something had its hands around her throat. 'Impossible,' she thought, 'No one's here!' Then she got the oddest sensation of a smell. It was very distinct too. She mulled over the idea then considered it mighty peculiar to be thinking of fragrances at a time like this. Whatever it was, it seemed so familiar that it distracted her away from her current peril. 'Talcum Powder…no…Baby oil…nah…I don't…think so…' then as she took her last breath, 'Musk oil…' she thought, '…definitely, m…m…musk.'

CHAPTER THIRTY-TWO

"You took the wrong turn, woman," Billy Earl told her. "Man, I did not make the wrong turn. Who drivin' me or you?" she asked with her lips in a severe pucker.

"It says Walker not Wallace…not Wallace…" Billy Earl shouted.

"Listen, man, you keep yelling and I'm gonna' drop your ass off on Wal-lace, not Wal-ker," Patsy Mae promised.

At that, Billy Earl turned back around and hummed under his breath because he wasn't going to give her the satisfaction of a response. Patsy Mae hummed too. She hummed as if her next move was to reach across him and open his car door. If he flew out while the car was moving, that would have been just fine.

They sat in silence for a while.

"You're gonna' have ta' look out the winda' and help me, you know," Patsy Mae warned him.

"Now, you need my help? What about leavin' me at the side of the road…?" he asked.

"Man, just look out the winda' and stop acting a fool," she told him.

"Why I gotta' be actin' a fool?" Billy Earl asked.

"Good God help me see the damn signs, man!" Patsy Mae shouted, "…or reach in that bag there and get me my good glasses. You know I can't see with these on, these my reading glasses."

Billy Earl fumbled down around his ankles to find Patsy

Mae's purse.

"If they your readin' glasses, why can't you read the sign? Now, you tell me you can't see," Billy Earl harrumphed.

All the while he searched through Patsy Mae's cluttered things.

"What in the world you got in here?" Billy Earl commented.

Patsy Mae stopped the car in the middle of the road and snatched her bag out of Billy Earl's hands. Then she just stared at him for several long uninterrupted seconds.

"Babe, we're in the middle of street. You can't sit in the middle of the street like this. We could get hit," Billy Earl told her.

"Man, I know where I am. That I know. The question is, do you know where you are? That's the question and if you like I'm gonna' give you an answer. Rest assured, you gonna' get an answer. You might not like what I have to say but I'm sure gonna' say it…" Patsy Mae ranted.

Then she took her sweet time getting her glasses out from her purse. Meanwhile, Billy Earl twisted his face into a question mark and kept jerking his head around to see if cars were approaching. He sighed loudly over and over again goading Patsy Mae to get the hint that something might happen to them out there all exposed. Patsy Mae had no intention of moving until she put her glasses on and carefully stowed the others deep within her purse. Once done, she swung the bag at Billy Earl's stomach for him to take it. He snapped his head in her direction and eyed her. Once the bag was safely underneath the seat again and not a moment before, Patsy Mae pulled off.

Then two blocks later, "Turn left! Turn left!"

"I'm turnin'. I am turnin'. Stop yellin'" Patsy Mae told Billy Earl.

"I wasn't yellin'. I just don't want to keep cirlin' round Bayside all day looking at these little tiny signs. Gees, you think they'd make 'em bigger seeing that no one can read 'em. Do they want us to come visit or not?" he joked.

Patsy Mae smiled too. She was happy that they were finally there. Between Billy Earl's nerves and those of her own, they both needed to get out of the car. They crept forward down the street.

"What they say thirty-seven, thirty-five…?" she asked.

"I believe it's…" Billy Earl started.

"Man, just look at the directions," Patsy Mae huffed.

Billy Earl unraveled a piece of paper from his shirt pocket.

"Oh, oh, here it is. Ah, thirty-five," he said then looked out of the window, "Right here. Right here," he pointed.

Patsy Mae hesitantly parked. The entire concept of having to be parallel with the adjacent car first, then back up, was lost on her. Instead she circled around into the spot, something that riled Billy Earl to no end. Yet, he wasn't going to bring it up. He sat patiently until the vehicle came to a complete stop then leaped out quickly, happy to touch earth.

"What's the rush?" she asked dramatically helping her own self out of the car.

"What?" he asked.

"Aren't you gonna' help me out?" she asked.

"Why?" he asked.

"Why? Why do I have to tell you why?" she asked poised to strike him if she had to.

"How long we been married?" he asked.

"What that got to do with anything?" she asked making her way onto the sidewalk.

"I'm just asking you a question now. How long we been married?" Billy Earl repeated.

"I don't know, man. Why you got to ask me silly questions like that all the damn time. Forever, that's how long, for-ev-vah'," Patsy Mae answered.

"You can joke but you still here, ain't cha'?" he grinned.

Patsy Mae stood very still on the lawn glaring at Billy Earl as he grinned triumphantly.

"Oh, now you think, you think it's 'cause of you, do you?" she grinned now.

Then she scurried pass him and proceeded up the walk way to the front door.

"T'aint got nothin' to do with the likes of you. You just here taking up space 'til…" she stopped suddenly.

She didn't want to completely crush him. She knew that if she said what she was about to say that she'd never hear the end of it.

"…Don't stop…'Til what? You can say it. I can take it," he told her pressing his feet into the ground with the whole of his weight.

"…If somebody betta' come 'long…" Patsy Mae said with her hands on her hips.

"Yeah, right," Billy Earl laughed and walked right pass her to the front door, "I don't know what you thinkin' but you stuck right here."

Patsy Mae reluctantly followed him up the stairs grunting in a way that showed she disagreed with his assessment.

"Look, if you think for one minute that I couldn't get another man besides you, you crazier than you look," she told him, "Now I can get a man. Don't worry 'bout me. I could have two, three of 'em sitting up looking at me if I wanted. Don't worry 'bout me and stop looking so pleased with yourself."

Billy Earl rang the doorbell.

"You ready?" he asked smugly feeling that he had made his point.

Patsy Mae adjusted her clothing, fluffed her hair then nodded yes to him.

Mid ring, Bernie answered the door like a schoolboy full of joy and anticipation.

"Hey," he sang greeting his new best friend.

"How you doin'?" Billy Earl asked hugging Bernie by doing a double hand pat on his back.

"How you doin,' man? Good to see you," shouted Bernie, then "Fine. Just fine," he smiled reaching around to Patsy Mae, "So, this is the lovely lady."

Bernie grabbed Patsy Mae's hand and shook it warmly. Lillie came into the foyer, apron on, wiping her hands into it. She was beaming just like Bernie excited to have company.

"Hey," she said joyfully.

Bernie stepped aside so Lillie could meet and greet their guests. Lillie enthusiastically shook both their hands.

"Hey there, Billy Earl…and this must be Patsy Mae," Lillie said smiling from ear to ear.

Patsy Mae looked surprised.

"Yes…" Lillie answered Patsy Mae's curious expression, "…he did tell us about you."

"Yeah, what he say?" she asked casually shifting her eyes

towards Billy Earl.

"That you are the love of his life, of course," Bernie reassured her.

Billy Earl gently backhanded Bernie.

"Man, come on now. You ain't got ta' say all that," he told Bernie, but underneath his breath, "…them trade secrets, man."

Patsy Mae grinned in Billy Earl's direction. Billy Earl tried to avoid her gaze, but eventually, secretively he did smile back at her.

"He's told me so much about you too, Lillie," Patsy Mae said warmly greeting her.

"Come…come sit down," Lillie and Bernie ushered Patsy Mae and Billy Earl into their living room.

With just a few slight changes, it was almost identical to theirs. They had a beige quilted sofa and two reclining chairs flanking it, a tasteful wooden coffee table with an inlaid glass top. Patsy Mae ran her fingers over the curved detailing of braiding across its edge.

"This is beautiful. We have one similar but I really like this top. What you think, Billy Earl?" Patsy Mae asked.

Billy Earl looked and nodded his head in agreement. Then he sat in one of the easy chairs while Bernie took the other.

"Patsy Mae, do you go fishing with Billy Earl?" Lillie asked.

"Not anymore, no," Patsy Mae answered.

"She used to go with me all the time when we was courtin' but not now…you know the kids…work," Billy Earl explained.

"Where are my manners? Ya'll want something to drink?" Lillie stood and ran into the kitchen.

"You need some help?" Patsy Mae asked while joining her.

As the women went into the kitchen, the men stretched back

in their chairs grinning.

"Nice spread," Billy Earl said.

"We call it home," Bernie beamed modestly.

They leaned even further back continuing to grin like two pampered cats.

"Let's check out what's on the news," Billy Earl suggested.

"You got the remote on that side," Bernie told Billy Earl.

Billy Earl reached down grabbed it and pointed toward the television, Sylvania floor model, thirty-two inch color. They could hear the news before the picture came on.

"How you doing with that fin?" Billy Earl asked.

"Man, that thing last forever," Bernie told him.

"Same here...same here. I think Patsy Mae done done everything with that thing, soup, salad, sandwiches," Billy Earl said.

"Same here," Bernie laughed, "I do believe though that she's 'bout tired of it now."

"Same here," Billy Earl said, "Same here."

Then they both cracked up over their women just as Lillie and Patsy Mae reentered the living room carrying trays. Lillie had iced lemonade on hers with glasses. Patsy Mae had an arrangement of crackers, cheese and fin-fish-dip, Lillie's own creation. Bernie waved at Billy Earl to help himself as soon as the trays were placed on the coffee table.

"Mummm...that's real good," said Billy Earl with a mouth full of dip on a Ritz, "Taste that, honey," said Billy Earl handing Patsy Mae one.

Patsy Mae tasted it and smiled, "Found another use, huh?" she asked Lillie.

The women nodded to one another empathetically.

Then they drank, enjoyed and chatted while the six o'clock news got going on the daily stories, most of it not very good. It was peaceful, but then suddenly, Bernie shot clean out of his seat.

"Hey!" he shouted pointing at the screen.

"What? What?" Lillie asked him while both Patsy Mae and Billy Earl glanced at the television set.

The announcer said, "…and in today's news Police are looking into the mysterious death of a young mother of six…"

There on the screen was a high school picture of a young Black girl with thick full lips and big bulging eyes.

"You know her?" Lillie asked Bernie, who was still staring at the screen with his mouth shaped in an 'O'.

Billy Earl and Patsy Mae glanced at each other.

"What?" Patsy Mae asked, now noticing the awed look upon Billy Earl's face too.

The announcer continued, "…A ditch digger made a surprising discovery this morning as he was driving into work…"

Behind the announcer appeared on a screen an elderly man looking physically shaken.

"He looks familiar too," Bernie whispered.

"Where you know them from?" Lillie asked him.

Bernie stared hard at the television set trying to recall.

"Don't you remember her, Pat?" Billy Earl asked Patsy Mae as the girl's picture was flashed on the screen again.

The announcer continued, "…Apparently, she suffered a massive heart attack…"

"Yeah, she do look familiar," Patsy Mae said, mouth agape.

"Jesus, she's too young for that..." Lillie said almost to herself.

"Yeah, she look 'bout twenty, but I don't think that was a recent photo of her," Billy Earl said agreeing with Lillie.

"I think everybody I see is someone from court, you know. It could be that," Bernie told them.

"That's true. It was a while ago you retired," Lillie agreed with her husband.

"That's true," Bernie concurred.

The announcer continued, "...in a mysterious chain of events, she was found at the grave of the late James Dubois, a man found murdered more than ten years ago..."

All four of them sat with their mouths hanging wide open now at the mentioning of Jimmy's name.

"Oh, my God! Sweetie, ain't that...that..." Lillie couldn't even bring herself to say it.

Bernie just sat nodding his head in disbelief. Both Patsy Mae and Billy Earl had finally realized why the girl looked so familiar.

"Oh, my Lord," mouthed Patsy Mae unevenly.

"That there's Jimmy's girlfriend...one of them anyhow..." Billy Earl said to a silent room.

"Oh, my Lord," said Patsy Mae.

"Oh, my God," said Lillie.

"Oh, shit..." said Bernie and Billy Earl simultaneously.

Lillie winced at Bernie and Billy Earl's foul language.

"I remember her from the funeral. She was really broken up, remember Pat?" Billy Earl said.

"How you know Jimmy?" Patsy Mae asked Lillie.

"Oh, I don't know him really. I only know what Bern told me about that there case," Lillie responded looking at Bernie to help her with her answer.

"Yeah, he was my last case…in court…" Bernie told Billy Earl and Patsy Mae.

"Bernie was down at Queens Borough Court. Worked there for, how many years, Bernie?" Billy Earl asked Bernie.

"Too many. When I started I had a full head of hair, right honey?" Bernie laughed nervously.

"Said it was a crazy case, right Bern?" Lillie asked.

"It was the nuttiest thing I'd ever seen and I've seen some doozies. Yeah, it was a murder trial. They caught the guy that did it," Bernie said.

"He died too, right?" Billy Earl asked.

"Sure did…mur...murdered, I...I believe," Bernie added.
Silence.

"She was really torn up at the funeral, right Billy Earl?" Patsy Mae added.

"What she do?" asked Lillie.

"Well, she laid down on the coffin practically the entire service," Patsy Mae said, "Poor thing."

"Really?" Lillie exclaimed.

"Really. Poor thing was messed up over it. I think she had a baby by him too. Poor thing," Patsy Mae said.

"Poor thing," Lillie repeated.

"Strange place to drop dead of a heart attack though," Billy Earl chimed in as everyone else was contemplating Debra's sudden departure.

Then they all sat contemplating what Billy Earl just said.

"Everything was strange about that there case. Nothing surprises me about it," said a very somber Bernie.

"Jimmy was a strange one all right," Patsy Mae told them.

"How did you know him?" asked Lillie.

"Oh, Jimmy stayed in our...in our..." he couldn't even bring himself to continue, "...in our basement...a short while, not long, not long at all. Why, we barely even knew he was there most times, right Pat?" Billy Earl asked with a strained grin.

Patsy Mae struggled to remain cool and calm as she eyed Billy Earl with her lips forcibly turned up. Billy Earl was now certain that although it had been over a decade ago, and although Jimmy was dead and long gone; this subject was definitely still a sore spot with Patsy Mae. At that moment, he leaned back and decided to relish whatever peace he had left during their little visit with Bernie and Lillie because God only knew what the ride home would be like. This time she might stop the car in the middle of the freeway.

CHAPTER THIRTY-THREE

No one was more traumatized than Jimmy. He floated rather grumpily over his own grave thinking that if it were not for the fact that he was already deceased, he might have just killed himself. For there she was, in all her spirited finery, looming too close a proximity to him for his comfort. He didn't know what to say, or think, or do. So, as per his usual initial response, he yelled.

"AAArrrrrrhhhhhh!" he bellowed giving her his fiercest scowl.

However, spirit to spirit hollering doesn't render much reaction. Debra merely looked back at him unmoved and unimpressed. In truth, she was on a brief mission of her own, wondering what had happened to her. At that point, she wasn't entirely sure. One minute she was clutching her chest and the next, she was above her body feeling calm and serene. The stomachache from earlier was gone, as was the fatigue she'd felt her entire life. In fact, everything in her was whole and operating well and as it ought. She couldn't get over this new glorious result. Suddenly, she was quite well with the world, except for the aspect of seeing her body on the ground with strange stuff spewing out of it. That part befuddled her somewhat and left her blanched. Then she faced the only source of sound she heard coming from the only other being present. She didn't recognize Jimmy right off. It was his odor that brought her to some awareness of who he was. All at once, it warmed her to have him there right beside her. She was comforted by him and yet still puzzled. She started to ask him what he was doing there. Yet, deep down, she knew. It was just as she had always suspected that spirits do linger near their gravesites. She smiled at him. Conversely, Jimmy didn't return a smile. Instead, he contemplated vanishing into thin air, even though that would have been redundant. So, he decided that he'd simply leave. He could do that if he so chose. After all, he didn't have to hang around her if he didn't want to. Surely, he had better things to do than pal around with a former acquaintance that he could barely tolerate in life and he wouldn't bother to in death.

Debra felt him withdrawing and called out for him to stay.

"Jimmy, wait!" she cried.

Despite Jimmy's best efforts, just like that, he materialized right back beside his headstone —again; this time angrier than before. Again, he yelled, but this time Debra practically laughed in his face. Then she stared at him pitifully. It took him a while, but he began to consider his fatal blunder. Now, he was going to be stuck with Debra for the rest of his miserable immortal life. He would have wept if he could but crying was not part of him in life, nor in death. He looked over at Debra, who was once again smiling. He knew that she could read his thoughts, his feelings, everything. In death, he was completely transparent to her. He loathed that aspect of their current condition never fully grasping that that was always an aspect of her skill as a woman. He lunged at her, this time to scare her away, seeing as he couldn't kill her all over again.

"Ahhhhhh!" he roared, growling and recklessly swinging at her.

Debra simply stepped back like a Kung Fu Master with an arrogant student and smiled ever more broadly. This was definitely not the response he was expecting. She was sparing with him. This annoyed him no end. How he had come to this deplorable condition, he couldn't fathom. Yet, there she was, the object of his annoyance mocking him, taunting him even. Since Jimmy was clueless, he couldn't possibly have realized that Debra had always been two steps ahead of him. She swiftly put together her predicament, knowing that she had come to a sudden demise at the hands of her dear, old friend, Jimmy. She also knew that he was still trying his hardest never to admit that he had any real feelings for her whatsoever. For that, he was in a perpetual state of denial. As she read through him like a piece of soggy toilet tissue, her heart began to ache though not entirely for this reason, but for want of her children. This sensation seemed to pour out of her like a mist of sorrow that grew brighter with every thought of them. Before she knew it, she was transported over her apartment seeking one last glance at her beloved offspring.

Jimmy couldn't have been happier. Debra was finally out of his sight leaving him to ponder his new ostensible problem in peace. He showered himself with praise. For in his egotistical mind, he thought that he had made her disappear. He reckoned perhaps that his tantrum had propelled her elsewhere after all. He loved thinking that his commanding essence had shoved her away as his hands once did in life. In fact, it warmed him deeply to think he had anything to do with her sudden departure as he had with her death. He looked down upon her expired body and tried as hard as he could to find something disgusting about it.

However, he now looked upon almost everything as picturesque. It was his godlike nature that betrayed him. He felt cursed by this particularity, or, as he would say, flaw. He noticed her rounded curves, her matted hair, the blank stare still fixed upon her face and he was actually moved to something akin to tears. 'That does it,' he thought, 'I'm gonna' find some other way to get rid of this woman.' Though he didn't have the faintest idea how, he had to once and for all cleanse himself of all things Debra. Having thought her name, to his dismay, she reappeared beside him. Then they both simply waited and watched her now rapidly expiring body.

"Wow, look at that," she said marveling at what she saw.

Jimmy couldn't face her because he didn't want her to see that he had been moved by anything other than revulsion. Meanwhile, Debra couldn't pull her attention away from what used to be by all accounts, her.

"Am...I...dead...?" she innocently and rhetorically asked yet knowing the answer with or without an answer from Jimmy.

Jimmy stood very still and didn't deny nor confirm. What was the point? They both knew the unshakeable truth. However, Debra needed confirmation anyway. Jimmy saw that in her sullenness. So, he reluctantly nodded. He could give her that much. After all, he did kill her.

"Oh," Debra replied very matter-of-factly.

Then she stood cooperatively waiting for every last bit of life to exit through what used to be her pores. It took a while. Jimmy didn't want to be there but he didn't want to be her little ricochet either. So, he watched and waited patiently same as when this happened to him.

CHAPTER THIRTY-FOUR

Otis knew why he was there, what with the love of his life unexpectedly dropping dead and all. However, something as simple as a whiff of the freshly cut grass made him lose all sense of concentration. This would have been the appropriate time and place for him to feel something, to cry out loud unashamedly. Yet he found it all too pretty, stunning even, with the scenic billowing hills rolling into eternity, not to mention the austere quiet - absolutely astounding. He hadn't heard silence like that even in solitary confinement. He was at some wonderful place called perfect peace. Angels couldn't whisper more softly. He caught himself enjoying this refreshing atmosphere and thinking however inappropriately, how awe inspiring it was. Periodically, though, he'd straighten up and look directly at the preacher. 'When in doubt, look at the preacher,' he thought. That's what he used to do as a boy sitting in Sunday school. He'd stare at the preacher meanwhile dreaming about the peanut butter and jelly sandwich he'd have afterwards. He'd think about the dodge ball he'd play with his friends, them all running in the middle of the street. He'd think about school and all the girls he liked, and some of the boys he'd like to beat up. There he was a grown man doing the exact same thing he used to do to avoid getting a swift back hand smack for too much squirming and fidgeting in service. Much older now, his thoughts were on more adult endeavors like all the attractive women sitting directly across from him. He tried not to make his ogling obvious but it had been eight years since his last conjugal visit, a birthday gift from the boys on his block. He thanked heaven that memories could last a lifetime because that was his reality. The fact that all the ladies wore black, his favorite color, and that they were looking all vulnerable and helpless wasn't helping his case at all. It was really difficult but he really had to keep his mind off of them because the slightest glance got him aroused. So he thought instead about how lucky he was to have made it out that day, with Warden Sanchez-Walker's written approval, no less. That was a mini-miracle, considering Warden Sanchez-Walker swore to him that he'd never see daylight from outside of the prison walls again.

Otis looked slowly around taking in the wide open air. It made him smile again, not a prison wall or barbed wire fence in sight. The State even bought him a new suit and tie, a white shirt together with loafers and new boxer shorts. Plus, he didn't have to wear any prison jewelry except a little electronic area ankle bracelet. His pant leg managed to cover over that, but if he left the county, they'd track him faster than flies to shit. His handcuffs were taken off by the reluctant Officer, whose job it was to drive him around all day in their State issued, non-descript sedan. His last ride with a Police Officer didn't go so well.   It was a black and white sedan and the entire neighborhood could hear and see it coming. Now, there he was with his very own plain-clothes Officer, both seated together amongst all the other fine people at the funeral. Poor Otis was one of them today, one of the fine people, looking just as fine as anybody else. No one could tell that he was a permanent resident of the State, a convicted man. As far as they were concerned he was a pillar in their community coming to say good-bye to one of their own. That made him laugh. He covered up the smile with a closed fist when some started to stare. Even he realized that he must have looked peculiar staring off into space grinning and carrying on so, not that he really, sincerely cared. He had a day off, a whole entire day, twenty-four fresh ones.

After the ceremony, prayers, funeral, etc., his baby-sitter was ordered to take him to the deceased's house. Apparently, Debra's mother, Bonnie, had organized a cookout in her late daughter's backyard. Everyone was invited back there for spare ribs, collard greens, potato salad, wings, hot and spicy, fried whiting, banana pudding, tomato and okra something and some other stuff that Otis overheard when the menu was being recited by someone to someone else in the crowd. In truth, Otis stopped listening after banana pudding and his mind wandered to how his mother used to make it, God rest her soul. It was his favorite. She used to say, 'It's the bananas.' Otis used to nod thinking his mother strange, but he didn't figure her intension until he was practically grown. One day Otis, Willie and TJ had just gotten their paychecks from the service station they worked in. The owner paid them in cash. It was just enough for a meal and they did just enough work to earn it. They were just about to order soul food from their favorite restaurant over on Sutphin Boulevard, when Willie got into an argument with one of the servers. She took another customer's order over his. He repeatedly told her that he was there first. She repeatedly said that he wasn't. Before Otis and TJ knew it, Willie was holding the customer down and punching him in the mouth.

Willie kept asking, "Who's next? Who's next? Answer me,

who's next?"

Next thing they knew, all three of them were thrown out on the street and told never to return. Otis was upset because all he thought about that day was how he was going to get him some banana pudding. That's when Willie came up with a great idea. He ushered his friends over to the back door of the restaurant, which stood wide open and empty, since everyone else now was up front tending to the bloodied customer. Both Otis and TJ were excited by all the unoccupied piles of food and proceeded to help themselves to everything they could grab. Meanwhile, Willie had an entirely different agenda in mind. He stood directly over the banana pudding and peed in it then he dropped his pants and turned around. Otis swore he'd never eat banana pudding again. 'It's the bananas, all right,' he thought with a suppressed smile. He now considered that that might have been an omen of Willie's character.

The backyard was average. The grill was one of those built-in jobs with hand laid bricks and cement. The furniture was a series of folding chairs; the church brought forty or so over for the occasion. The tables were of the poker game variety equipped with paper tablecloths draped over each. They were scattered about in no particular order, so everyone immediately rearranged them around to their liking. Otis also helped with the seating then he sat by the fence, with his chaperon, of course. Bonnie handed him a full to overflowing plate. She also offered one to his plain-clothed Officer. She was the only one other than Otis, who really knew who he was. The Officer declined Bonnie's offer then stretched his neck towards the grill more times than Otis could count.

"Thank 'u, Bonnie," Otis said.

Bonnie lowered her head leaking tears from every part of her face it seemed. Otis lowered his too, in sympathy, but when his nose fell to the plate, he couldn't see Bonnie, his Officer for a day, the backyard, nothing. All he saw was food and all he wanted to do was eat. If he had it his way, he would have walked into the house, turned on the soaps and sat contently for the remainder of his life. Thankfully, he managed to restrain himself for a second or two and place a sorrowful enough demeanor to his expression for Bonnie's sake. Bonnie nodded her head up and down, then she shook it from side to side as if words failed her, so at a loss was she for her daughter. Then she glided away on those imaginary wings of a woman in mourning. Otis watched her leave trying to hold onto the sympathy he had mustered in her honor. It was difficult though with the savory aroma of the food in his lap just beckoning him to dig in. As soon as Bonnie arrived at the serving table, Otis dived into the potato salad, then the chicken, then the collards and so on and so on. He couldn't get enough. He hadn't had a home cooked meal in such a long time that it felt foreign and wonderful on his tongue as if he was experiencing it all over again for the first time. State issued food was like all things state issued, plain, anti-individualism and one size fits all. He thought it best not to delve on the State. Instead he chewed slowly and deliberately with unsurpassed joy in every mouthful.

To think, he was awarded this lovely little day trip for one reason and one reason alone; everyone in prison believed that he was the father of all six of Debra's kids. Otis had never said such a thing to a living soul but that's what they all believed.

Only Otis and Debra knew the absolute truth. This little rumor or flat out lie was started by none other than Debra who apparently traveled by bus, of course, from place to place visiting the many daddies of her babies. Being a good Christian girl, she thought it was the right thing to do. They'd sit together, eating something she store bought. She'd show pictures of all the children of which Otis didn't see any resemblance to him. She'd tell him about her little piece of a job here or there. He'd listen because prison life, like nothing else, had taught him to listen. She'd tell stories about this person or that person that Otis could or could not remember. In truth, he didn't want to remember any of them. They didn't come around and since he might never see them again, he didn't want to have updates on how wonderful their lives were on the outside. As far as he was concerned, they were dead or was it him? Prison made him disappear and sometimes that was the only thing that got him through his day. He didn't mind Debra coming around but he never felt the need for her to keep him up to speed on every little aspect of what could have been his life had he not been party to shooting a man in cold blood. To his shame, he didn't even really know Debra until he was incarcerated. She was the one who told him he was a father. She was the one who told him where and how she came to that conclusion. He remembered her but nothing of that night that made a baby. For him, drunk and hung-over, he could have been with anyone. She was the one who said that it didn't matter whether he could support the child or not. She was going to be both mother and father to their child and that's all Otis needed to know. He never really gave the child much thought after that. Even with Debra coming around monthly, and with the child's pictures hanging up in his cell, he never really thought about his kid.

Then Bonnie reappeared before him, again she had floated there as if by magic. Behind her stood someone half her height. The little person clung to her dress. All Otis could see was the side of his tiny face and the shine off his Sunday polished shoes. There were kids all over the yard and Otis didn't give any of them a second glance but he nearly choked when he realized that there was absolute purpose in Bonnie's stance before him. Otis' mind began to race trying desperately to remember the child's name among other things. What does one say to someone whom they should know? What does one say to someone who wants answers and actually is deserving of them? Otis felt flustered and when placed in that position wanted to lunge and strike. That wouldn't be appropriate no matter the provocation. He managed to breath, though uneasily, but he did it. Then he prepared for the worst. Suddenly, he hated Debra and every woman alive, including Bonnie who stood right next to him with peacemaker written all over her sorrowful face. Otis resisted the urge to shove her and the kid out of his way as he made a dash to the front gate. This panic all took place within the course of several uncomfortable seconds, just before Bonnie spoke.

"Otis, I'd like you to meet…" she began.

Otis could feel the lard from the collards coming up into the back of his mouth, not to mention the fat back. Any minute he would have to excuse himself entirely.

"…your son, Otis, Jr.," Bonnie sang in a fanfare.

Otis nearly dropped his plastic plate while standing to extend his arm to a little boy who oddly enough didn't remind him at all of himself. As he shook his hand he examined him discerningly, trying to see if he could find any kind of resemblance. He could find none. He tried to see some of Debra in the boy as well but could scarcely see any of her in him either.

Bonnie's smile began to fade with every inquisitive gesture Otis made, every frown made her hot between her shoulder blades.

"He's yours…" she stomped, leaving the boy behind as she continued her rounds amongst the guests.

Otis watched her with a mixture of bewilderment and fear. Then his eyes went down to meet…

"Uh…ah…ah…" he stammered.

"O-tis," the boy sang shyly.

Little did he know, but Otis, Jr. felt apprehensive too. Otis could barely stand he was so completely altered. When his chaperon slanted his eyes at him as if he were a punk, then Otis straightened up and took some courage.

"Hi, there, Otis," he squeaked, cleared his throat then went on, "And how are you today?"

"Fine," Otis, Jr. said obediently.

Then both Otis one and Otis two searched the yard as if each needed a way of escape.

"What grade you in now?" Otis one asked Otis two.

"I'm going to the third grade…soon…" he said trailing off fidgeting with his Sunday best braces.

Otis didn't have a follow up question. He never attended third grade when he was in school, preferring to hang out in the schoolyard instead. He tried to remember what courses were given so he wouldn't have to stand there and look dumbfounded. The Officer smirked observing Otis' discomfort. Otis, Jr. didn't look much better pulling at his tie and scrapping one shoe with the sole of the other.

Their discomfort was abated when Bonnie and some other women came out of the house carrying pies and cakes. As soon as they got to the serving table, a crowd emerged around them. Now the two Otises had a new source of which to relieve their uneasiness, each wanting to pull away unobtrusively; neither one knowing how.

"Otis, get me some chocolate cake, would cha'?" the Officer asked clearly trying to save himself from the collision of Otises.

Both Otis senior and Otis junior slowly made their way over to the table and stood on line with everybody else. As Otis, Jr. eyed the enormous supply of goodies, Otis, Sr. began to see their one resemblance, they both loved food. In retrospect, he wished he'd been attentive to Debra while she was alive. She'd tell him stories about the boy all the time and he'd drift off thinking about other things until she'd change the subject. He never thought he'd ever see the kid. If anyone ever asked, he would have told them that he'd be dead by now. He had no idea that events would have led him to this moment where his own flesh and blood would be standing right next to him. He looked at Otis, Jr., admirably. Though, he didn't think he looked like him at all physically there were other things that caught his attention, like the way they both stood. Each slouched and leaned on their right leg. Otis noticed that right off and smiled.

"What?" Otis, Jr. asked at the grin on Otis, Sr.'s face.

"Nothing. Nothing," Otis, Sr. said beginning to feel more at ease with the concept of being a father.

He couldn't help but think that maybe his life sentence might not be so bad if his son would write to him from time to time. He could keep progress of his growth and give him whatever wisdom he possessed. Otis, Sr. thought that he might like that after all. Then he realized that this new situation only occurred on account of Debra dying. He couldn't really reconcile that part of the equation. Somehow it didn't seem fair, Debra seemed so full of life. No one believed she died of a heart attack regardless of what the doctors said.

"What would you like?" Otis, Sr. asked Otis, Jr.

"Pie," little Otis replied.

Otis, Sr. nodded to Bonnie.

"Two, please," he told her and she handed them to him with two forks.

"I see you two are getting along," Bonnie winked.

Otis grinned, then remembered his chaperon and got a slice of chocolate cake for him.

Then father and son walked back by the fence and sat down. Otis watched and waited for Otis, Jr. to get comfortable before digging into his dessert. He paused noticing that Otis, Jr. sat surprisingly just like him. He could feel his Officer for a day boring his eyes into the back of his neck. He knew that there was a similarity between him that they couldn't deny. Otis was okay with that, he thought. He didn't know Otis, Jr. at all but what did that matter. Otis, Jr. would be someone to give his dreary days ahead some purpose. He'd write to him and ask him for pictures. He'd watch the progression of his education, his career. He'd have something to talk about besides *grits and eggs again, didn't we have that yesterday* to his fellow inmates. The more he looked over at his son, the more okay he was with the idea. Now, he could also see Debra in Otis, Jr.'s face. That fact brought him back to the backyard, the Officer over his shoulder, Bonnie's periodic glances, all the beautiful women present he couldn't lay a hand on and, ah yes, jail.

"I thought you had a whole mess of kids?" the Officer for the day asked Otis rhetorically with a slight grin.

CHAPTER THIRTY-FIVE

Clark stumbled out of bed. She stubbed her toe on the dresser and then smacked her knee against the bedroom doorframe while walking blurry eyed to the front door. The racket in the hallway might have been going on since dawn. By all accounts, she thought, this had better be an emergency. She had no idea how long the extremely enthusiastic knocker had been slamming their fists into the metal security door, but by the strength of it, hours had passed. She hated the fact that they, them, whoever, awoke her out of a virtually perfect slumber.

"...old...yo..ur...orses..." she slurred, propping her hands against the hallway walls for support.

Meanwhile, the banging continued through her reply. 'Who is this uninvited guest,' she pondered, hoping the building wasn't on fire or worse, because even with that panic swelling within her, she still couldn't will herself completely awake.

"...wh...o..?" she inquired hoarsely to the door.

No answer came, just a ruffling sound from someone on the other side. Clark leaned upon the door this time, eyes still shut, mouth ajar in deep, deep repose. She had forced herself to stay up all night believing that she was once and for all going to deal with the evil lurking in her bedroom. Now, feeling hung-over with grogginess, she felt sure that her plan needed some adjusting. The knocking began again.

"Who?" she yelled angrily this time.

"Me," a woman replied indignantly.

Clark placed her head against the peephole and flickered her eyelids rapidly in an effort to clear her cloudy lens. Just barely recognizing a familiar face, she opened the door.

"Oh ma' Gooaawwd. 'U sleep like 'u dead…I wasn't sure you were e-vin home but I saw yu' carr…" Arlene said loud enough to stir everyone else in the building, rushing pass Clark. Then she headed straight toward the kitchen and swung open the refrigerator before Clark managed to close the front door. Arlene proceeded to help herself to whatever she could grab, orange juice and some left over pizza. She threw the entire box into the microwave and pressed start. Only after she got herself a glass from the cabinet and sat at the table did she look at Clark, who literally seemed to be melting.

"H..elp your..self…" Clark mumbled, just barely maneuvering to find a chair with her eyes in a squint. Then she plopped down into it, resting her hands upon her face, and her elbows on the table.

"You don't look so good," Arlene told her sipping and nodding again and again with emphasis.

Clark couldn't look at her, mainly because her head wouldn't lift. There was an aching that threatened to spread all over her body. Currently, the aching hovered about her head and at the back of her legs. It hadn't reached her feet yet. So, she braced herself for that inevitability.

"…huh…Ar…lene…ah…what…?" Clark asked now really feeling the pain of her lack of sleep.

"Yeah…yeah…wow…girl…ah need to tell yu' somethin' right away…" Arlene paused to get her pizza out from the microwave, "…wow…it's hot…ouch…" she said while grabbing the box and flinging it onto the table.

Clark wanted to laugh but she had discovered that now her stomach muscles were hurting on top of all her other bodily issues. Meanwhile, Arlene wouldn't begin her story without at least three to four bites of the nuked leftovers.

"...momm...y...ah...didn't...git...nah...sleep...last...nite ..." she said smacking her lips and tugging on the rubbery cheese.

Clark listened, having little energy to do anything but.

"...he...came...chu...no..." said Arlene clutching at her chest and heaving heavily, nodding up and down as if Clark should easily know what she meant.

Clark looked as droopy as the day old pizza.

"...he...him...yor...him..." Arlene said in a panic.

"Peter?" Clark asked wondering why her ex-boyfriend would have stopped by to see Arlene.

With that thought, her mind began to drift to all the possible reasons, which would have led him there, none of which made any sense.

"Nooooo-a, not Petah'..." Arlene said rolling her r's in a drawl, "...That thing...that thing that's attached to yu'a," she said so matter-of-fact that it took Clark completely by surprise.

She knew that Arlene had special insight into these things but she had no idea that she had any inkling about her little problem in particular. She took a breath, realizing that she hadn't for several moments. She was in shock.

"Yu' didn't think ah knew...." Arlene laughed through her nose and then coughed from the thick breaded crust stuck in her throat.

Clark was ashamed at how little credit she gave her. Now,

Arlene had her full attention. She was all ears, while Arlene leaned back, smiling, open-mouthed, food still inside. Then she nodded up and down, side-ways and then finally eyed Clark very, very seriously. Clark was speechless.

"Lis-sen, yu' need to git rid of that thing, yu' hear mey…rid of that thing," Arlene told her sternly.

"Arlene, what happened to you, I mean…did something *happen* to you?" Clark asked though slightly nervous of actually receiving an answer.

Arlene stopped chewing and placed her pizza slice back down on the box. She was all at once sullen and introspective. These were new expressions for her. Suddenly, Arlene's youthfulness aged ten years. Clark worried that she might have inadvertently had something to do with this sudden paleness.

"Well…chu no that what it is ain't human no more…" she started.

Clark leaned back and tried to listen without showing a surge of sheer panic that had been bubbling up for days.

"What did you see…exactly…?" she managed to ask Arlene, who was still stiff and sallow.

"Ah wake, yu no…and ah'm like, ah have a shortness of breath, yu no…in…my chest, right here…" she said pointing to her sternum.

Clark couldn't move for she too had awakened many times, that same way.

"…Ah'm wondering what's going on, yu no, like am ah'm having a heart attack…or something. Ah don't no, yu no, what's going on…and ah'm scared because hubby's out working and ah don't have any family, yu no, here…in New York…Anyhow, ah'm out of breath, so ah try to breath slowly…so ah don't die. Ah tell yu, ah thought ah die, right there in my own bed, by my own self, as God is my witness…" she made a cross from her shoulders to her chest and chin then rambled in Spanish what sounded like a prayer.

Clark still blanched, watched and waited, wondering all the while how she could just make it all stop.

"…When ah opened my eyes…" she gulped, "…there he was…" she shot a stare at Clark as if they both were there.

Clark shifted in her chair realizing that at any moment she could have fallen off.

"…He was sitting, yu' no…" she nodded as if Clark knew exactly what she meant.

Clark didn't but was afraid to ask.

"…They sit, yu' no…on your chest, yu' no…" she said slowly and deliberately as if pealing an onion with a chain saw.

"On your chest…" Clark repeated.

She had seen for herself this position and had already concluded that she hadn't really seen what was right before her very eyes. Only now, with Arlene's testimony, had she begun to acknowledge her own denial of this entire situation. Arlene was like the catalyst bringing her screaming back into reality.

"They sit on your chest because they're trying to push your soul out of your body," Arlene said so articulately that there was no mistaking the meaning.

Clark's body was in a rigid pose, back tilted forward, forehead protruding up and out towards Arlene. She suddenly felt as if she couldn't breathe. It was the undeniable fact that her life was indeed in danger that made her pause in unyielding contemplation. She now knew this to be true or as true as she could bring herself to believe and that this thing actually had a name, Jimmy. There it was; the truth. Jimmy was trying to kill her.

"This son-of-a-bit-tch is trying to kill me…ah think that's what it was…but ah'm protected, yu' no," Arlene told Clark.

"Protected?" Clark asked wanting desperately to find out how.

"Yeah, girl," Arlene said, once again eating pizza and drinking her orange juice, "This stuff is good. What kind is it?" Arlene asked about the juice.

"Mario's, Pathmark's, Walgreen, whatever, protection…pro-tec-tion?" Clark inquired with emphasis and urgency.

"Yeah, yeah…my mother gave me this," Arlene said reaching for a necklace, an amulet with an oval shape and some sort of sword up the middle.

It looked like the top part of a streetlight.

"What's that?" Clark asked, both intrigued and disappointed.

"AKhanda. It's said that when yu' wear one of these, mom-miee,' can't nothing get to yu', yu' no. Ah don't even take this off in the shower. And ah take off my wedding ring there, yu' no," she laughed heartily.

Clark sat back completely bewildered at what she just heard. Was this Jimmy character haunting her friends now too? That thought boggled her mind. Why? And, did Arlene just tell her that a piece of costumed jewelry saved her?

"Yu' don't believe me, do yu'?" Arlene asked seeing the look of disbelief upon Clark's face.

Clark couldn't hide her curious expression.

"Look, ah'm still here ain't ah? Yu' mey not believe in my

mother's magic but yu' do have this thing attached to yu'. He's probably come after me 'cause ah'm spiritual. He probably saw that on me…'cause ah'm your friend, yu' no," Arlene said matter-of-factly.

Clark grew suddenly really, really tired. And, although Arlene was making sense, she didn't want to sit and listen to her any longer. She didn't want to know anymore about Jimmy and his antics, or Arlene and her charms and powers over evil. She stood up and went over to the bathroom. At first, she was just going in there to get away from Arlene for a moment; before she knew it, she was in the shower allowing the water to wash away everything she just heard. Especially, the part about this thing, dead and gone for more than ten years, trying to kill her; that part was not what she wanted to hear at all.

"Hey, mommy, ah'm leavin'," Arlene yelled at the closed bathroom door, "And call Priestess Enomwoyi to get rid of this thing!"

A few minutes later, the front door opened then closed and Clark's apartment was silent again, save for her pounding heart, which ricocheted off the walls and drowned out everything except her fear.

CHAPTER THIRTY-SIX

Everything about her day, in a nutshell, was bizarre. After her little chat with Arlene which left her head spinning, then a pitiful excuse for a shower where the water spurted one moment then trickled the next; she felt ill at ease and ill prepared for her day. Tossing and turning all night, then essentially being dragged out of bed, would hardly qualify as restful. She was fitful, on edge and sensitive to everything. The sunlight bothered her eyes. Her lazy pupils refused to adjust. The school kids playing across the street from her apartment bothered her; the courtyard acting as an echo chamber amplifying the sound tenfold. The insufferable heat of the Subway was torturous. That morning her hair was beautifully coifed with a slick bang gelled down with Dep and a mass of soft spiral curls framing her face. Now, it clung to her cheeks affixed there with the help of tiny beads of sweat. The air-conditioned train car, freezing, and frigid, made her teeth chatter, with her head wet, she felt like she was coming down with a cold. When she walked up two double flights of stairs and finally exited out of Pennsylvania Station, New York City's busy throngs impeded her every step. If she had any energy left, she would have pushed more than a few people out of her way. She felt down right violent. Unfortunately, this haggard, miserable replica of her normal self was the last thing she needed for this latest job, a national photo shoot. This would be her first one. She was hired to pose next to four Caucasian teenage graduates for a coveted spot in a United Negro Fund print advertisement.

She was cast to represent an equal opportunity society, the lone Black girl standing beside four Whites, having the same educational privileges as them. Ironically, the caption, above her head would read, '*A Mind Is A Terrible Thing To Waste*'.

When she arrived, her mind, her spirit, her very soul felt just that - wasted, hung-over and the fretfulness inside of her had all but hardened into a kind of extra skeleton. Try as she might, she couldn't bring herself to understand what the photographer was asking of her at any given request.

"Stand on the left side! Right there!" he shouted, his eyes querying the Director for an explanation for Clark's apparent lack of knowledge of the English language.

The Director gave Clark a scornful look several times indicating that had it not been for lack of time, she would be kicked back home faster than the camera shutter closing. Clark steadily stared at the photographer for several uncomfortable seconds before coming to the recognition of his words. It was difficult to decipher anything with a splitting headache, a knot in her back, ailments resembling a fever and a crippling dread of the future, which was unrelenting. Not to mention, the extreme exhaustion, which was sheer physical pain leaving her riddled with tension. Her body absent from her mind, now stood before a room of strangers, all wanting something from her, awaiting her full attention. This job would establish her as a model. Her image would be plastered from New York to California, on buses, trains, and billboards. She sincerely needed this break and wanted to do her best but her own body wouldn't yield even an inch to help her accomplish the goal. It took a few seconds but Clark finally moved left and posed with a perfectly phony smile together with the rest of the bewildered girls. Clark hated most of all that this was yet another very important moment in her life that she couldn't enjoy.

How could she? She was being hunted down, but not by anyone, but by someone who didn't even exist anymore. She wondered if any of what Priestess Enomwoyi or what Arlene said to her was even true or possible. Maybe, what her mother told her was truest of all, that there's nothing the dead can do but rot. However, she knew that there was indeed something wrong, something unearthly, something threatening. Of that fact, she was convinced. As she changed positions and grinned like the hopelessly idealistic graduate she was pretending to be, she came to the realization that she wasn't exactly trying very earnestly to get to the bottom of this predicament. In fact, she knew for certain that she had been running away from it all along. She hated to admit that Arlene had moved her out of her comfort zone, as it were, not to mention Priestess Enomonyi's little get-together with her undead relatives. She was discovering that she needed to be more than just a casual observer in this dilemma. She needed to be an active participant. She needed to dig down deep and despite her crippling fear, fight for her life.

"Ah!" she gasped out loud.

"Good, good," the photographer told her, "Finally, some life out of you."

'Yes, there is still some life in me,' she thought, trying to receive the compliment with some kind of dignity, meanwhile knowing full well that everyone in the room knew that she was the weak link, holding the others hostage.

It took every ounce of energy she had left, but she did finally manage to pull herself together. She had to pretend that everything prior to the photo shoot never happened. She had to pretend that her life was as promising as the teenagers to her right, all genuine smiles and pearly whites, naturally shiny everything. She had to pretend that she didn't have to go fight a demon afterwards in order to reclaim any sense of normalcy. She had to pretend that she had some clue as to how she was going to accomplish this feat without supernatural power. She had to pretend that she wasn't really scared to death about the whole thing, and that thought almost broke her, almost. Instead, she smiled and stopped thinking about it for the next hour's work and though some peace came, it didn't last long.

CHAPTER THIRTY-SEVEN

Jimmy wasn't scared, though he knew where she was heading, and what she intended to do once she got there. In fact, he knew everything about it, all the cozy details. What surprised him though was how much strength and courage she possessed. He did everything he could to wear her down, spooking her apartment, lying with her at night, pressing down on her with all his might. She was definitely not like all the rest. Good old Busta was a breeze. All he did was scare him a bit, and boom; he was dead. And, he didn't even want to mention Debra, mainly because she might show up, but, all things considered, she was easy too, but not Clark. She had been his supreme challenge. Though this fact annoyed him, he knew deep down that it was only fitting. After all, she was also his greatest love. Throughout his experiences with Debra, he knew that love too easily won was not worth having. Debra proved this by being a clinging leach in life and so far the same in death. He sincerely regretted all of their little trysts. Not with Clark, though. Clark was a feisty young thing worthy of the chase. She would be his success story, and eventually his reward. Together they would be unstoppable. For all intents and purposes, he believed that they were already wed. In his imagination, they had an enviable, grand ceremony. Everyone who was anyone was present. Clark wore white, of course. He wasn't hypocritical. He forgave her all those other men. That was before he came into her life, a real man. The rest were mere boys. Now, that he was on the scene, like birds in winter, they scattered. One by one they ran.

Leaving her just the way he preferred, all to himself.

Neither was he worried either. Sure, she was on her way over to the Yoruba Priestess's house, or YP, as Jimmy referred to her. He could still remember how he was so unceremoniously harangued by her relatives at their last encounter. It made him smile now just thinking about it. He knew how to get even. He was not some wimpy, spineless mutton to be run out of town screaming like a little girl. As far as he was concerned, he wasn't going to let go of Clark until he had her very life. Until that day, he wasn't going anywhere. To think that the little witch doctor from Brooklyn was going to thwart him was blatantly preposterous. Jimmy left Clark that night for one reason and one reason only. He was bored. It wasn't exactly a party like Clark's silly friend, Arlene, told her. They were dancing to conga drums. Jimmy laughed, thinking that he had heard better music in an elevator. Then when the other spirits came at him the way they did, he was downright tickled. It was pointless, really. They knew he had the ability to go wherever he pleased. He'd but wish for it, and he'd transport himself wherever in less time than it would take him to think about it. It was sheer jealousy. This he knew. That's why they wanted to take her away from him. They could never have the kind of existence he had with her, the kind of intimacy they shared nightly. She was his and he was hers. It was a divinely inspired relationship, that couldn't be squelched even in death. No man or old has-beens could change that no matter what they did. It did upset him to see that Paulo guy again, though. He had forgotten how attentive he was to Clark that last time. He gave Paulo a little headache by placing his energy on both sides of his head, then squeezing. He made sure to do it whenever he spoke to Clark. It was subtle but effective, not that Paulo was a threat. Jimmy just didn't like the guy. Anyone with that much hair on his head was clearly more interested in a mirror than in a woman. Jimmy figured that that's why he was having trouble with his girl, YP.

Boy, she irritated him too, with her holier than thou attitude strutting around like a queen. He did what he could to trip her, but she was surrounded by her ancient relatives all the damn time. They acted as a fortress shielding her from him. He would have killed her too for sport if given the chance. It bothered him to no end that she would purport that she could send the dead packing. He could so clearly see that she had no more power than a piece of yarn. She had only what was woven into the fabric of her ancestry. Without them, she was completely useless. He saw her with the chicken and couldn't help but laugh at the sheer theatrics of it all. Had he really wanted to, he would have done away with the whole loony household, including the children, the future bloodline. Admittedly, though he did have a curiosity about the whole charade. He mainly watched and waited as she, the Yoruba Priestess began her show. 'This should be amusing,' Jimmy thought. He was right there beside Clark. Before he knew it YP was chanting some long ago forgotten scriptures and prancing around the room with the bloody sacrifice in hand. The more she danced, the closer Jimmy drew to Clark. He could feel Clark's heartbeat quicken. He wanted to tell her not to worry, that this was nothing to get all worked up about, that they would be leaving soon enough, going back home together, but she wasn't responding to him the way she normally did. She paid him no mind. He could tell, to his astonishment, that YP was distracting her. Her eyes were wide staring blankly across the room. She scarcely thought she knew he was there. So, he decided that he'd enter her. He'd done it many times before, but those were on happier occasions. Now, she seemed distant and he felt that he needed to intervene. She was his and he needed to protect his property. He went right in, but as he did, YP's relatives came clamoring right beside him. Now, they were offering their protection to Clark too, crowding Jimmy out. They were next to her body hovering closely. Jimmy grew impatient. This was his territory not theirs and they had no right to her. He remained right there by her heart listening to its sweet rhythm. He loved her. He stroked her hair. He adored her. It would take more than a few incantations to remove him. He would fight for what was rightfully his.

Though, it didn't take long before he realized that something was terribly wrong. He had the oddest sensation forming around him. He looked down and saw that he was beginning to literally disappear. Little by little he felt like he was no longer rooted to this plane, called earth. There was a spot in the corner, just beyond YP's kinfolk and Clark. It stood there growing in size and as it did, so he grew fainter. The light that was him, once shimmering like a bolt of electricity seemed dimmer and dimmer. He growled at the menaces before him, each with their necks stretching to get at him. He thought himself too clever for this bunch, but there was something pulling at him. He could now hear Priestess Enomwoyi screaming at him. Though he did not know what she was saying, each word acted as daggers piercing him. He was at an impasse, wanting to fight but still holding onto Clark. He didn't know which was more important.

He could sense that she was so frightened and in his soul, he wanted to be with her always. So, he began to push down on her. He would have her. He would take her with him, even if he were forced by this black magic out of this world. He knew himself to be a god and that if not here on earth, he would still exist somewhere else. He hunkered all of his energy into the pit of his being, and released it onto Clark. She gasped and he knew that he had her. He did this a few more times and then finally, thankfully she yielded.

He rose above her towards the ceiling and, to his astonishment; she came drifting up right along with him. He smiled but it was done prematurely in triumph. As he did so, his connection with her stopped working and Clark descended downward, back to her stiff body. He saw life awaken within her. Again, her face went flush. Still the relentless chanting continued, slowly soaking mysteriously within Jimmy's state of being. He snarled at the Priestess and shooed her troublesome relatives away. Momentarily, they halted their practically military formation. It was just long enough for him to reach into Clark and grab hold once more. Before he knew it, they were again ascending. This time he held fast to her as well as the excitement, which was so intense, it had him radiating like a star. He kept telling himself over and over again to calm down and to be patient. All he needed was a few more lousy minutes, just enough time for Clark's connection to her flesh to be permanently severed. He couldn't believe that the Priestess and her crew were actually helping him get his beloved. Again, holding his emotions together, he made sure never to lose contact with Clark. He was not about to let go, not now, when everything he'd ever hoped for was finally in sight. 'Just a few more seconds,' he thought, relishing the painful sweetness that swept across him. Finally, in all his miserable life and death, he was going to get what he always wanted, his precious Clark – his beautiful, true love.

CHAPTER THIRTY-EIGHT

If the floor was cold, that would have been a blessing. As it was, Clark would have to thaw out in order to breathe again. Her bones were stiff and aching. And not just because of the relentless draft coming from underneath the two doors that led into the living room, turned ceremonial chamber. It was seventy-eight degrees outside. Brooklyn was enjoying what seemed to be the last few days of Indian Summer. Still Clark shivered in a way that all too well showed her nervousness and apprehension. She was at wits end. She hadn't many choices left. She would have to grin and bare the shame of this latest decision. Coming to someone for help was bad enough but when one does so, on one's hands and knees, pleading, well, what's left of their dignity. It took her just fifteen minutes to drive from Downtown Brooklyn to Bedford Stuyvesant. It took her two hours to make it to Priestess Enomwoyi's front door. During this lapse in time, Clark sat in a diner not more than five blocks away sipping on coffee and gnawing on a sesame bagel. It wasn't that she wanted to make sure that she was on time. It wasn't because she didn't want to see Priestess Enomwoyi again and dreaded another meeting. Those items were only a part of it. The other part rested in the fact that she simply didn't want to stay at home alone anymore. If she could have, she would have camped out in front of Priestess Enomwoyi's overnight. Unfortunately, her apartment had become down right eerie. Not only was she seeing things during the night, but now even as the sunlight soaked through her windows, the spirits would come.

Arlene kept telling her that she had really developed and finely tuned her gift. Clark still didn't think it a present but a curse. She would have preferred not see things being trapped, as Arlene told her, between life and death. She was afraid to sleep unless she had four to five blankets covering her face. She didn't want to have to wake in the middle of the night having seen through the cracks of her eyes shadows passing by. She had a difficult time in the shower too, thinking that these ghosts were watching her disrobe, especially since Jimmy seemed to always be around her when she was naked or in bed. She was young when she had known him, but she would never forget how he was in life, simply perverted. She never really liked or trusted him and wouldn't have thought of him romantically no matter the context. She had always considered him a dirty old man, which made him equivalent to a slug. In earnest she knew that she had tried everything she knew how to rid herself of him, this unearthly attachment. This procedure with Priestess Enomwoyi was her last hope. She never thought she'd end up under going something like this. But there she was at Priestess Enomwoyi's lying bare back on the floor trying to find the peace that was promised to come through the circle of fire surrounding her; thick white lit candles all melting into the planked wood. Clark had sent Priestess Enomwoyi a five hundred dollar check, all she had left in her bank account. Arlene swore that this was the only way - essentially an exorcist.

Earlier, when Clark had finally arrived, Paulo had given her a lukewarm greeting. She got the impression that he was actually saying good-bye. It was just a feeling, but he did seem distant and moody. 'If this ritual works,' she thought, 'Priestess

Enomwoyi, Jimmy, and, alas, Paulo, would all be but a faint memory.' Clark sighed at that bittersweet thought. Jimmy, of course, had to go, and she definitely didn't want to run into Priestess Enomwoyi again. She wasn't planning on being another one of Priestess Enomwoyi's groupies. She wasn't going to hang around one minute longer than she had to once all this was all sorted. Priestess Enomwoyi made sure to remind her that she had told her that this wasn't over. Priestess Enomwoyi would accept nothing less than Clark's complete and wretched debasement. Clark was made to grovel and beg. Clark obliged knowing that she didn't have much choice. Now devoid of shame, she laid on the floor, trying to settle herself, and to calm her nerves. She prayed to the sun, the moon, the stars and the earth gods, having no clue what she was doing. She had doubts, sure, yet she lay there still enough for the business of getting rid of a ghost to be conducted. If she weren't so mortified and scared, she would have scoffed at the whole notion of life after death. Despite everything, the idea of haunting still wasn't completely sinking in. Though, she had seen him, Jimmy, all over her apartment, felt his presence in her very bed, and had awaken to his smoky figure; she couldn't suppress the doubts that would come at times of normalcy. When everything was fine and he wasn't around, she would always begin to surmise that she must have dreamt the whole thing, that maybe she was losing her mind, that he was just the substance of her imagination. She was an actress, after all, prone to fits of mental imbalance. It was harder, though, to rationalize the bruises and scratch marks and the chilling shortness of breath arresting her sleep, or the fact that both Priestess Enomwoyi and Arlene had seen him too. Those truths were not so easily dismissed. There was so much she didn't understand; didn't want to believe.

As she turned her head to the side, desperately trying to get a crick out of it, she could see Priestess Enomwoyi seated in repose, trance like. She was humming and singing something slowly and softly. She looked as spooky as she had the night of their little fight. Clark tried not to pay too much attention to her. She thought that if she did, she might be tempted to get up and run out of there, naked and all. Then at that precise moment, off in the distance, she swore she heard what she knew to be a live, cocking chicken. It sounded as if it was coming from the kitchen, but it might have been the backyard. It, apparently, knew its fate. Priestess Enomwoyi's apartment reeked of death. Clark could smell something rotten right beside her but whenever she looked over, the odor disappeared. At first, she thought it was Priestess Enomwoyi, but she remained stationary, while the odor, it seemed, moved about the room. Clark didn't like the fact that she had to remove her hands from her breasts and private area in order to hold her nose.

"So…" Priestess Enomwoyi finally spoke.

Clark only then realized that she hadn't said a word all morning, only nodding in greeting and directions of where Clark should stand and wait. Paulo had told her to disrobe and lie in the center of the room. Clark wouldn't have obeyed had he not seemed so indifferent towards her. Contrary to their last meeting, now he made her feel like she was in a doctor's office.

"…If it weren't for your friend…" Priestess Enomwoyi said sternly, purposely allowing the innuendo to do her talking for her.

Clark knew exactly what she meant. She knew that without

a doubt, she wasn't entirely welcome; just barely being tolerated really. She also knew that the payment sure did help Priestess Enomwoyi's pain and suffering. Clark was glad when Priestess Enomwoyi left the room altogether. She had further preparations for their ceremony. She exited into the back of the house, and Clark took a deep breath for the first time since her arrival. In truth, she didn't want to look at her or talk about anything other than the business at hand. She wanted her to do her thing and let Clark go back to her life unencumbered. Clark hoped that once this whole spooky mess was over that she would be a free woman again, free to pursue others things like men, having children, a career, anything that life had to offer. So, instead of concentrating on her predicament, she lay there contemplating future possibilities. That's when the chicken really began its cocking or crowing or possibly crying. Clark tried not to think about that either.

Then, there was silence. Clark turned her head and listened. Nothing. She couldn't hear the chicken anymore. Then she heard footsteps coming in her direction. She decided to close her eyes. She figured that she'd keep them shut like when she'd go to the dentist, not wanting to see what was going on with the drilling or extractions. All she wanted was to sleep through the entire procedure and wake up again without something dark and ugly attached to her.

"You alright?" Priestess Enomwoyi asked her knowing full well that she wasn't.

Clark could see the smirk upon her face still. It was the same one from the last time she was in her house. Clark nodded, yes, but what else could she do? She was without pride and deprived of rest. When she did sleep, it was with her whole system buckling under and colliding with the bed. These deprived nights had affected her work performance, her friendships and definitely her mental health. Of course she wasn't alright and Priestess Enomwoyi only asked that question to be cruel. They both knew this and yet pretended otherwise.

"Okay, I want you to put your hands out to your sides," Priestess Enomwoyi instructed.

Clark obeyed, though this position made her even more exposed.

"This is going to seem a bit odd, so, hold still," Priestess Enomwoyi warned.

Clark bit her lip, trying hard not to say, 'And what else is new.' She appreciated the fact that now Priestess Enomwoyi was clinical and professional.

Priestess Enomwoyi grabbed the now dead chicken from a bucket. Clark realized that she had just carried it in. She raised it above her head and recited some incantation. Clark noticed that the chicken was headless. Before she knew it, blood dripped everywhere but the bulk of it made its way onto Clark's naked body. Clark tried not to be grossed out because it was so slimy. It was heavier than she thought it would be and as it struck her, it pelted her skin like an out-pouring of hail from the sky. Before she knew it, she was covered with it. Priestess Enomwoyi continued her unearthly discourse, stomping about the circle of fire and shaking the chicken upside down, draining the life out of it. Clark knew that anyone looking on might have thought it humorous to witness, but up close, it was frightfully paralyzing. Then the floor beneath her began to shake. She looked over and thought she saw someone or something enter the room.

Clark looked around but could see nothing except Priestess Enomwoyi and, of course, the chicken. Then they came, the same spirits from Priestess Enomwoyi's party. They just appeared in the room and gathered around the circle of fire. Clark's immediate response was to stare blankly at them. Her entire body was frozen with fear especially knowing that Priestess Enomwoyi had summoned them. Now they too began pelting at Clark's flesh. It was like being slid through a sewing machine. The pain of it was unbearable, as well as humiliating. She just knew that they were drawing blood but with so much of the chicken's on her, she couldn't be sure whose was whose.

"Ahhh…" she sighed finally able to make a sound.

Her cry came out heavy and throaty. She looked over and saw Priestess Enomwoyi dancing manically, her eyes rolling back into her head. The floor thundered in a roar, as the room grew dark and misty. Clark realized that the flashes of light, looking more like lightning, were actually the spirits racing in and out of her body. They popped in and took her breath away. They emerged out taking with them a part of her soul, leaving her weakened and hollow. She didn't like the sensation at all, yet she couldn't move. She was literally pinned to the floor. It was the ringing in her ears that really got her going though. She could hear these apparitions also chanting and speaking spills, all of them sounding off at the same time. She felt as if her head couldn't contain so much information. She was near faint.

Priestess Enomwoyi reached down and pressed her palm against Clark's forehead, still speaking in a language Clark did not recognize. Clark began to cry frightfully wondering what in the world was coming next. She looked into the whites of Priestess Enomwoyi's eyes and could now see tiny droplets of blood moistening them. The blood appeared like sweat rolling across her cheeks. As Priestess Enomwoyi pressed, Clark could feel something clinging to her chest. It was a suctioning of some sort that seemed to be pulling her heart right out of it. Her entire upper body began to burn in agony. Then the same shape she had seen for days on end was right there before her. It was Jimmy. She was horrified lying there helplessly watching him as he stared peculiarly down at her. Suddenly, Clark knew where the chill she felt earlier was really coming from. Jimmy had a frosty film surrounding him that hung over her like frostbite. His face was at first smooth and eerily perfect. She noticed his hands reaching down pulling at something within her chest. That's when she began experiencing a shortness of breath. Her body convulsed as if she were having a heart attack. She was petrified. This had been the same position she had awakened to nightly. Priestess Enomwoyi was screeching at him, gesturing frantically to let Clark go. Yet and still he continued to wrench at something between her breasts. Then he hissed at Priestess Enomwoyi, and an odorous film sipped out of him resembling thick, blackened sludge. Priestess Enomwoyi and her cohorts hissed right back. And when they did, Jimmy's face transformed into a vicious, decomposing creature. Now this scaly, pus erupting haggard thing was nose to nose with Clark. Clark squirmed away from him but he was inescapable. Then as Priestess Enomwoyi's voice grew louder, Jimmy's face as well as the rest of him began to drip down onto Clark. Jimmy's matter felt like acid smoldering into her skin. She tried to cry out but there wasn't anything left in her. Suddenly, she heard whimpering coming from a distance. It was guttural and sorrowful. Later she would discover that it was her own thin voice that she heard. Jimmy's grip loosened ever so slightly and Clark took in as much air as she could, tensing for his next round. He didn't want to let go of her but Priestess Enomwoyi was just as determined to send him on his way.

The more Jimmy and Priestess Enomwoyi fought, the freer Clark began to feel. At one point she actually knew that a weight had been lifted off of her. She was all at once light. The painful burning had ceased and she was elevated upward, seemingly right out of herself. Then back again down plummeting, it seemed, to the floor. This happened several times before she noticed that each time she descended, vomit had spitted out of her mouth. Now she was covered in blood and bits and pieces of her breakfast, Jimmy still hovering, making her feel as if she were trapped in a coffin lying underneath his deceased body. It was horrifying. Then, when she sincerely thought that she just couldn't take anymore, that she would join him in the hereafter after all, Jimmy gasped one last time. Then ever so slowly he quietly evaporated into thin air. Clark watched as pieces of him dissolved right up and out into the atmosphere. Thankfully, the cold chill went with him, as did Priestess Enomwoyi's guests. Right after that Clark could hear street noises, cars passing, birds chirping, and passersby. Clark envied them. It was altogether difficult for her to tell what was real and what was imagined. She sort of felt as if she had stepped back into the world, coming from a foreign place that isn't subject to time or space, a parallel world. Priestess Enomwoyi said nothing for what seemed like an eternity. She was hutched over, drained and disoriented too. Clark sat up for the first time since Priestess Enomwoyi entered the room with the sacrifice. She would discover later that day, that her session had taken three and a half long hours.

CHAPTER THIRTY-NINE

Priestess Enomwoyi muttered, "That was one arrogant son of a bitch…" She'd been washing her hands in the guest bathroom for over twenty minutes. First she used half a bottle of the Dawn disinfectant dishwashing liquid. Then she moved on to some Dudu-Osun Black Soap, for good measure. Next she was going to shower a few times, and then wash her hair until it squeaked. Then she'd sit in the tub filled with scalding, hot water. She was no longer the picture of grace and elegance. She was now a woman suffering from an obsessive, compulsive disorder.

"…but I used his ego against him, you see…" she smiled, "…silly fool…"

She tossed back her head and laughed while using a scrub brush this time on her hands and forearms all the way up to her elbows. Her hair was mated with dry perspiration, and chicken blood. Her eyes were black and puffy. Her normally smooth skin was filled with creases, as if it was actually chipped in several places.

"…You saw him, right?" she asked, for the first time in a long while looking over at Clark, remembering that she was there.

Clark was laboring into her clothing, still feeling uncomfortable and uneasy with all that had transpired. She nodded her head, wondering why she wasn't immediately feeling released from her burden.

"It's going to take some time," Enomwoyi told her, reading the exhaustion in her hunched shoulders and syrupy movements.

Clark nodded in agreement. She was too tired to contemplate how Priestess Enomwoyi knew what was on her mind. Priestess Enomwoyi leaned outside of the small half bath, resting her head upon the doorframe, hands still soapy with lather. Now she was looking directly at Clark. Clark couldn't bring herself to return her gaze. It wasn't just her physical tiredness; she longed to get away from all things spiritual. She had had enough.

"There's something else about him that you need to know…" Priestess Enomwoyi started.

Then she turned back around and rinsed the soap from her hands.

"…It's about your grandmother…" she continued.

"What about her?" Clark snapped, promptly interested in their conversation for the first time since the ritual.

"He knew her," she said.

"Knew her?..." Clark asked, "In what way?"

"Fair question, but that's not what I mean," Priestess Enomwoyi came back into the doorframe and lowered her head.

Clark watched her patiently wondering if anything could be worse than what they both had just been through.

"She was with us today," Enomwoyi told her.

"Why would she be with…" Clark started to ask then remembered the last thing said to her by Grandma Olivia.

It didn't take her long to figure that he must have been attached to her then and that Grandma Olivia must have seen him.

"He didn't…" Clark asked, then leaned forward and vomited on the hallway floor.

Priestess Enomwoyi tossed the towel she was holding down and wiped it up with her foot.

"It's going to be alright. She was very sickly," she said patting Clark on the back.

Clark was listening but nothing, absolutely nothing was giving her the relief she sought.

"How…what…he did?…I don't understand…" she now sobbed.

Priestess Enomwoyi was gentle now, lifting Clark's head and handing her some tissue for her eyes.

"She's happy now. She isn't feeling any more pain," she said to Clark, looking off in the distance dreamily.

Clark finally allowed that fact to infuse her troubled spirit. She knew that her grandmother did not have an easy life. She liked hearing that the after life was faring much, much better.

"She wants you to do something in her honor," Enomwoyi said.

"In her honor?" Clark repeated.

"Yes. She would like you, when you're all cleaned up, of course, to put some roses in a glass and toast to her," she told her, "She asked me to tell you that."

Clark had a lot to absorb, least of all drinking flowered flavored water, but she agreed by nodding. Then she continued to dress, putting on her sandals, and fastening her baseball cap back on her head.

She stood up, noting immediately her wobbly limbs.

"It takes time," Enomwoyi reiterated.

Again, Clark nodded that she understood but not much more than that.

"…There's…one…more…thing…" Priestess Enomwoyi said turning on her heals and walking back to the sink.

The hand washing was in the double digits now. Clark wanted to criticize Enomwoyi's manic behavior but after what she'd been through, decided it was best to let it go.

"What?" Clark asked shouting over running water.

That's when she noted how hoarse her voice was. The sound came out gravely, and from the back of her throat. Enomwoyi dried her hands again and stepped outside of the little bathroom. Again, she leaned her head on the doorframe and sighed.

"I wouldn't be worth my Priestess title if I didn't warn you about the dangers of not taking care of yourself now that the operation, so to speak, is over," she said contemplatively.

She finally walked out into the hallway and now leaned against the wall facing Clark. Clark lifted her head and waited, unsure whether she wanted anymore of what Enomwoyi had to say. It sounded ominous, therefore spiritual, and she was sick of that.

"Now that that lunatic is gone, you're going to need to fill the space now," Enomwoyi told her, matter-of-factly.

Clark's eyes looked glazed over.

"I know, I know, it's not easy to understand some of these things. I grew up a Priestess in the making, come from a long line of them. My mother and her mother before her. My family tree is deep rooted with them, from generation to generation. But you...do you go to church?" she asked.

Clark hesitantly shook her head no.

"You need to," Priestess Enomwoyi advised her.

"I do?" Clark asked.

"Well, that's what I'm trying to say. You see the two worlds here on this plain, human and spirit, exist together. We're in one world and that fool was in another. See, he was not supposed to be in this one with us. Sure, they visit but when this life is through, you go on to the next. Well, now things have changed for you. You can now see both worlds. You're what they call, open, like a doorway…an open door. See, right now, I've cleaned you with the help of my guides. We work hard for you today, trust me. He not want to leave easily. Him say he love you, love you, huh…fool, that he is. Him can't love no one but himself, but that's 'nother story," she laughed.

Clark didn't. She was sure she didn't like anything said so far.

"Anyway, now you must fill yourself, with good stuff. You had bad stuff. Now you need good stuff," she said nodding slowly agreeing with her own statement.

Clark was at a loss. She kept wondering what 'good stuff' meant. She had already experienced bad stuff apparently, but this antithesis baffled her, though it sounded sort of intriguing.

"See, God knows you. He, himself saved you. He has a reason for your life. He don't want you taken away like that, with someone who don't know he dead and damned. That was not for you, okay," Priestess Enomwoyi finished with a double pat on Clark's head.

Clark felt like she was being sent away to fight lions and tigers with nothing more than a pre-game speech. Her mind was in a knot. Locked within, she knew was some sort of unraveling recognition of an understanding as to what Enomwoyi was telling her. She wanted to make certain that she left with instructions but she also wanted to simply leave.

She stood up again, and this time her legs supported her. Then, with one head nod to Priestess Enomwoyi, she walked silently to the door.

"Remember, to church," Priestess Enomwoyi told her.

Clark waved and nodded in acceptance and agreement of her marching orders as she opened the front door to exit. The mid-afternoon November sun nearly blinded her. She had forgotten how beautiful a day it was. At Priestess Enomwoyi's house the shades were drawn shut. Before Clark knew it, Enomwoyi appeared beside her once more.

"Make it a Catholic church, okay," she told her.

"Catholic..." Clark curiously asked.

"It's an ancient religion. It would be better this way...at first, Catholic, okay?" she said.

"Okay," Clark muttered, then left.

She never saw Priestess Enomwoyi again.

CHAPTER FORTY

It was a time of thanksgiving. Though, New York City, among other cities, had failed to meet acceptable standards for healthy ozone levels, and as a result, a hole in the atmosphere loomed about threatening to annihilate mankind. There upon them also was a mysterious disease ravaging the country, called Acquired Immune Deficiency Syndrome a/k/a AIDS. It had cast a black cloud from shore to shore, nearly grinding public parties to a halt, nearly, but not quite. After all, this was New York City. By all apparent circumstances it was a scary time. Though many decided that rather than dwelling on the gloom and doom of the current issues they'd seize the opportunity to live life to its fullest, finally realizing that tomorrow wasn't necessarily promised. The City's resilient nature became its new sparkle and shine. Macy's Department Store spent its sixty-second anniversary filling giant, hot air balloons and parading down Fifth Avenue to hoards of contented spectators. Meanwhile new foundations sprung up all over with an agenda to raise funds to research or to combat this or that disease or environmental cause. A celebrity without a mission outside of their own career began to seem heartless and shallow.

Likewise, Clark was beginning to feel a bit transformed as well. Like her city, she was in a scant state of recovery and redesign. In her case, she had a lot to think about, to reflect upon. With everything she'd learned, she could now look back and see some of the things in her life with much more clarity and understanding. One thing in particular was the subtle connection between her spotty love life and Jimmy's hold on her, once believing she was the main reason men left. Now, she knew otherwise. Although Jimmy was invisible, he was obviously perceivable. She also knew that he was determined to move what he believed to be obstacles out of his way, be they her friends, lovers, or even her family. She was still wrapping her mind around what he did to Grandma Olivia. That part stung bitterly and would forever haunt her. She purchased two roses, stuck them in a glass of water and drank in Grandma Olivia's honor, just as Priestess Enomwoyi had instructed. She cried too, thinking that maybe she might have had more time to get to know her, had it not been for the likes of Jimmy. Her only comfort was in knowing that Grandma Olivia was now smiling down on her. She too was finally free of her own burdens, of her own entanglements. As Clark continued to mull over the many aspects of her life, pre and post Jimmy, the phone rang. It was Patsy Mae.

"You coming?" she asked her.

"Yeah. Yeah," Clark replied.

"What time? I may need some help before everybody else gets here," Patsy Mae informed her.

"Oh, I don't know...around three-ish, I guess. I have something I need to do first," Clark told her trying hard not to say what.

"To do?" Patsy Mae pried, "I thought you said you had the day off."

"I do...it's just that...well...I told you what Grandma Olivia said to me before she died right?" Clark asked.

"Yeeeeesssssssss," Patsy Mae answered curiously.

"Well, it has something to do with that. Well, I just need to go to church first...a Catholic church," Clark told her mother.

"Church?" Patsy Mae asked bluntly now more curious than ever, "You?...Church?"

"Yeah, well....I...well..." Clark stammered.

"One of my kids is going to church without me poking them there with a stick?" Patsy Mae asked with a hum of complete disbelief after.

"I know. I know," Clark said in disbelief too.

There was a defiant pause as Patsy Mae waited for her daughter Clark to now relay the truth.

"Well?" Patsy Mae asked.

"Well...what?" Clark replied perplexed.

"Well, I guess you don't have to tell me what you're really up to if you don't want to. After all, I'm just your mother. Lord, knows, I'm the last to know. Whatever it is, I'll see you later," Patsy Mae told her.

"What?" Clark responded but by then she could hear the receiver click before she could tell Patsy Mae that she wasn't lying. She would need proof now, like a note from the Pastor or something.

Clark only knew of one Catholic Church, which was located in her old neighborhood in Jamaica, Our Lady of Perpetual Help. It wasn't too far from her house. In truth, she didn't know anything about it except where it was and that it always seemed to be a bit on the creepy side, that assessment given from having passed it by bus on the way to school everyday, and it had been a long time since then. Yet, when she parked across the street and looked into its entryway, she still caught a chill. It reminded her of a tiny fortress that didn't look like it could protect anything even in its inception. She honestly wanted to complete the mission she was on, but now she began to have some serious second doubts. She stood outside for a long while contemplating Priestess Enomwoyi's ominous warnings about open doors and filling up spaces and such. She wavered in indecision longing never to have any more to do with any of this. Then she decided that it must be nerves and as she'd done at all of her auditions, she'd wing it. So, with that in mind, she walked up the steps to the large, wooden front doors all the while thinking to herself that she wasn't a member. She wasn't even Catholic. She hadn't been in a church since her baptism at age five and then one or two times thereafter during various holidays. As these thoughts swam in her mind, she mustered some courage and went inside. It took her eyes a moment to adjust. Given the fact that they hadn't seen the likes of her in such a long time, she figured that that was only fair. Yet, even as her vision became clearer, she still couldn't see much. She figured that that was fair too, symbolic even. The lights were dimmed, the pews empty, and there were candles burning on either side of the entrance. Ahead was a single aisle, straight down the center. Now that she was completely inside, she grew even more apprehensive. It wasn't that long ago that she walked down a similar pathway, one that had a deplorable end. She was reticent to go down another. She looked around and saw a small gold plated sign that simply read, "Mass in the back." Though she had never been to one, she knew that mass meant church meeting of some sort. And, although, she couldn't see a single soul, she could hear the voices. 'It could be the Priest' she thought. Right off she could tell that he was speaking in another language followed by a chorus of sound from about twelve or so people who seemed to be repeating everything he said.

So, off she went down the long aisle towards the sound of hushed voices. She didn't like the fact that the floorboards creaked under her weight. Now everyone back there would know she was coming. As she approached, she saw heads turning at her intrusion. There they were, a young White Priest heading a small circle of congregants. All save a few peeping at her, had their heads down and their eyes shut. He, the Priest, waved Clark over to the gathering, ushering her to join in. Clark shot into the closest open space not wanting to further disturb.

"In the name of the Father, and of the Son, and of the Holy Spirit," the Priest said.

"Amens" filled the space, mostly in whispers.

"In nòmine Patris, et Fìlii, et Spìritus Sancti," the Priest said.

Again, "Amens" came, this time almost silently.

"The grace of our Lord Jesus Christ, and the love of God and the fellowship of the Holy Spirit be with you all," said the Priest.

"And also with you" the congregants answered nonchalantly.

"Gràtia Dòmini nostri Jesu Christi…" the Priest continued in Latin.

As his monotone voice echoed against the columns and pillars, and the ancient statues of saints, Clark all at once began to have a visceral reaction to each and every word. It all began as a slight tingling in her fingers and toes. At first, there was no reason to be alarmed, but this sensation began to grow in intensity. That's when Clark's eyes shot open. She stood frozen waiting for the worst. She was now set on edge and terrified.

She couldn't help but to remember Jimmy and his afterlife pursuits. Though, within moments she began to notice that this was not entirely the same; this was a warmer feeling, as if she were being hugged by someone.

"…et càritas Dei, et communication…" he said.

Then her chest tightened as if someone grabbed it. She twisted uncomfortably from side to side as her upper body began to ache. There was a force, some kind of weighted pressure pressing down upon it. It burned too, from the inside out, and her temperature elevated thusly. Something deep within, told her to look down. As she did so, obeying her inner voice, she saw something unusual beginning to happen at her feet.

"…Sancti Spìritus…" the Priest said slowly.

She was now standing in something, something liquid. She immediately thought that she must have had an accident. On closer examination though, she saw that whatever it was, it was colorless and odorless and it moved with the consistency of Jell-O. It was similar to a small puddle of water, but it was globed together as if solid. She began to think that her mind was playing tricks on her, because all at once it began to rise. In one fluent movement, it lifted clean off the floor. She gasped and started looking around the room to find other witnesses of this phenomenon. None saw, all had their eyes closed; their ears focused on the Priest. She squirmed to get away from it. She tried dodging and ducking, everything short of fleeing, but as she did so, it seemed to follow and anticipate her every step. She could see it more clearly now too as the liquid bubble floated in mid-air, creeping ever so slowly up towards her head. Worry and panic nearly choked her. She staggered back, yet it stayed put like it was a part of her. Before she knew it, the water was level with her chest, right around the area of her heart, which raced ahead of reason. She gasped again, this time more audibly. Although, the Priest and some congregants then opened their eyes and looked directly at her, she couldn't understand why they didn't seem to see the liquid wonder moving about. Then swiftly, magically even, suddenly the liquid blob simply slid straight inside of her. She watched as it infused itself through her very skin, seamlessly flowing through bone and marrow, cartilage, everything. She thought she might faint.

"…sit cum òmnibus vobis," the Priest said slowly.

The congregants all answered in unison this time, "Et cum spiritu tuo."

Before Clark could register what just happened, tears came streaming down her face, and suddenly she was covered in sweat. The weeping poured out of her, gushing like an unruly fountain, replacing the puddle that had just been at her feet; that had just entered her flesh. She looked down at herself and felt as if she was witnessing a flood. The crying that had begun in her, without permission or prodding, was irrepressible and her body shook spastically with volcanic release. With it any anxiety, angst, or frustration over the past years, melted away in a pool of slobber. It was an ugly cry too, the kind that's so tangible, others can feel the weeper's pain. It was loud too, for everyone in that little section of church, opened their eyes and now stared at Clark. She was doubled over, holding her face in her hands, trying to stop the leakage as best she could. None looked more uncomfortable though than the Priest. He had stopped cold in a panic. He looked around stunned at Clark's reaction, thinking that it was too dramatic a response for his latest routine sermon. It never occurred to him or to Clark that it could be something taking place on the inside, beyond the earthly realm, in the spirit. Consequently, neither knew what to do. He looked up to Heaven for answers, while Clark stood alone struggling to get a hold of herself. Beside her, an elderly woman reached into her purse, pulled out a tissue and gently enfolded it into Clark's shaky, wet hand. Clark nodded a thank you, then quickly tried to clean herself up. It was impossible.

"Are you alright?" the Priest finally came over to ask her.

Clark nodded yes, though completely unsure. Yet, the burning sensation slowly subsided with each wipe of the tissue. And, her breathing slowly transitioned back to normal. A minute before, it was all rapid sniffles and sighs. Now that she was feeling more and more like her herself, she stood wondering sincerely what everyone else thought. Especially, since they all looked around stunned and perplexed about what to do next. They seemed anxious, in a flux as to whether they should leave her alone or escort her to the nearest hospital. She didn't have an answer for them. She kept wondering about that too. While driving over to Patsy Mae's, she continued to wonder, though, she was sure that the Priest's words had something to do with it. Since she didn't understand most of what he actually said, it was hard to determine what part uttered touched her so.

At Patsy Mae's, she was greeted by Tara at the front door, then came the delightful smell of sweet potato pie, and glazed ham, collards and potato salad. The house was covered in a thin, warm, layer of good cooking that descended upon her like rain forest mist.

"Wow," Clark said breathing in all the marvelous aromas.

"Yeah, Ma's been cooking all day. Oh yeah…and she's been

drinking too," Tara whispered whimsically closing the front door with her hip.

"That you, Clark," Patsy Mae called out merrily.

"Yeah, Ma," Clark said winking to Tara and stepping into the kitchen.

Patsy Mae grabbed them both gingerly and hugged one with one arm and one with the other. As she did so, Lillie came to the doorway carrying an empty tray.

"Oh, isn't that nice," she said looking at them with their arms enfolded around each other.

"These my babies," Patsy Mae said proudly, practically tearful, pushing Tara and Clark forward to greet her new friend.

"Hi, girls," Lillie said smiling widely at Tara and Clark.

"This is Ms. Lillie," Patsy Mae told them.

"Hi," both Tara and Clark said simultaneously.

"They're both so pretty. You didn't tell me you had such lovely girls, Pat," Lillie told Patsy Mae.

"Well, look at their momma," Patsy Mae replied grinning from ear to ear.

Then she poured herself some more Crème de Mint. She didn't bother to offer any to Lillie. Lillie had an ice tea she'd been sipping since breakfast.

"Am I late?" Clark asked hearing what sounded like a house full of people.

"No. No, you're right on time, ain't she, Patsy Mae?" Lillie said smiling.

"Lillie and Bernie came over early to help out. Then Tara showed up. It's okay. I told everyone where you were…church right?" Patsy Mae chuckled.

"Ohhh…" Lillie said, "…Which one?" she asked.

"Uhh...uhh...Lady of Sacred...Help...something...I..."
Clark felt a little embarrassed.

"Oh, Our Lady of Perpetual Help?" Lillie asked to clarify,
"Who did the mass?"

Patsy Mae lowered her glass and humorously awaited Clark's
next response, still skeptical. Tara, who hadn't closed her mouth
since the topic of church came up, continued to stare at her sister.

"Ah..." Clark started feeling like she was on a witness stand,
"...ah..the Priest was a White guy...named...named. He..."
Clark strained trying to remember, "Oh, yeah, they called him,
they called him Father Tom," she finally blurted.

"Oh, Father Tom," Lillie said in recognition of his name,
"Nice man. Nice man. Did you enjoy it?" she asked Clark.

Clark nodded yes all the while avoiding both her mother's
and sister's goofy grins. At least they no longer looked shocked,
but now quite possibly proud as if she had done something
unimaginable.

"Yes. Yes, it was good," Clark said to everyone present.

"You need to come over to mine one Sunday," Lillie said
extending her invitation to both Patsy Mae and Tara at the same
time.

Both were silent for a moment then Patsy Mae finally said,
"We'd like that."

She looked over at her girls and reiterated, "We'd – like -
that," she said as if it was no longer a request but a firm
command.

Tara and Clark eyed each other aware of that fact.

"Yes Ma'am," they said in unison.

"What about Melanie?" Tara asked.

"What about Melanie, what?" Melanie asked while stepping

into the kitchen.

Patsy Mae grabbed hold of her too and commenced to give her a squeeze.

"What's all this about?" Melanie asked.

Tara nodded towards the Crème de Mint. Melanie giggled beneath her breath.

Billy Earl and Marlin's conversation spilled out over from the living room.

"Man, that thing was as big as me…bigger," Billy Earl shouted followed by loud raucous laughter, "Right, Bern? It took two of us to pull that dag-gone thing onto the boat! I was sweating; that thing weighed so much. Peeeew! Sweetest thing I ever did see."

"Sweetest thing, but I think I chipped a tooth pulling on her, but she was worth it, right Earl?" Bernie joked.

"You said it was in the bay?" Marlin chimed in.

Lillie turned and gave Patsy Mae a knowing glance.

"Don't worry. Fish is not on the menu today," Patsy Mae told her.

"Thank God," Lillie replied.

"Please, please, no more fish!" Patsy Mae said loudly.

"I hear ya'll in there," Billy Earl shouted from the living room.

"We can hear ya'll too and that's the problem!" Patsy Mae shouted back.

All the women in the kitchen laughed heartily as the men came tracing in.

"Woman, that was some good eatin' I'm hear to tell ya'," Billy Earl bellowed with Bernie not far behind snickering.

Marlin stood along the counter's edge shaking his head from side to side. He had been listening to the big fish story since he walked in the door. His now wife, Karen, was on her way from work. He couldn't wait for her to arrive so he could use her as a human shield against it. Marlin just wanted to eat and sleep and not necessarily in that order.

"Marlin, man, help me out here," Billy Earl asked him for support.

Marlin shook his head again willing it to spin around and come completely off if that would stop the inane chatter.

"Man, please. You and that big fish," Patsy Mae chuckled and sipped.

"Billy Earl, you got those pictures they took of us?" Bernie asked.

"Had 'em blown up. I didn't show you?" Billy Earl anxiously asked him, "Oh, man! Take a look at these."

With that the men exited back into the living room for the viewing.

"I put 'em on a slide show. Wait 'til you see this," Billy Earl told an enthusiastic Bernie and a reluctant Marlin.

"Oh, brother. A slide show?" Lillie rhetorically asked Patsy Mae.

Patsy Mae looked toward the ceiling while nodding yes. Clark, Tara and Melanie were in tears they were laughing so hard.

CHAPTER FORTY-ONE

It was practically a miracle to have the entire family in church on a day that didn't have holiday in its name. Just like old times, Clark sat sandwiched between her two older sisters. More than fifteen years into adulthood, yet they maintained youthful seating assignments. Their eyes focused on Billy Earl, who had been fussing with his shirt collar and mumbling underneath his breath since he got dressed that morning.

"Woman, what you tryin' to do to me?" he grimaced at Patsy Mae.

Patsy Mae snapped her head around toward him.

"Don't let me get to cussing at you this morning, Billy Earl," Patsy Mae warned, through gritted teeth.

She was studying him as if he were a misbehaving two-year-old. After a very long pause attributed to her patience, she reached round his back and yanked his shirt down which allegedly was strangling him. Their conversation about the pros and cons of too much starch had filled the car like a comedy routine. Clark and her sisters were still laughing over it. Billy Earl finally settled down into his seat insisting on overtaking the armrest as if battling for territory. Meanwhile, Marlin had opted to sit in the next row quite a distance away from the family. In his mind, he was in a complete state of protest. He would have been fine if his VCR was working and he could have taped the football game, but since it was on the fritz, so was he. Both Patsy Mae and Karen had insisted Marlin come to church with the family instead. His arms clasped around his body, his lips protruding in a pucker, as far as he was concerned if the Pastor wasn't reciting the football score, he wasn't listening. He responded to them by repeating Billy Earl's sentiment on the subject word for word.

"I'll go, but I won't like it."

Lillie and Bernie had finally taken their seats diagonally across the aisle from Patsy Mae, Billy Earl and their family. Everyone's arms were tired on account of the amount of handshaking they'd done with both Lillie and Bernie parading them around then shoving them into an introduction. It was entirely possible that Bernie and Lillie knew every single soul in their twenty-five thousand plus member church.

Once seated and with the service having officially begun, everyone for the most part in the Green family found themselves actually enjoying Lillie and Bernie's church. To their surprise, it was extremely progressive. With Lillie and Bernie's old-fashioned sensibilities, they assumed that their place of worship would be similar in nature. Instead the whole place was modern, beautifully decorated with Italian leather sofas, fine wooden cabinetry, with dramatically stunning artwork that matched the décor perfectly. The sanctuary was enormous, the seating comfortable and wide, flat screen monitoring devices nicely spaced throughout, telecasting the platform, not to mention announcements as well. The Pastor was equally surprising. He was young, good-looking, well spoken and shockingly personable, not at all what they had expected. Church was nothing like Clark remembered from childhood with the *thee's* and *thou's* of the ancient Bible. Now, the Pastor seemed more like a motivational speaker than a preacher. One who could really get his audience hyped and excited by relating to them funny stories and anecdotes. He seemed a cross between President Clinton and Malcolm X in the charisma department as he preached about healthy vs. unhealthy relationships. Clark felt sure that she finally got to see the great speakers of the sixties, who had important messages to relay, ones that would ultimately change people's lives for the better. She found herself laughing and soulfully imbibing the many life lessons he offered as examples. It astonished her how many she could relate to. It all struck a cord in her but especially when he began a discourse on the law of attraction. According to his words, there was something in each person that acted as a magnet to others. She could live with that theory so long as she was not the cause of Jimmy's arrival in her life. She couldn't imagine what particular creepy aspect of her being carried him to her door. Just as Clark was feeling good and uncomfortable with the present course of the discussion, the Pastor excluded children. She was relieved. It would be many, many years before she'd fully understand how personal responsibility factored into every equation.

Occasionally, Patsy Mae eyed her child, Clark, with stealth-like curiosity. Clark could feel her gaze penetrating the back of her neck. She knew that her sudden transition perplexed her mother. She couldn't bring herself to explain all of the ins and outs of everything that had transpired. Patsy Mae would have to wait until she herself had more of it sorted out. Tara and Melanie also stared at her from time to time, most likely curious as well. It wasn't that long ago that Clark was anti-church, anti-God or else acting like a Buddhist, or a mystic. If her family needed an explanation, they would all have to wait. It would be another twenty years before Clark uttered her life's story to another living soul. For the longest time, she wouldn't quite know how to brooch the subject.

It was an hour later after the sermon was over, she would find herself down at the altar giving her life to Christ. At least that's what people told her she was doing. In truth, she had no idea the significance of her actions or, for that matter, what everyone else was talking about. All she knew was that reoccurring again was that same burning sensation in her chest, this time accompanied by a fire that started at the soles of her feet and rapidly moved upward. Next thing she knew she bolted from her seat and ran, at first, in no particular direction. In her mind, she was trying to flee from the flames. Before she knew it, she went down a long flight of steps facing the church platform, tears trickling from her eyes, drool coming from her mouth and with the same overwhelming pains she'd experienced at the Catholic Church, pounding within her. Again, the weeping was uncontrollable, her knees weak, pulse racing and for the tears, she couldn't see straight in front of her. She actually didn't know where she was at that precise moment. She didn't even know how she had gotten there. One minute she was seated and the next she was standing in front of Lillie and Bernie's Pastor, thankful that she had finally stopped. Then the Pastor, who had been speaking earlier as if directly to her, suddenly appeared before her. Without warning, he reached up and touched her forehead with something wet. Next thing she knew, she was on the floor, struggling to get back up. She knew that he hadn't pushed her or anything, but something or someone had. As if on cue, a complete stranger came out of nowhere and grabbed hold of her. Their quick thinking cushioned her fall. That's when she heard screams coming from some of the other people in a similar position as she, all were crying, all looking spent as if positively exhausted. She glanced across and saw them all appearing as if they'd been rescued from a vicious, monstrous storm. She felt a sudden kinship to each of them, survivors all and unashamed of the toll. In her entire life, she had never been so unguarded, so exposed, so unaffected by anything or anyone, so free. In the midst of that realization, there was a surge of exhilaration stirring within the entire church. Tambourines were being clanged, music roaring, and a frenzy of shouts from congregants that sounded similarly to cheers. Behind her, Clark, witnessed a party going on. This was further confirmed when she, and those who joined her at the platform, were guided out of the sanctuary to the sounds of people applauding, expressing heartfelt salutes and giving standing ovations. Clark cried at such an honest out-pouring of emotion. Just as she had floated from her seat, this too took on that supernatural eminence. She could not feel her feet touching the ground. It was as if the warmth she was receiving literally supported her, spirit, soul and body. From that moment on she felt as if she'd been wrapped in a blanket of it. Even after the church helpers handed her a booklet to read and made her repeat the confession they recited, she still wasn't sure what had taken place. In continued confusion, her brothers and sisters teased her in the car ride back to Patsy Mae's.

"You got religion now, huh? You and Jesus forever, now, huh?" they said such to her and similar.

She didn't know what was really intended by their words. All she knew was that the burning sensation had now become more like an after glow, the fire at her feet, now clouds. Gone were all remembrances of it all. Suddenly, she felt wide awake, not the sleepless kind, but as if she was seeing absolutely everything for the very first time. It was hard for her to be anything but brilliantly conscious. When the trees rustled along the road as they sped by, Clark felt as if she were making them do so. She did a double-take to the sky thinking that the flock of birds overhead had circled into what appeared to be a heart-shape. Even the air seemed crisper and more vibrant somehow. It was as if she discovered that she had until that moment spent her entire life monumentally asleep, never fully present anywhere she'd actually been. Like a sleepwalker, she had trod through her entire life and could recount numerous times of not enjoying it because unbeknownst to her, she wasn't really there. She was either sick with worry at auditions, or mentally out on tour whilst with Peter or in imaginary relationships like with Alfonso. Now, every breath seemed to come to her as a blissful little present, all gift-wrapped and precious.

Months later, still with the new state of consciousness, she had awakened to the idea of actually forgiving Jimmy, though he was dead, though he could care less, though he probably thought that he did nothing wrong. She had come to terms with all of that. Like her mother had told her, *"The dead can't hurt you, they dead."* Patsy Mae was right, but Clark now knew that there was so much more to it than just that. She had discovered that there was one thing the dead could do. After fifteen years with Jimmy, he had wasted a lot of her time. He had stolen some of her youth, years she could never get back. And most importantly, she also knew that she couldn't have defeated him all on her own, using her own strength. That would have been impossible. She had none to combat the likes of him. Someone rallied for her along the way, of this she was absolutely certain. She could now look back and see a delicate helping hand every step of the way. She had had divine help; the kind of supremacy that made air and everything that breathes. For the war waged against her was beyond sanity, past human existence. She couldn't have done battle with man-made weaponry. She needed an advocate on the other side, someone who set the laws of the universe in motion and could stop the earth revolving with a thought, someone, some being. Who could it be? She had been told by Patsy Mae and even by Priestess Enomwoyi, but to know for one's self. It floored her to think it, but she knew that she had God on her side. God! She would now thank him for the rest of her life. She knew that quite possibly she'd been looking for him all along and just didn't know it. She thought she was trying to get rid of a ghost, but instead she had found God as if by default or was it the main plan? She would look back and see him all over her past, sprinkled there like baby's breath in a bouquet, but she hadn't even taken notice of that fact until very recently. She would sleep with her Bible beneath her pillow for months now, knowing who wrote it, loving the comfort of it. She would read it from cover to cover thereafter. For her, it was a love made in heaven, one that had actually seemed to have restarted her life all over again, anew.

As for the other one, the one made in hell, as for Jimmy, that one was marvelously and thankfully over. She grabbed her purse, scooted out of her apartment, locking the door behind.

Then she joyfully sailed down the stairs into her future. She burst through the front door and allowed the world to kiss her face with its springtime dew. Every drop of sunshine was savored. She loved the smell of the freshly cut grass and the sounds of birds chirping with delight at migrating out from the cold. She knew how they felt. She felt reborn, knowing that troubles would come in life but after what she'd experienced, she knew that she'd be able to overcome them all. She took in a deep breath and held on to it for a while, loving the very fact of being able to do so without fear. Her date waved to her as she exited through her front gate. He was in his Jeep and bade she come join him. A few weeks prior, they had reconnected at a party of a mutual friend. She hadn't seen him in over two years. First thing he said to her was that he had broken up with Priestess Enomwoyi. He had mentioned that tidy little fact before saying hello. It was as if he knew what she was thinking, as if they had picked up where they had left off. She liked that about him, among other things. Clark walked slowly towards Paulo, determined to hold back on some of the excitement she felt as she looked into his deep, brown eyes. She practically had to restrain herself from leaping into the man's arms, at least for now until they went on a few more dates together. After all, she wasn't a nun and as she had discovered quite recently, she wasn't dead either. **THE END.**

I know thy works: behold, I have set before thee an open door, and no man can shut it: for thou hast a little strength, and hast kept my word, and hast not denied my name. (Revelation 3:8 KJV)

- on sale now -

www.blackcurrantpress.com
www.amazon.com
www.barnesand noble.com
Dare Books
Nicholas Brooklyn
Brownstone Books
Christian Cultural Center Bookstore

About the Author

Beverly A. Burchett placed second in the Billie Holiday Theatre Poetry Contest and thusly her love of writing was spurred. She's a graduate of the famed High School of Performing Arts, and has acted in a number of national commercials as well as a few popular films, including "Fame", and "Joey Breaker." Her latest works <u>Queen Kinni</u>, <u>Smart, Sexy, Spiritual, Strong</u>, and <u>Random Arts of Kindness, a journey</u>, are available in stores and on-line at www.blackcurrantpress.com. Beverly's also a published lyrist, who resides in New York.